GALACTIC CLUSTER MZB

Writing is a solitary and lonely profession, but every now and then writers do meet, join their fates, and weave their visions together.

The literary mainstream world still speaks with awe of the Bloomsbury group of Virginia Woolf. The science fiction world is strongly influenced to this day by the Futurians of the "Ivory Tower" days. And now another such galactic cluster has arisen around the home of Marion Zimmer Bradley and her friends and associates—the house known as Greyhaven.

There, at Greyhaven, is the Earthly terminal from whence the lore and history of Darkover is launched. From there also arises fabulous tales of other worlds and other magicks, spun first to other writers, then put onto paper and sent out to enhance the fantasy cosmos.

This is truly a unique anthology. As with other such groups, you may meet here first some of the names that will grace the magazines and book racks of the eighties and nineties—and some that already do.

—Donald A. Wollheim

GREYHAVEN

An anthology of fantasy

Edited by
MARION ZIMMER BRADLEY

DAW Books, Inc.
Donald A. Wollheim, Publisher
1633 Broadway, New York, N.Y. 10019

FIRST PRINTING, APRIL 1983

1 2 3 4 5 6 7 8 9

DAW TRADEMARK REGISTERED
U.S. PAT. OFF. MARCA
REGISTRADA, HECHO EN U.S.A.

PRINTED IN U.S.A.

DEDICATION

To Robyn Elisabeth Cook

In loving memory of our dear
and cherished Robert Cook,
"our obedient humble Serpent"
who did not live to see this
anthology in print; as part
of the legacy he left.

Et lux eterna luceat eis.

CONTENTS

GREYHAVEN: WRITERS AT WORK

What is Greyhaven, and why is it the title of a fantasy anthology?

On the purely physical level, Greyhaven is a huge, grey-shingled house in the Claremont district of the Berkeley hills. On a subtler level, it is a "household," an extended family, a state of mind. On still another level, it is the center of a circle, a literary school of writers, both in Berkeley and through the world of fantasy and science fiction.

It began with a sister, and her two brothers—one by blood, one by adoption—all three of whom were aspiring writers. It was the sister—myself, Marion Zimmer Bradley—who first became known as a professional writer. The two brothers married women who were college friends; one wife became a selling author in her own right, the other began a small literary agency, being possessed of a talent even more rare than writing skill; the ability to tell where a given story falls short and what should be done to fix it.

Time went on. Children were born to all three marriages. The family outgrew even the enormous house called Greyhaven, and established House Greenwalls. Through the two households passed a great number of young people—as friends, visitors, babysitters and what have you—and since like attracts like, a large number of these people passing through turned out also to be aspiring writers, who were given houseroom, and even more importantly, writing space, use of typewriters, encouragement, and the company of their peers.

About three years ago, sitting at afternoon tea in the big dining room at Greyhaven, we were counting up the number of professional and semi-professional writers whom we looked on as "family" and one of us said, "Good heavens, we're a literary movement all by ourselves!" Someone else quipped, "Who needs to go to a writer's conference? We've got one right here around this table!"

It's true; several "literary movements" have begun with fewer people than the writers who gather around the Greyhaven or Greenwalls table at teatime on Sunday, or at one of the "Bardic Revels" given at Greyhaven. It seemed inevitable that we should turn out an anthology of writers whom we regard as "family."

Every writer in this anthology has, with two exceptions, actually lived at Greyhaven or Greenwalls; the exceptions are close personal friends who have taken writing courses at Greenwalls or worked in close collaboration with one or more of us. Yet the stories in this anthology are very different. Perhaps the one thing we all have in common is a genuine love of the speculative in fiction, and a love of the writer's craft. We spend many, many hours talking about our various works—in fact, whenever any number of us get together, around the teatable at Greyhaven, or in the hot tub which is the major attraction of Greenwalls, before very long, the conversation inevitably turns to writing.

Who's writing what? How is the new book coming? Oh, wow, you made a sale, we'll have to give you a publication party! Did you see the cover on my new book? Hooray, or Horrors, depending on the editor or art department involved. I just got this rejection slip, what do you think the editor meant by *that*? And so forth and so on, far into the night, while the hot-water jets bubble, or the cookies vanish and the coffee pot or teapot get filled and refilled. Deadlines, contracts, plots, dénouements—endless shoptalk comes and goes where we are all professionals—or devoted amateurs, in the case of those who do not yet make their living by writing.

The company of our peers. That is what it's all about. Friends and family to share the rejoicing at a success, to share the disappointment or disillusion at a rejection slip, to talk over the plot that won't jell, the choice of a new subject, the happy or unhappy ending.

The family that writes together stays together? I hope so. Inevitably, some day, I suppose some eager doctoral candidate—now that Speculative Fiction is regarded as a serious academic concern—will do a thesis or dissertation on the

Greyhaven School of writers through the sixties, seventies and eighties. This book may provide him, or her, with a place to start. But even more, I hope it will give you a picture of what it's like to be a member of a big household and instant family whose members all share an overwhelming common interest. Greyhaven is, therefore, a state of mind; and a wonderful place to write. And out of that state of mind came the many stories in this book. . . . and as the oldest, and so far, the most successful in the family, I have the privilege of introducing my writing family.

Marion Zimmer Bradley

About Diana L. Paxson and
Kindred of the Wind

Diana Paxson, who is, in private life, the wife of my adopted brother Don, is proof positive that writing is contagious. I knew Diana as a deft costumer, an expert in English literature, a poet and even a musician, writing her own songs and performing them, first on the mandolin and then on the Irish harp. She was the founding genius behind the first tournament of the Society for Creative Anachronism, she spent many years writing school curricula which would help Native American children to retain a sense of cultural integrity in the Space Age. She has also taught at Mills College.

However, no one was more surprised than I when she confided to me that she had actually begun a novel. Eventually the novel was finished, but I thought it quite unsalable, and said so. I was, however, sufficiently impressed with the setting and characterization to encourage her to continue writing.

There is one thing about being a selling writer with many aspiring-writer friends; you are always getting asked for advice and critical comment, and I have learned that the best way to deal with these people is to give them what they all say they want, but very few actually *do* want; a completely honest evaluation. (It has lost me a few friends, but they are not the kind that I regret very much.) My maxim has become the one quoted by Harriet Vane, in Dorothy L. Sayers' classic *Gaudy Night*: "I'll do anything for anybody except tell them their beastly book is good when it isn't." It is often a painful task, and I usually feel like a brute; beginning writers are a sensitive breed, and at the stage where I first see their work, they have not yet developed the first necessity of a professional, which is a tough and objective view of their own writing; rejection is the first experience of almost every would-be commercial writer, and they must learn to stand the heat, or get out of the kitchen.

Diana's ability to be objective about criticism, to go away and rewrite instead of defending her own imperfect work, convinced me that she was worth encouraging; and, as I had foreseen, a day came when she sold her first story, then her second. Eventually the time came when I counseled her that she should no longer listen to any criticism, except for that of the fellow who is going to sign the check—not even mine.

By now, Diana has had a round dozen of short stories in various anthologies, including my first two (*The Keeper's Price* and *Sword of Chaos*) as well as sales to *Millennial Women*, the recent *Hecate's Cauldron*, and by the time this anthology sees the newsstands, her novel, *Lady of Light and Darkness*, will be in print from Pocket Books.

This particular story, in a very real sense, was the genesis of the idea for the *Greyhaven* anthology. Some years ago Diana showed me the first version of this story, and asked what I thought. I was very impressed with the story, though after its first rejection I gave some hints for rewriting—mostly a matter of convincing the then-inexperienced Diana that a story of this length could not sustain three separate viewpoints. She rewrote the story, and the rewrite seemed to me not only competent but excellent; I was as angry and disappointed when it didn't sell, first time out, as Diana was herself. In fact, I told her that if I ever edited an anthology, I would buy it immediately; and the very day I signed the contract for this anthology, I telephoned Diana to tell her that I was now in a position to honor that promise.

But when it arrived, I felt a little trepidation. Diana had since sold several short stories, her writing had improved enormously, and I was infinitely more experienced as an editor. Would I still like the story, and what would I say if I didn't? I even gave myself an out by asking her to submit a couple of her more recent unpublished stories, so that I could have a choice. Yet on re-reading "Kindred of the Wind," I felt again all the story's power and passion; I think the editor who rejected it was completely in the wrong, but after all, her loss is our gain!

Diana wrote about this story:

This is the only story I have ever written that began with a dream, which in this case provided the central character and conflict, and more important, the atmosphere. Like many other people, I have also had my share of dreams about flying, and in the story I was trying to convey how it feels. It would be interesting to do an informal survey of how many people have flying dreams, and what techniques they use.

THE KINDRED OF THE WIND
by Diana L. Paxson

Anakor paused, almost motionless in the eye of the wind. East of the mountains below him, he could have seen, if he willed, the ruins of the Barilan Empire, where the wizards had created his kind. A smudge in the western sky marked Tarrant, where now a new Empire was rising. His eyes, so much keener than the eyes of those who were merely human, could have seen over the curved edge of the world. But his whole being was focused on one speck of life toiling over the slopes directly below.

He did not need food. The young blue-buck he had killed the day before hung roasting over his fire. But he was hungry for vengeance, and he knew that the speck he watched was a man.

Anakor waited patiently, for from the air he saw that a fall of rock had broken the trail. It was a hard path to climb—it would be almost impossible to get down again. The speck crawled upward, and Anakor shifted the angle of his wings and began to descend in slow circles.

Orik struggled up the path, panting in the thin air. Until now he had been able to cling to the side of the mountain when the trail faltered, but he wondered how much longer he could endure. His wound was hurting badly now, throbbing in time with his laboring pulse.

The boy had been climbing for several hours. It was his third day of travel, mostly without food. His pursuers would not overtake him, now. It was like an evil dream—the discovery, and his flight, and this terrible journey. He had escaped death, but if those he sought were legend as he had been told, death lay before him as well.

He clambered a few feet farther and rounded an outcropping in the cliff. And stopped. His legs gave way unbidden and he sank to his knees, for the path had disappeared.

This was not the perilous slippage to which he had grown accustomed, but a sheer gap, as if the ledge had been scooped away by a giant spoon. The mountain rose in a sheer wall above him and fell many thousand feet to a rocky canyon.

For a long moment the boy's mind simply stopped, and in that moment Anakor struck.

Orik cried out as great talons drove into his shoulder. Then he clutched at the ground with his good hand, struggling madly against the buffeting of the mighty wings. He screamed, and the sound blended with the harsh cry of triumph his attacker gave.

The power of Anakor's beating wings lifted them a little off the ground, and Orik felt each lift move him closer to the edge. He twisted convulsively, and one of the creature's claws, dislodged, tore through his bandages and down what had been his arm, piercing him with a new wave of pain that brought him close to unconsciousness.

And then all movement ceased.

Orik's breath came in harsh gasps, his good hand still dug into the ground and his eyes, unfocused, stared over the edge. As his head cleared he felt the murderous talons slowly release, and then the sound of heavy flapping as the great weight lifted from his back.

Slowly he turned his head. On an outcrop of stone a few feet away he saw a great bird, larger than any winged creature on Reveuse. It was considering him intently with hostile yellow eyes. Orik stared back.

An eagle . . . Legend supplied the name, and after a moment, hope. As he watched, the outline of the bird seemed to waver, to break up as a reflection breaks when a stone is thrown into a pond. Orik gazed, and presently he realized that he was no longer looking at a bird, but at a man, naked and shaggy, who crouched upon the rock. The man spoke in a voice harsh as if from disuse.

"You are one of us!"

Orik nodded dumbly, and then he fainted at last.

"No, father, no! I can change it back; put away the knife!"
Orik had shrieked. The torches flickered madly and the
drums throbbed in his head. He felt a sharp pain as the first
stone hit, then another, and another, as the crowd closed in.

"But it's only me, Orik—you've known me all your lives! I
haven't changed. Why are you doing this?" He stared wildly
around the circle of faces, and knew that they were all
strangers. Behind him waited the woods, dark and threaten-
ing, and beyond them the mountains, where the were-eagles
lived. He looked once more at the log village that had been
his home, and shielding his head against the stones, he ran.

Orik groaned. His leg hurt, and his arm. Where was he?
Were they stoning him again? He shuddered and opened his
eyes. He had been dragged away from the edge of the cliff,
and his limbs straightened. He was safe.

His wound still throbbed dully; the bandage, clumsily re-
wound, tightly constrained the limb. He rolled his head to
one side, for the first time able to look at the feathers which
showed from beneath the rough cloth with neither joy nor
fear.

This was his own, an eagle's wing where his arm should be,
and the only unnatural thing about it was the fact that the
rest of his body had not followed in the change. A harsh sigh
from behind him told him that the other was still there.

"Can you teach me the rest of the Change?" Orik asked,
voicing the question that had driven him for the past three
days.

"Yes. . . . It will be difficult, old as you are, but I see
that you have courage—you can learn . . ." there was a
short pause, ". . . if you live. I have a cave across the valley,
sheltered, with a good fire. If I could get you to it I could
nurse you there. But eyries have no footpaths to their doors,
and if I lifted you my talons would injure you more."

Orik rolled his head back, his mind moving sluggishly.
"Could you take care of me here?"

"I could bring you everything but fire. We are very high,

and it is early in the year. I do not think my own warmth would be enough to keep you alive."

"Do you have some kind of blanket? If I lay on something and you lifted it by the corners, or the corners were tied to your legs, could you carry me?"

"You weigh less than a buck, and I have a sorbal skin in which I might lift you, but eagles fly high, and if it slipped, you would be smashed. It is too dangerous."

The boy thought for a moment. "We must try. . . . You have said it yourself. When the evening cold comes I will die. I was as good as dead anyway when you found me. To fall would at least be quick. I free you of responsibility for my fate."

Anakor's eyes were as expressionless in his man's face as in his eagle's form. Without further speech, his outline began to waver and shift as it had done before. Orik watched, fascinated, as the form of the eagle replaced that of the man. Anakor made his way to the edge of the precipice, launched himself, and was gone, rising in dizzying circles and soaring across the valley until he disappeared in the blue mist that veiled the other side.

Orik closed his eyes. It was done. Perhaps the were-eagle was right and he would soon be dead on the rocks, but he had achieved his goal and found his own people at last.

"But *when* will you teach me the transformation spell?" said the boy, his voice still querulous from the fever that had taken a week to pass. "Am I to remain half man and half bird for the rest of my life?"

Anakor poked another stick into the fire and grunted. "I have told you, it is not a spell, not even magic, no matter what your superstitious neighbors said. You must train the mind. A mind weak with fever cannot master the pattern of the Change. The mind must be absolutely clear, completely calm. Our one weakness is that if emotion clouds the mind before the transformation is complete, one becomes human once more."

"What about after the Change has taken place?"

"Even then. That is why it is so dangerous. If you should Change in flight you would be killed. I have known such a thing to occur, when I was young and our people were many in these hills." Anakor paused. When he went on, his voice grated, though his face remained unmoved.

"I had a friend, and he was competing with another for a mate. There is a ritual for such contests—we fight on the ground with knives, for even were it safe we would not so misuse our gift. But the other was reputed very good with a weapon, and my friend loved the woman to madness.

"They were hunting, and a fury came on him. He attacked, not the jouri they had spotted, but his rival, the other eagle. The Change came on him in midair." Anakor stopped, and began to stir the fire. "I saw what was left of him on the rocks below. That was why I hesitated to try to carry you here."

"I am sorry. I did not understand." Orik wondered if that fear had been enough to trouble the older man's self-control. Such a death seemed more terrible to him now, when he could feel life tingling in his limbs. Anakor's face was as always, closed and calm. Orik remembered his family's easy tears and laughter, and thought that this discipline would be hard to learn.

His training began the next day. There were hours of sitting on the ledge before the cave, concentrating on some small point on the other side of the vast gulfs that separated them from the distant peaks, or memorizing the landmarks of his new home. In the evenings, the firelight replaced the hills, and he practiced emptying his mind of conscious thought as he described the pictures he saw in the flames. Breathing, strictly controlled, was a part of it too, and he began to achieve an awareness of bodily processes he had not known existed before. Anakor told him he must know how to make every cell in his body respond to the imprinting of his mind.

"How early do our people usually begin learning this?" he asked after a particularly frustrating day. He had begun to wonder if he would ever know the freedom of the vastness over which he gazed. It was a beautiful view, but he did not want to spend the rest of his life sitting on a ledge. His pinion was nearly healed.

"When the infant is old enough to focus his eyes he begins," said Anakor with a rare smile. "And he hears the music of the high spaces with his mother's lullaby. But the Change has been learned by those who are older. Once, men brought us their sons and daughters when they found them to be of our kind." He looked over at the boy.

"It is not so now," Orik said bitterly. "If the Change comes on them in the cradle they are burnt, and such births become rare. Do you know of others who have come late to your people, like me?"

"Not in my lifetime. The brotherhood of the skies diminishes each year, for we also do not always breed true."

"What happens to the children who . . . who are not . . ." Orik faltered.

"Who are not of the eagle kind? Many of them die—no, not at our hands, but it is a hard life, with many accidents. We take those for whom there is no hope of the Change to the edge of some settlement of men by night, and leave them." He stopped, his features suddenly imprinted with some ancient pain.

"It sorrows you to speak of this—can you tell me why?" Orik said softly.

"We had a nestling once, my mate and I, with whom it was so." The yellow eyes were veiled once more, and the older man turned away.

Orik began to speak, but stopped, now knowing what to say. Only he swore to himself that for the sake of the man who sat on the other side of the fire as well as for himself, he would master the Change.

"Now, tell me once more how you felt when your arm changed to a wing . . ." said Anakor. They had come out of the cave into a morning like the beginning of the world, with air so clear it seemed they could see each needle on the trees in the forest below, as an eagle flies, full ten miles away.

"It was a morning like this," said the boy. "I had gone after a strayed goat. There was a wind, and as I reached the top of the hills I forgot about the goat and could think of nothing but the sky and the wind. I felt a little drunk, and I leaned forward into the wind and spread my arms as if I would soar upon it.

"Suddenly there was a tingling all through my arm and shoulder, and then the wind caught me, and I was half lifted into the air. I lost my balance and was frightened and fell back to the ground. When I opened my eyes I saw this—"

and he lifted the eagle's wing that hung where his right arm should have been.

"That is the inebriation of the air, the drunkenness proper to our kind. That is how you must feel today. Stand up and lean into the wind—I will be here to see that you are not blown away—and cast your mind out into the heavens. Imagine the lift of the wind under your wings, the sun on your back, and say in your heart, *I am free of the heavens, and the heavens are free of me. I am the eldest son of the north-wind, and the air is my element and my true home.*"

Orik gazed into those amber eyes, that were always the eyes of an eagle even when Anakor was in human form. Then he nodded and stepped to the edge of the cliff. Slowly he stretched his ill-matched limbs until the wind, catching at arm and wing, swayed him, and Anakor grasped him around the ankles lest he should indeed be borne away.

But Orik did not feel it. His awareness had gone inward, transforming skin and muscle and bone. His heart and soul took flight, and as the wind surrounded him, he felt the tingling go through him.

"Open your eyes, my son, and look out upon your heritage!" said Anakor.

And Orik opened his eyes, and saw.

They sat before the fire in the cave, feasting on a mountain jouri. Orik leaned back, still so dizzy with elation that he scarcely heard what Anakor said. He had flown! Concentrating furiously, he had flung himself upon the bosom of the wind, imitating Anakor with each filip of feather, shift in weight, until he began to relax against the air, following his master in great circles over the crazy quilt of greys and greens stretched out below. Eventually, fluttering madly, he had sat down on the narrow ledge once more, but his heart was still in the sky.

He roused enough to eat the meat when it was done, and realized that Anakor had called him "son," once more.

"Did you mean that?" the boy asked. "I thought I had given up all hope of kindred when I escaped from my village."

"I told you that I once had a nestling whom I lost. You

have come to take his place. If your heart agrees, be a son to me." He smiled, and Orik grinned back.

The seasons passed. Orik gained in strength and size—a strength of corded muscles stretched tautly over slim, enduring bones. Hair and plumage were thick and glossy brown, and always his eyes, as yellow as Anakor's, kept their piercing, slightly hooded look.

Once in all those years a summons came, and they left their lonely kingdom to attend a meeting of their kindred. Men were increasing in numbers again, and they came into the mountains, seeking gold and silver, timber, game . . . and land. The eagles, with their long memories and longer traditions, remembered the ruined cities on the other side of the mountains, and the sorcerers who had bred and tinkered with human-kind until it was sundered, and the race of were-eagles born.

They had played with other powers too, until disaster came. The peasants of the plains called their ancestors gods, and thought them legend. But as the generations passed they called the eagles demons, and killed them when they could.

The eagles debated killing in return, but the decision was to leave men alone, at least for a time. There was plenty of room.

Anakor, who had counselled attack, fumed all the way back to the cave, and Orik, who despite his exile sometimes remembered wistfully the hearthfires of a human home, tried to understand his foster father's passion.

"It is not because of me, is it, father?" he asked when they had reached the cave.

"Because they cast you out? No, although it adds to the score." Anakor was silent for awhile, and Orik did not dare to speak. "I will tell you, my son, why I hate earth-bound men." he said at last.

"I told you once that I had a child, and what became of him. But I did not tell you the fate of my mate, his mother. Her name was Lanaka, and she was the fairest of our maidens. At least I thought so, and so did my sworn brother, for it was me he was attacking when through jealous rage he lost hold on the eagle-form and fell to destruction.

"She and I were happy together, and even happier when

we had the child. But when we had to send the child away her joy went too. Sorrow dulled her plumage, and she became fixed in the idea that perhaps we had been wrong about our son, that if we had waited, he might have Changed. She blamed me, although it was not my decision, but our people's law, and she began to watch for men, sure that at last he would discover his true nature and come back to us.

"One day hunters came to the edge of the forest, seeking the spotted cat, and one of them fell and was injured. Lanaka saw, and came down out of the air to see if she could help. They shot her. . . .

"They did not think she was a bird of prey—I could forgive if they had thought she meant them harm, but she had made the Change. It was in her body of a human woman that she met her death—it was because she was a were-eagle that Lanaka died.

"And so I know there can be no peace between us and men. Their fear turns them against us to do what evil they may, and the only way to deal with them is to fulfill their fears so they will trouble us no more. The Council may decide for the others, but on my territory, no earth-bound man shall set foot and return unscathed!" Shaking with rage, Anakor turned and began to throw wood on the fire as if he would put it out.

But it was Orik, searching the forest for game, who saw the little group of men, moving antlike beside the faintly gleaming stream. Orik was thankful that Anakor had chosen to spend this day at the cave. He dreaded what the other could do to these creatures if he caught them at a bad place on the trail.

He did not hate the men. He did not want anyone hurt. Slowly, almost lazily, he began to descend.

Orik stood, hidden by the fringe of trees at the edge of the clearing, and watched. His nostrils, long unused to anything but the scent of roasting meat, flared as the odors of their cooking reached him. And there was their own scent, the scent of man.

But they were not quite like the people he had known. Their garments were all the same, not like the rough and colorful garb of villagers. Their speech was different too, and their women worked alongside the men. They were five—a big man with silver hair who seemed to be the leader, two other men, a stocky darkhaired woman, and one other, a tall girl, with hair that shone as sunlight glimmers on a mountain pool.

Orik watched, trying to understand them, and again and again his eyes rested on the bright-haired girl.

The falling shadows reminded him that Anakor waited. Taking bird-form once more, he made a quick and clumsy kill of a young bounder-doe, and bore it homeward, wings beating heavily in the dusk, wondering if Anakor would discover the intruders, and what would come if he did.

The steady chuckling of the little waterfall filled the air, masking the noise that Orik, unused to travel on the ground, made approaching the pool. Late afternoon sunlight slanted through the tall pines that stood round the water like a line of guards, and sparkled golden in the droplets clinging to the skin of the girl who bathed beneath the fall.

Orik watched her, moving backward into the bushes as she made her way to the bank and began to dress. Still watching, and stepping unaware, he trod upon a dry branch that snapped with a loud crack. He grasped wildly for balance at the nearest tree, and recovering, turned and found himself staring into her eyes.

"Hello?" she said after a frozen eternity.

Orik, with vague memories of taboos against nakedness, pulled the branches around him. He gazed at her, unable to think of any reply.

"Who are you? Do you understand what I say?" she asked, relaxing perceptibly as he made no move.

"Yes." he was able to get out.

The girl looked at him, frowning, and mechanically began to pull on her boots.

"You and your people, what do you here?" Orik asked suddenly.

"Well . . ." she began uncertainly, humoring him, "we are collecting things—plants and flowers and rocks—and making pictures of the animals and insects that we find."

"Why?"

"No one from our country has been in these mountains for a long time. We have only legends in our records, no real knowledge at all. We will take our samples and our reports to a place of learning where there are others like us—people who desire to know about the world and what it contains." She paused. "I didn't know anyone lived up here. Are you from a village nearby, or a hunter from the plains?"

He looked away, unable to meet her eyes. "I am . . . hunting," he answered at last.

"I must go—it's time for our evening meal. Would you like to eat with us? My name is Idella. Tell me yours and come meet my friends," she added, holding out her hand and smiling again.

Slowly, he stretched out his arm and enclosed her hand in his.

"No," he said. "I cannot come." He released her and turned away. Then for a moment he faced her once more. "I am Orik. Perhaps I will see you again." He smiled hesitantly, then darted behind the trees and was gone.

For a long moment she looked after him, her hand still hurting from his grip. Then she sighed a little, picked up her towel, and turned toward camp.

"They have been in our land three days, and you knew it, and were silent! Why?" Anakor's voice was harsh with anger hardly controlled. Orik opened his mouth to deny and then shut it, wondering how much his foster father knew. He bowed his head and let the storm beat about his ears.

"Three days ago you came home late with a lame story of scarce game and a poor kill. Yesterday you were gone again, and offered no story at all. You sit by the fire, and your thoughts are far away. You know my will—this land is forbidden to men! Why did you say nothing?"

"The men are on their way out of our territory . . . they will soon be gone. I know how you feel, but they seek to do no harm."

"They are men! It is their nature to do harm, just as it is ours to fly. Well, if they have discovered the way into my country, at least they will find no way out again!" He glared at Orik, challenging him to reply, but the young man was silent, and turned away.

The wind blew cold on Orik's bare skin as he and Anakor emerged from the cave. The east was buttressed with clouds from which an angry muttering could sometimes be heard. It was an evil day to be abroad, and likely to become more evil still. Orik shivered, and turned to his companion with sudden resolve.

"Father, I beg you not to do this!"

"No." Anakor did not turn his head.

"Then I will warn them!" Orik cried, taking a stride forward.

"Orik! Control yourself. You cannot fly like that, and you must not let them know what you are. I will not have you killed before my eyes!"

"Has it occurred to you that if they have weapons they may kill you instead?"

"With two of us, and the storm, and the place I shall choose, I think not!" and Anakor laughed.

Orik sobbed and fought for control. This was the father of his spirit, to whom he owed his life, and yet the face of the girl with the shining hair rose up before him as she had haunted his sleep.

Anakor laughed again, then stilled, and made his Change. In a moment he was launched upon the wind and winging swiftly southward. Orik, still battling with himself, swayed against the cliff wall. He forced himself to quiet, and gradually cold determination replaced his passion, a sense of purpose bleaker than the chill in the air. For a moment he poised, then the Change came upon him as well, and he followed Anakor.

Thunderheads filled the sky. The climbers, about to scale the last ridge, shivered in the cold wind. The barren and glacier-scoured wasteland that lay above the timber line had not even a bounder trail to lead the men and women who had ventured into it, and they must depend on their leader's eye for country to find a way through and down again.

Above them floated an eagle, as it had so often during the

past days. As the climbers reached the crest, a second joined it, hovering above it and a little behind.

Roped together, the humans were toiling downward now, toward the great rift that plunged a full mile from the peaks to the stream that cut its way still deeper into the cleft. It was faced with slide and slip and tumbled stone all the way down, and it was the only way out of the high country.

The noise of the waterfall echoed from the walls of the gorge, intermittently deafening as the wind changed. The climbers must pick their way beside it for fifty perilous feet before striking off across the face of the cliff once more. As they began their move, the first eagle began, in careful circles, to descend.

Orik watched Anakor go, saw him glide closer, closer, and then, with folded wings and talons outstretched, shoot toward the girl who was inching across the slippery stone.

Idella. . . .

She sagged against the line and cried out, her scream mingling with the hunting eagle's harsh cry. One stiletto talon hooked her tunic, ripping it from shoulder to waist. Her grip loosened, and scrabbling furiously, she slid toward the edge. Inches away, her partner hauled her up short, began to pull her toward the comparative safety of his ledge. Her hood had fallen back, and the wind whipped her hair about her like a flame.

Anakor swept away and up again to repeat his attack.

Orik saw her hair, and remembered the smooth perfection of her body beneath the waterfall. Anakor was oblivious of his presence, oblivious of all but his prey. He was beginning his terrible stoop once more. . . .

With a clarity outside of time, Orik was aware that he had folded his own wings, and felt the bitter air ruffle his feathers as he slashed between Anakor and his prey.

The attacker saw him and soared away from the cliff-face with a croak of rage. He sliced by Orik so near that their wing-tips almost touched. Then he had reversed, and was dropping like a falling star.

Orik wheeled as well, his smaller size giving him the advantage in the limited space. In that small corner of awareness that was all he knew of himself he felt as cold as the air.

But Anakor's eyes glowed like coals as Orik hurtled towards him. They struck, and then Anakor's form blurred and he screamed.

It was a scream that could only have come from a human throat.

Orik's eyes fixed as the outspread wings below him became the outflung arms of a man, flailing vainly as he plummeted toward the mists below. Orik's own momentum carried him away from the cliff, his paralyzed wings holding him steady as the wind lifted him.

Anakor had disappeared.

The wind whistled briefly in the silence. Then Orik's croak of despair echoed from the canyon walls as he folded his wings and dove downward after him.

The girl, still clinging to the cliff, watched uncomprehendingly as he vanished in the shadowy vastness below.

The eagle beat upward through the shimmer and swirl of the mists and past the rush of the falls, fighting the moisture that weighted his wings.

The climbers had made their way across the rock face and disappeared into the forest long ago, but Orik did not even pause to look for them. Upward—he must get higher . . . He strove toward the clean sky as once he had struggled up the mountain path.

He had piled rocks to hide Anakor's broken body, built a cairn to mystify any reasoning creature that might someday venture there. But still he saw the rage in Anakor's eyes as he fell, and the emptiness in them when Orik had ended his pursuing plunge beside the body at the foot of the falls.

The mountains dwindled beneath him. Orik caught an updraft, let it fling him past the lower clouds. And only then, when he was beyond all but the unveiled light of the sun, did he grow still, motionless in the eye of the wind.

Somewhere below him Idella and her companions were creeping toward the plains, easy to find if he willed. No one would forbid him to follow her now. No one, and nothing, but the image of Anakor's falling form.

And yet he would not return to the empty cave, and he had never really known the others of his kind . . .

Involuntarily he twitched a feather, slowly turned. Below him the world curved away like an upturned bowl.

Orik had no home now but the skies, and no kindred but the wind he rode. But he saw suddenly that all the world was his. For a few moments longer he hung in place.

Then he soared eastward, following the sun.

About Joel Hagen and *They Come and Go*

So many people pass through Greyhaven in any given year that I never learn all their names. One of the people I saw quite often at Greyhaven parties was a tall, blond look-alike for Luke Skywalker, who was introduced to me simply as "Chang" and whose real name I never knew.

In Phoenix, at the World SF convention (Iguanacon) while passing through the art show, I was attracted greatly by one of the exhibits, containing, among other small strange sculptures, the skeletal "bones" of a miniature winged man, complete with Latin taxonomy (*Homo aerialis*, or something like that). That year, two Greyhaven writers, myself and Randall Garrett, had been nominated for the Hugo awards; Randall's story "Laurelin" had been nominated for Best Short Story, and he was sitting in the enclosure kept for nominees, very dressed up with a ruffled shirt, with Vicki, whom you will meet later, holding his hand, and my *Forbidden Tower* had been nominated in the Novel category and I was sitting in the enclosure with Diana holding *my* hand. Despite the stress of the moment, I was pleased to hear that the winged-man exhibit had won the prize for best 3-dimensional art in the show, and asked Diana "Who is Joel Hagen?" As he came up the aisle to accept the award, she pointed him out and said, "You know him—that's Chang!"

Which goes to show that the talents of Greyhaven are not limited to science-fiction writing, and over the years I have seen a good deal of Joel's excellent artwork and sculpture. But when I asked Tracy Blackstone, who serves as agent for most of the Greyhaven writers, to send me anything she felt might serve for this anthology, I was astonished to find this odd, cryptic little story.

One of the tests I use for choosing material for an anthology is this; I read all the stories sent to me, and of those which I do not reject on sight for incompetence or some unsuitable quality, I try, two or three days later, to recall the story without re-reading it. If I cannot remember anything about it, I reject it.

"They Come and Go" remained clear in my mind, with its biting surreal images, for much more than the three days. For reasons which will be obvious when you have read this story, it reminded me of Richard Matheson's classic *Born of Man and Woman*.

I find this story quite unclassifiable, though I think it is more horror than fantasy . . . or is it? But I also found it quite unforgettable.

THEY COME AND GO

by Joel Hagen

Here comes that bug out of the kitchen. He shines like a penny when he flies. Maybe I could put him in a jar with some sticks and leaves.

I feel sick now. She must be trying to come through. The plaster on the wall is getting wet and part of the rug in front of it. I move the green chair away and stand across the empty room, because the smell of whatever wets things is so bad. I see part of her floating in the air, wet and pink, and throw newspapers under it so the rug won't get so messy. The rest of her comes slowly. Her eyes and mouth are stuck shut again and she sounds awful, wheezing and slopping trying to get her mouth clear. Her hands don't work good yet so I have to wipe her eyes and mouth with wet rags. Her eyes are real far apart and big, but I think she is a pretty lady.

She can talk now and has me draw the lines I know on the wall. She never touches that wall and I sure don't like to. As I finish the lines they look blurry, then I can't really tell where the wall is. I am so dizzy I can't stand up, and crawl around with my eyes closed to find the chair.

I sit in it and watch her talking in the middle of the floor. A place glows where her backbone ends, and another near her shoulders. She moves her arms in slow circles but her fingers dance like flies and leave scratchy lines dark in the air.

I hear a pop like a lightbulb breaking and one of the black things comes shooting out of the space in the lines and smashes into the back wall. It is messy and dead and ugly and she has to say other things and make new lines before the rest come through.

I know the big one. He came a year ago in the winter and wore my shoes and walked backwards by the ocean watching his footprints. He is the one ate my dog and then gave me his knife when I cried. Knife's no good anyway. I can't hang onto it when it's out of its bag, and I get cut whenever I put it back.

She got five through this time not counting the big one and the dead thing. I watch them move in the room and put themselves into old clothes and hats. Most of these can't wear shoes like some of the ones from winter, but it is dark out and only a few blocks from here to the Whitman house. I wish they hadn't changed Johnny Whitman. I liked to play outside with him before, but he won't do anything fun now. Just goes to stores to buy sugar and vinegar for them. Now there's that bug again. I wish I had a big jar. I wish I had another dog.

About Vicki Ann Heydron and *Cat Tale*

Vicki Ann Heydron entered the Greyhaven circle when she shared a taxi with me, enroute to Bill Crawford's Witchcraft and Sorcery Convention (later *Fantasy Faire,* since the previous title attracted too many occultists, Satanists and the like, whereas "Witchcraft and Sorcery" was simply the title of one of Bill Crawford's magazines!)

Vicki happened to hear me saying to a taxi driver that I was enroute to the hotel where the convention was being held, and asked to share my taxi. She was a little overawed at discovering that I was the Guest of Honor, but we quickly became friends, and later that day I introduced her to my brother Paul, and somewhat later to Randall Garrett, author of the well-known "Lord Darcy" fantasies.

While she was living among us, she and Randall discovered that they could work together and write together; one of Randall's best stories, "The Horror out of Time (a non-humorous pastiche of H.P. Lovecraft) was begun by Randall and continued by Vicki, then completed by Randall, in such seamless fashion that not even those well-acquainted with Randall's work could tell where Vicki's work began and Randall's left off. Sound familiar? Yes; it takes an expert to tell which of the stories published under the many Kuttner pen names in the fifties and sixties were by Hank Kuttner and which by Catherine Moore Kuttner. Pragmatically, like the Kuttners, the Garretts signed these works with Randall's name—as an established writer, he commanded a higher word-rate than did novice Vicki. Likewise, Vicki's first solo story, "Keepersmith," published under a joint by-line (to give Vicki credit) was marketed as by Randall *and* Vicki, for a higher word-rate from *Isaac Asimov's Adventure Story Magazine.* By this time it was obvious to Tracy Blackstone, agent for both Garretts, that Vicki's writing was fully as competent as Randall's, and during the prolonged hospitalization that interrupted their first novel—when Randall was, for a considerable time, in a deep coma, and then recuperating at length—no one had any qualms whatever about allowing Vicki, alone, to finish the novel they had begun together and discussed at length. *The Steel of Raithskar,* published by Bantam in 1981, is a splendid novel—I had read a part of it when Randall showed me the first four chapters, and on finishing it, my comment was "If Leigh Brackett were writing in the eighties, this is the kind of thing she would be writing!"

But even when she is not collaborating with Randall, Vicki Heydron Garrett has an equally sure hand with fantasy, with adventure, and with humor . . . as "Cat Tale," written for this anthology, certainly shows.

CAT TALE

by Vicki Ann Heydron

I

Katherine Christopher was wakened from a sound sleep by the deep-throated hunting growl of her Siamese cat, Martinique. It was coming from the balcony, through the sliding glass door that was always left open as an evening exit for the cat.

She got up and stepped quietly out into the moon-silvered night. Martinique was crouched on the side balcony railing, staring intently into the tree. Where he looked, the branches quivered as something caught there struggled and twittered with a sound Kathy had never heard before.

The cat's dark-tipped tail had been lashing with anticipation. Suddenly it grew still. Kathy lunged forward, catching the cat in mid-leap.

"Whatever that is," she scolded the loudly complaining cat. "It's trapped. That's not fair game."

She pulled Martinique's claws out of her bare arm and threw the Siamese lightly into the bedroom, sliding the door closed before he could dash out again. Then she leaned against the railing and looked up at the shadowed figure in the tree.

A disease of some kind, caught and arrested in its middle age, had redirected the topmost growth of the tree so that it leaned closer to the corner of the building. One of its stronger branches grew parallel to the outside railing of Kathy's balcony, about three feet just above it. Last year many of the encroaching branches had been cut away, but she had asked that this one be spared. It was convenient for Martinique as a private entrance to her second-story apartment.

The high-pitched twittering came from a dark area above and beyond the "doorway" branch, where new growth from the cut branches had created a dense green tangle.

"I knew this would happen sometime," Kathy said aloud. "Those stupid Miller boys—there's enough of their kiteline in this tree to snarl up an elephant."

She lifted the long skirt of her nightgown and stepped up to the seat of a white wrought-iron chair, then stepped cautiously to the top of the wide wood-trimmed railing, testing it with her weight, holding the branch for support.

Now she could see *where* it was; a dark silhouette moving against the slightly lighter background of the matted inner branches of the tree. She had thought it must be a bird, from the twitter-chirp sounds it made—but the silhouette was too long and too thick.

She glanced down, regretted it instantly, and looked back at the trapped creature.

"I can't leave you here!" she told it impatiently. "If Martinique doesn't get you, another cat will."

She curled her toes over the edge of the railing, then braced her hips against the lower branch and reached with both hands for the moving shape.

"Take it easy," she said to it. "Don't bite, or scratch, or sting or anything. I'm really trying to help."

As though it understood, the small figure quieted. One of Kathy's hands closed gently around it.

It wasn't a bird. It was warm and furry and . . . odd. A gust of wind whispered through the tree, raising the flesh on her arms.

Kathy supported the strange creature with one hand and

with the other pulled at the line which had it trapped in the web of branches.

She was thoroughly uncomfortable. The bark of the tree was rough on her thighs through the thin nylon, and the strain of the awkward position was making her arms and legs ache.

She thought, belatedly, of the sewing scissors in her bedtable drawer. *Too late now,* she moaned silently. *If I ever get down from here safely, no way would I ever get back up!*

So she struggled one-handed with the stubborn string. Just as she began to fear that she really *couldn't* do it, the last strand broke so abruptly that she lurched forward. She doubled over and clutched the branch with all her strength, closing her eyes and holding her breath until the swaying stopped. And, just for good measure, a few years longer.

Then she oozed down off the railing to sit blankly in the chair. Her head was throbbing, her heart was pounding painfully, her thighs had been badly scratched on the branch, and every muscle ached.

The creature, which she had carried carefully even through her own danger, lay quiet and trusting in her hand.

At last she could breathe again. She looked down at the bundle and hastily began to unwrap it. When it was free of the last bits of string, it flew from her lifted hand to hover lightly in front of her face. She stared at it.

Clearly visible now in the moonlight, the thing she had rescued was about ten inches long, and shaped like a man—with wings. It seemed longer than it should be, as though a man had been shrunk and then stretched. Its feet were like hands; they had opposing thumbs. It was covered with a fine, shiny softness—she had thought, when touching it, that it was fur. But it might be down.

The wings were thin, almost transparent membranes, visible only in their reflection and refraction of the moonlight. Oval eyes that looked like opals were set at 45-degree angles in its smooth, graceful head.

It was watching her with interest. She smiled at it and said, "You're . . . more than beautiful. You're exquisite."

She had a flash vision of finding this lovely creature *after* Martinique had reached it, and she shuddered. "I'm so glad that you're safe."

She *felt* from it. A sense of friendliness, a clinging, caressing warmth, altogether pleasant. Its words came directly into her mind.

"*You valnish our gratitude and ferdingly a lollom until lunar-solar rejuxtaposition thersh.*"

Then it flew away.

II

Katherine was exhausted and shaky from the physical effort and the intellectual shock of what she had seen. She walked back into her apartment in a daze and sat down on the bed, pulling the bloodied nightgown away from her skin to examine the scrapes. They were ugly but superficial, and they had stopped bleeding. She decided she could tend to them in the morning; she slid under the covers with a sigh of relief.

When the sliding door had been opened for him, Martinique had streaked out to the tree and sniffed around in disappointment. Now he jumped up beside her, nosed her cheek, and wandered down to settle himself on the foot of her bed.

Suddenly Kathy wasn't sure it had really happened.

Wouldn't she feel almost exactly like this if she had just wakened from a dream?

Some dream, she thought fuzzily. *A gorgeous little creature that can't exist, and which thinks a language I can almost understand. That's fantasy. But then there's an element of reality, too. Me doing exactly what I would actually do in that kind of situation: nearly break my fool neck.*

Her mind was moving in that comfortable wedge between sleeping and waking where the truth is sometimes clear and seldom frightening. She clung to the mood, knowing that it was in these periods that she learned a great deal about herself. She let her thoughts wander in and around the "dream."

I suppose my subconscious is trying to tell me what I already know but won't admit—I'm stuck in a rut which is slowly destroying me. I need a change, something different.

And this damned vacation isn't it! It was a mistake from the beginning. Hawaii—this year of all years, when I'm twenty pounds over my normal overweight. Remember trying on swimsuits that day? I looked in the mirror and couldn't

*find my waist. I was so depressed I stopped on the way home
for a double caramel sundae.*

She was more awake now, but she fought to keep the
stream of insight flowing. She had recognized the symptoms
these last few months—overeating, lethargy, continual nervous headaches—of a problem she couldn't identify . . . or
wouldn't face.

*How "different" will this vacation be, anyway, from my
daily life? Like all the rest of them—a tour, with visits
planned and sights preselected to see. A vacation pro-
grammed for me—the way my job is run by other people.*

*I can't blame Mr. Lodge for preferring the system he
created. But I'm the one who has to work the extra hours
necessary to keep modern volume flowing through twenty-
year-old purchasing procedures.*

*I've put a lot of time and thought into the design of the
new system. It will process purchase orders in half the time
and leave me room to set up the automatic recorder program
Mr. Hodges keeps saying we need.*

*But he says the transition will take too much time, and he
won't let me . . .*

WON'T LET ME?

*I've been there six years now, I'm thirty-two years old and
a hefty hunk of a woman, I know I'm right, and . . .*

*I'm chicken. I'm afraid to lay it on the line: my way—or I
QUIT!*

I'm just too damned comfortable. *I make enough money
there to keep this nice place and do a good bit of traveling. I
don't want to "rock the boat." Even though I could do a better job or—let's be honest—maybe enjoy my traveling more
if I had the courage to make my own decisions and take the
chance of being wrong.*

She moved restlessly in the bed, disturbing Martinique.
With a flip of his tail that was the dynamic equivalent of
"Hmph!" he jumped down to the floor, trotted out to the bal-
cony through the open door, and disappeared into the tree.

A cat doesn't care, she thought, watching him. *Martinique
does things his own way all the time, without wondering
about the decisions he makes.*

*Perhaps it's only this that separates men from animals—
that men must consider the consequences of their actions.*

Suddenly she smiled. *So that's what's been bothering me. I'm a human being who wants to be a cat. Or at least to acquire cat qualities. Beauty. Independence. Grace. Confidence.*

The smile faded as she remembered finding Martinique ready to destroy the pretty life caught in the tree.

What about savagery? Is that part and parcel of the other, more humanly desirable qualities?

She turned over on her side and scrunched the pillow comfortably under her head.

An interesting problem. The only way I'll ever find the answer is to be a cat myself. For a moment her sleepy mind played with the idea, and she concluded, *I think it would be worth it. Worth the violence to have the other things. I do wish that I could find out what it's like to be a cat.*

As for what happened tonight, she decided, *in the morning I'll look and see if my legs are really scraped. I could do it now—but I want to believe in my beautiful friend a little longer . . .*

She drifted off into sleep.

At twelve-eighteen and one quarter, the moon was exactly full.

III

The shrill scream of the alarm clock galvanized her into wakefulness.

That idiot thing has gotten louder!

She lunged to the side of the bed, reaching for the clock, but her hands felt clumsy and her legs were oddly tangled in the bedclothes. She overbalanced at the edge of the mattress, and fell out of bed, scrabbling at the nightstand for support.

It toppled too. A half-full glass of water flipped backward and shattered against the wall, leaving a large wet stain. The bedside lamp fell outward and then was jerked back by its cord. It lay on the floor, its shade crooked, its bulb miraculously intact. Two cone-shaped bottles of nail polish rolled in random curves on the thick carpet, finally stopped.

The wind-up alarm clock was lying on its face and still producing its nerve-jarring shriek.

Katherine heaved herself around and slapped angrily at it.

The glass over its face crunched and a welcome silence arrived.

Good! I've always hated that thing.

My God, what a way to wake up! How stupid to fall out of bed—I haven't done that since I was five years old.

And why did I do it this morning? I feel so odd . . .

She looked at the hand which had smashed the clock.

It was a paw.

Her first reaction was, *I'm still dreaming!* but she rejected it instantly. Not because the experience felt particularly real. In fact, the room around her had that sharp, extra-clear quality that sometimes occurs in dreams. But she always dreamed in color—and this world was sharply focused black and white.

Scent provided the variety lacking in her visual perception. Strongest was the sweet fragrance of the planter-grown alyssum on her balcony. From the kitchen came the sharpness of onion remnants, and from the bathroom the light scent of her bath oil mingled with the earthiness of Martinique's litter box. She caught a whiff of "tangy green" from the leaves of the tree that loomed over her balcony. . . .

And she remembered.

So that's what the little whoozit said! It granted me a wish (listen to me talking in fairy tales but what else would explain this?) and I didn't even know it!

She felt indignant. To be given a chance like that in such a haphazard, unfair way. . . .

Or was it unfair? This way there was no conscious striving for what might be artificial goals. She had been allowed to make her choice on the totally impractical basis of desire.

And last night I wanted so much to be like Martinique. Do I look like him? she wondered, through a kind of hysterical calm. *Sleek and dark? Maybe longer fur?*

Ooomph!

She wanted to go around the end of the bed and look in the mirrors on her closet doors, but when she tried to stand up, the long nightgown jerked tight around her neck, throwing her off balance. The thud she made on the carpeted floor seemed, to her newly sensitive ears, hugely loud. The lamp jumped, and the nail polish bottles rolled a few inches.

A small nudge of doubt took root in her mind: Of course,

she couldn't imagine Martinique ever falling over his own feet, but if he did, she was certain there would be no such floor-bouncing.

Suddenly she was very anxious to see what she looked like. She stood up cautiously and tried to back out of the soft folds of her nightgown. When that didn't work she rolled on her side, pulling at it clumsily with all four feet. At last she stood free of a mass of shredded nylon that her memory told her was a bright yellow.

It was well past dawn and sunlight streamed in from the balcony doors as she finally looked into the mirror and saw the image of what Kathy Christopher had become.

There was one endless moment during which she balanced on the edge of panic. But then her sense of humor surged upward through all the strangeness.

Laughter rumbled softly in her throat as she stared at the creature in the mirror. Its jaws opened and a long tongue fell out, and that seemed funny. Its tail whipped back and forth, and the mind of Kathy Christopher shrieked with laughter.

She was not hysterical, but delighted.

Empirical proof at last that a person can't change her true nature! I may be a cat now . . . but I'm the same kind of cat that I was a human!

That's *why none of those transformation stories I heard when I was a kid seemed real to me. A prince into a frog, indeed! A prince is a hundred times bigger than a frog— where does the rest of him go?*

It made perfect sense. She had wished for the beauty and grace of a Siamese cat. But she had become . . .

A plumpish mountain lion.

She paced back and forth in front of the mirror, growing accustomed to the horizontal movement. She experimented with the spinal muscles that sent her tail whipping—what a sense of power it gave her! She felt generally stronger and, in spite of her incomplete control, more graceful. She felt and looked—comparatively—lighter than she had been.

That puzzled her until she reasoned it out. The musculature of a big cat is quite different from that of a human, thicker and more efficient. Some of her extra human weight had been absorbed into the denser muscle tissues of the cat, leaving only a relatively small roll of fat around her middle.

Her hair had been a dusty blond, a nice color, but rather drab, it had seemed to her. Watching the play of gleam and shadow along the side of the moving mirror image, she was sure that the color was just right for her lion's fur.

Her eyes were large and luminous, as mysterious as Martinique's. Her own eyes had been a bluish-green—had that color transferred? Was it the right color for a mountain lion's eyes?

Reflex had brought out her claws when she was trying to free herself from the nightgown. Now she extended them deliberately. It gave her a shivery feeling.

She began to scratch at the thick rug, clawing at it in exactly the same way she was forever telling Martinique *not* to. Hind legs stiffly vertical, forelegs and chest nearly on the floor—the delightful pulling sensation ran clear to her shoulders.

She froze at the sound of a step in the hallway beyond the living room. Someone knocked softly on her front door.

IV

"Kathy? Ready to go, hon?"

Marcia! Oh my God, she did insist last night at dinner that she would help me downstairs with my bags. And I gave her my extra key so she could water the plants and feed Martinique.

If she finds me in here, she'll have a stroke! What can I do?

"Kathy?" the voice said again, then fell into a mutter. "Probably still in the shower. Well, we've got plenty of time yet—" The key slipped into the lock and turned. "I'll surprise her with some coffee."

Kathy looked around wildly, noticing in passing that the round-tipped ears of the cat in the mirror were turned back, almost flat against the wide, smooth head. Seeing no other choice, she dived to shelter on the floor on the side of the bed away from the partially open bedroom door just as her friend stepped into the living room. She heard Marcia catch her breath as she saw that the bathroom was empty.

"Kathy?" There was a tremor of nervousness. "Kathy? where are you? Answer me!" She came slowly toward the bedroom. Kathy pushed herself as close to the bedframe as she could. Her whole attention was focused on Marcia.

Martinique padded in silently from the open balcony door and hissed at the huge tawny bulk cowering beside the bed.

Kathy screamed with surprise, leaped into the air, and landed on the bed facing the mirrors.

Martinique, you idiot!

Marcia peered around the door, stared in shock and horror. She looked from Kathy, crouched defensively on the bed, to Martinique, backed against the glass of the door with fur on end and ears laid back, and finally to the shredded, bloody nightgown on the floor. Then she slammed the door shut and ran screaming across the living room toward the hallway.

Kathy heard another sound from Martinique and turned to see him ready to launch his twelve-pound body at her. It was touching, and frightening—she knew that Martinique might hurt her badly before she could summon the control to defend herself. And then she might have to kill him.

She lunged at the Siamese with her best snarl, and he gave way. With a last defiant hiss, he fled out the balcony exit.

Marcia will call the police for sure—I've got to get out of here, and fast! She'll take care of Martinique for me.

She considered following Martinique down the tree, but rejected it when she remembered how the branch had swayed under her weight. No, she would have to get out of the building in human fashion—through the hallway and down the stairs.

She ran to the bedroom door and spent a frustrating few seconds trying to turn the knob with her paws. Then she told herself savagely, *Stop thinking like a human, damn it! Use what works!*

She stretched up her head and caught the faceted glass knob between her teeth, turned and pulled, backing away awkwardly. A paw caught the door open, and she was in the living room. That door, too, was closed. She tried the knob; it turned. She took a deep breath.

Well, here goes. Let's make it fast, catgirl.

She pulled the door open and ran through. There were people in the hallway, whispering. Now they screamed and scrambled for their own doors.

"My God, it really *is* a mountain lion!"

"Poor Kathy!"

The voices followed her as she raced down the hall toward the stairs and the elevator. Then a man's voice cut through the rest.

"Get outta my way, all of you! Give me a clear shot!"

Shot?

She remembered that Fred Hastings had boasted about his security, his shotgun.

SHOT?

She dug her claws into the carpet to make the last sharp turn into the stairwell, banging her head painfully on the swinging door. The shotgun fired just as she lunged through.

"I've got another load—I'll get that killer!" she heard Hastings shout as he ran down the hall after her.

Her head was ringing from the blow of the heavy door. She tripped on the top stair and rolled bumpily down to the half-story landing. The door above her swung open and she dived recklessly down the next set of steps, using the twisting stairs themselves as cover.

She barrelled out into the lobby and skidded to a stop.

The security door! I can't get out without a key!

Hastings wasn't the fool he seemed, for he paused at the lobby landing and pushed the swinging door slowly outward. She launched herself, timing it this time so that her steel-springy forelegs would strike the door first. She slammed through it, knocking the man backwards, and her leap carried her halfway down the last flight of stairs. The man swore, sat up and fired again, but she made it around the landing. Then she was in the parking level, following a departing car up the ramp and out through the automatic door, running through the streets of San Francisco in a nightmare of panic.

V

She lay in a weedy field beside a broken board fence. A black and white car pulled up beside it. She gathered herself to bolt, but the policemen didn't get out of their car. They rolled down the windows, checked in Code 7 on the radio, and started complaining good-naturedly about brown bags and the remaining distance to payday. She settled down, glad beyond words for the unknowing human company.

"Hey, Frank," one of them said suddenly, "why are we looking for that cat?"

Silence. Then: "You *want* a mountain lion loose in the City?"

"No, I mean, why us? The sheriff's got bloodhounds—why not just track it down?"

Good question. Frank? What's the answer?

"*In* the City? With all the cars. The stink of gasoline would cover up anything else, but it doesn't have to. One whiff and a dog's sense of smell is paralyzed for hours."

"Oh. So bloodhounds are out." The other detective sounded disappointed. "What the hell is a mountain lion doing in San Francisco, anyway?"

She could almost hear Frank shrug. "Who knows. Maybe it's somebody's pet, Bert."

"Maybe," Bert said, in a solemn tone that frightened her, "maybe it's rabid." He waited out a short silence, then added, "And maybe we'll find it tonight and bring this case to a rabid conclusion."

"Aw, shut up and eat your peanubutternjelly!"

When they drove away she laid her head down on her forelegs and tried to relax. *No bloodhounds* was welcome information. The suspicion of rabies, however lightly stated, was not.

With part of her mind alert for sound or scent which might signal her detection, she tried to examine what had happened to her.

Transmutation. She was awed by the power it must have taken. What was the small flying creature she had rescued? A "fairy"—something real that formed the basis for all the legends and the children's stories?

Or an alien? Someone with perceptions and powers that had no relation to the natural laws which apply to humans?

I'll never know.

What was it that it said to me? "*You*" something "*our gratitude*" . . . *and something else. Obviously it meant that if I wanted to be a cat, why sure thing!*

She sighed, and smiled inwardly.

Thanks anyway, little friend, for your good intentions.

At dusk she rose and set out to satisfy the hunger that had been growing steadily more acute. She had been some hours

in that field and had considered a number of methods of se-
curing food. She wasn't yet hungry enough to go digging in
garbage cans, and she could hardly walk into Fred's sandwich
shop and order a poorboy sub.

She located a supermarket and waited near the back door,
concealed in the shadow of the empty crates. When the shift
changed and people came out the bar-latched double door,
she crept close enough to catch the door before it closed. She
slipped through, crossed the crowded stock room, and made
her way to the butcher's back room.

A man was there, chopping chickens and packaging them.
Just this side of him was a rack with the biggest, juiciest T-
bones she had ever seen, and the smell of the fresh meat almost made her crazy.

She forced herself to wait there nervously, hoping the
butcher would go out front before somebody discovered her
in the stock room. Instead another man in a soiled white
apron came in from the front, stacked the packaged chickens
on a tray, and carried them out to the meat counter.

The butcher picked up a loin of pork, turned away from
her to the electric saw, and began slicing chops.

I'm not going to get a better chance.

She crept into the room, keeping the central chopping table
between her and the butcher as long as she could. Then she
dashed to the side counter and caught a couple of the steaks
in her jaws.

The butcher turned around and yelled out in surprise.

She ran for the door, but her paws slipped on the slick
linoleum, and her strength was wasted in a panicky scrabbling. Suddenly she felt a sharp, stinging pain just behind her
left shoulder. A bloody cleaver thudded into the wall beside
the doorway.

She dropped the steaks and whirled, snarling her outrage.

You son of a bitch! You tried to kill me!

He was yelling something, and his face was deathly white
behind a heavy black mustache. She gathered her feet under
her and sprang for him—but he had fled through the front
door. She almost followed him.

What am I doing? I've got to get out of here!

She snatched up one of the steaks and ran out the back
way, pulling down on the inside bar to release the catch on

the door. She couldn't stop to eat the steak now, even though its tantalizing juice seeped out around her sharp teeth and trickled down her throat. The alarm was out again—she needed to find a safe place.

So for the second time that day she was running full speed through the city streets. And this time not fear, but anger drove her. Not even stupid Fred Hastings and his shotgun had created such a rage in her. They had *both* been in a panic then, and Hastings had believed—wrongly, but sincerely—that she had killed someone.

What did I do to that butcher? I took a couple of lousy steaks from a stack of hundreds. He certainly knew I wasn't going to hurt him—I just wanted enough food to keep alive.

Probably afraid for his job if somebody steals from him. So he throws a cleaver at me, damn near cuts my head off. The bastard!

Her shoulder was hurting her, but she ran and fumed, keeping to the darkest streets she could find. The few hardy souls who tried to follow her were soon far behind. When she thought it was safe, she paused in a deserted alley to catch her breath.

There was a ladder leading to the roof of the one-story building on her left. On her first try, she found she wasn't built for human-style ladder-climbing; she dropped to the ground and backed away, then took a running start and jumped as high as she could. Her forepaws steadied her against a step of the ladder, her hind paws groped, found solid footing, and propelled her upward, onto the roof.

There was a skylight in the roof, and a wavering light in the darkened room underneath it. A whisper: "Help me with this TV, for chrissakes! We gotta be outa here in ten minutes!"

She padded softly across the roof to the next building. *Sorry*, she told the unknown owners of the TV, *but this time it's true: I really can't afford to get involved.*

The buildings here were jammed together shoulder to shoulder with their roofs more or less even. She moved down the block along the alley, jumping up or down a few feet at each joining, until she came to the last roof. Then she collapsed, releasing the steak to rest on her forepaws. Hungry as she was, she had to rest for a minute.

Blood had clotted over the wound in her shoulder, shielding it from the air and making it sting less. She tried to reach back and lick at it, but it was too high on her back.

If it were that bad, she assured herself, *I wouldn't have been able to run.*

Now for the steak.

She knew perfectly well that she ought to clamp the meat to the roof, spear it with one paw, and start tearing chunks from it. But the roof was filthy, grimy with settled smog and the portable litter of the higher hills.

Raw steak I can live with. I refuse, however, to eat dirty raw steak.

She sat on her haunches and held the steak between the claws of her forepaws, nibbling at it as delicately as she could.

Some mountain lion, she chided herself. *I feel more like a squirrel.*

Besides, this steak isn't going to be enough. I should have taken that loin of pork.

Or, better yet, the butcher.

VI

The thought startled her. And the feeling that had come with it. A thrill of . . . anticipation.

She finished the steak and dropped into a crouch to gnaw the bone. She flipped the small sharp edge of it from one side of her mouth to the other.

She tried to summon and analyze the fiery rage that had taken her when the cleaver cut through her shoulder. *I was ready to kill that man. I wanted to kill him.*

And not because he hurt me. I could cope with a simple reaction to pain, if I believed that's what it was. But I don't believe it. A natural cat would have been frightened by the pain and run even faster.

No, I turned on that butcher for a totally human reason. He offended me by throwing that cleaver.

And I was worried about the savagery of a cat?

She tongued out the bone and began to pace.

I've got to get out of this city. If I don't, they'll kill me, or . . .

The conviction rang through her that if she ever succeeded in killing a man with teeth and claws, the last shred of her humanity would leave her.

What am I thinking? Am I human now?

The answer was there before the question was properly formed, and it sent her purposefully to the edge of the roof.

Yes! I may look like a mountain lion, but I am a woman named Katherine Christopher. I can reason. I can make choices.

And I choose to get the hell out of this city before somebody gets hurt!

Thanks to the hilly contours of San Francisco, on this end of the block the roof was four stories high. She eased herself over the edge and started down the stairway-styled fire escape that zigzagged down the wall. The metal grids that formed the steps were sharp and hurt her paws. She made it down to the first landing and had almost decided to go back up to the roof when a police car pulled into the mouth of the alley and stopped right below her.

She shrank into the shadow below the dimly lighted window, risked a quick glance into the room beyond it. An elderly black couple were "watching" television—the man was asleep on the sofa and the woman was dozing in her rocking chair.

Footsteps on the roof, then a voice called out from directly above her.

"Jensen!"

A man got out of the car below her, looked up and moved to get his line of sight clear of the fire escape.

"Got 'em?" he called.

"Yeah. Just the two of 'em. All clear."

"Right. See you later."

The car drove off and footsteps retreated from the edge of the roof. She discovered she could breathe.

"There were twelve sightings reported today of the mountain lion . . ." The voice from the television set drew her back from her intention to leave.

There was a brief report of the encounter at the supermarket. There was no confirmation of the butcher's opinion that he had fatally wounded the mountain lion. That incident was, however, unlike the other reports, documented by other witnesses.

"In response to a request from the authorities that our viewers receive accurate information about the size, coloring and probable behavior of pumas, reporter Jerry Rogers is right now with Dr. Kenneth Lawson in his Wildlife Research Institute in the mountains near Santa Cruz. Jerry . . . ?"

"Thank you, Bob. I'm here with Dr. Lawson in his home, which is also the main building of the research center . . ."

She looked through the window at the TV screen. The flickering hurt her eyes, but she got an impression of a comfortable panelled room with two men in chairs near a huge stone fireplace.

"Have you any idea, Doctor, how a mountain lion could have arrived unseen in the middle of San Francisco?"

"Only unnaturally."

Boy, is that *an understatement!*

"I mean to say," the Doctor continued, "that it is impossible that a puma could have wandered into the city by itself. Someone must have brought it in as an illegal pet."

"Perhaps the woman in whose apartment it was found? The one it is believed was——"

"The one who has *disappeared,*" the doctor interrupted. "There is no evidence which satisfies me that the woman is dead, much less that the puma harmed her."

You tell him, Doc!

"What about the butcher who was attacked?"

"It seems likely that the cat was drawn into the market by the smell of meat, and the butcher surprised it in such a way that it was terrified."

"Are you saying, Dr. Lawson, that this mountain lion *isn't* dangerous?"

"By no means," answered the deep baritone voice she was beginning to like. "Especially since we have no way of knowing how badly it was wounded, and a wounded cat is more suspicious, more easily frightened.

"What I *am* saying is that the puma is naturally shy of man. It has unbelievable digestive powers; it can eat almost anything and survive." *I'll remember that.* "There is no reason to expect it to attack men unless it is directly threatened by them."

The camera zoomed in on the doctor's face, and she strained to get a clear picture of him through the flickering. He seemed young, with thick light hair and a neatly trimmed, curly beard. He looked directly into the camera, and she couldn't avoid the impression that he was talking specifically to her.

"This animal is a member of a highly endangered species, and it would be a waste to destroy it without first making every effort to capture it alive. We have plenty of room here, and facilities to care for it properly. I'm sure that I speak for the Institute in offering to shelter the puma until its origins and owner, if any, can be determined."

The camera pulled back again as a huge mountain lion padded into the room, causing the reporter to sit up straighter in his chair. Dr. Lawson reached out to scratch the cat's neck.

"This is Sir George," he introduced the cat, "who was raised here from kittenhood. From what I understand from the eyewitness reports, your puma is considerably smaller than George and a lighter tan in color. Probably it is a female."

She didn't listen to the rest of it. She had already known that she had to leave the City. Now she knew where she was going.

She went down the stairs with reckless speed, the cold metal frame quivering and ringing as she caromed around the tight square helix. She reached the first floor landing . . .

And stepped off into empty air.

Too late she remembered that these old apartments had a swing-down arrangement for the last few feet of the fire escape. She twisted frantically.

Cats always land on their feet. Don't they?

The reflexes were there; she did all the right things. But there was too much mass and not enough reaction speed. Her one-eighty slammed through a haphazard pile of cardboard boxes and she hit asphalt solidly on her left side. The boxes splashed out of her way and littered the alley, some of them coming down on top of her. She might have been grateful for the concealment they provided—if she had been conscious.

She woke up in a panic, gulping for air. She lay still and tried to breathe more steadily, and the burning pain in her side eased a little.

She moved cautiously. She hadn't broken anything and she hadn't stiffened up, so she guessed she hadn't blacked out for very long. She could hear street noises and voices—mostly women—laughing and calling out. But no evidence that the disturbance in the alley had been noticed.

She slipped out from under the boxes, suppressing a groan as she stood up. A glance into the street confirmed that at this late hour the neighborhood was the prowling ground of a different breed of cat. A few minutes of careful walking brought the soreness under control.

In spite of the pain she was feeling better. For the first time since this incredible thing happened to her, she had a definite goal.

Keeping to the darker streets and avoiding people, she began her journey to Santa Cruz. And Dr. Kenneth Lawson.

VII

It was important that none of the widespread reports of her sightings be reinforced by someone *actually* seeing her. She decided that she couldn't afford pride.

She investigated garbage cans, over the protests of their regular clientele. She managed to eat one cricket. She swiped a grocery bag from the back of a half-unloaded station wagon and feasted on raw eggs and milk.

Once, driven by the smell of *cooked* food, she leaped a six-foot hedge to snatch an enormous roast from an unattended rotisserie barbecue. It burned her mouth—but it tasted so good!

Mostly she just didn't eat. She discovered that trying to track a straight line through a maze of suburbs and across open country was a very different proposition from driving along the highway.

Finally, one afternoon she followed the sun west to the ocean and began to move along the shoreline. Eventually she reached Santa Cruz, and another two days of sweeping ever-wider half-circles inland brought her to her present position.

She wasn't sure what she had expected of the Wildlife Institute. But as she looked down on it from the hillside, she knew she *should* have expected this. A zoo. Large cages to be sure, constructed to be as comfortable and environmentally suitable for their occupants as possible. But cages nonetheless.

But I wouldn't be shot at, she told herself. *I'd be safe.*

Safe—inside a cage? another part of her mind sneered. *Still willing to sacrifice anything for security, aren't you?*

In the largest compound, uncovered and cleverly bordered with impassable ditches of smooth concrete, was George. He was lying on a large flat rock in front of a man-made cave. The large puma's head lifted and turned toward her. He stood up, sniffing the air, making sure of her scent. Then he called out to her, a fierce and beautiful sound that brought her to her feet and sent her down the hill to stop, confused, just outside the open gate in the stone wall which circled the Institute.

Beyond the gate was a large green-lawned area, and beyond that a house. A man came out of the house, looking toward the big cat. There was a wire-enclosed run which led from George's living area into a row of cages. Kathy guessed it must be his feeding cage. The man called out, and the puma came down off his miniature mountain and into the cage.

Kathy had recognized Dr. Kenneth Lawson. She listened now to the warm voice she had heard via television signal as it spoke to Sir George in comforting, affectionate tones. But though the cat rubbed against the wire fence to permit the man's touch, he remained restless.

"Something's got you stirred up," said Dr. Lawson. "I think I'll go take a look."

He started back for the house, tamping ashes out of his pipe. "Charlie," he called. "Get the jeep out . . . Holy . . . !"

He stopped dead still when he saw her, crouched uncertainly just beyond the gate.

"Scratch that, Charlie. Get the sleep gun and stay out of sight. We've got a visitor."

Dr. Lawson in person was even more impressive than the image she had strained to see on the TV screen. He was tall and Nordic, in T-shirt and jeans; she could see that he kept himself in good physical shape.

A flicker of movement at the edge of the house gave her a glimpse of Charlie: black hair and sunglasses.

"I've got a clear shot from here," he said softly.

"Not unless she spooks," said Dr. Lawson. "Look at her. The condition of her fur. That ugly scratch must be where the cleaver got her. No, I'd bet my career this is the first time she's been out on her own. She *wants* to trust us. She's used to humans."

He squatted down and held out his hand, even though they were some ten yards apart. "Come on in, girl. We won't hurt you."

She hesitated. She knew she had come here because of Dr. Lawson, because his had been the only voice raised in her favor. She was exhausted and hungry and desperately in need of the comfort she would find here.

Yet—the long ordeal of her journey here had wrought a change in her. She had become accustomed to *avoiding* contact with humans. And George's welcoming cry had stirred a restive wildness in her.

George called again and pressed against the wire of his cage.

The man smiled. "Come on, Lady. Come in and stay awhile."

She decided.

The strong fingers of the man's hand searched out a spot just behind her left ear and began scratching gently. She lay down on the fragrant lawn and rolled over. He laughed with delight and rubbed the fur on her chest. In a momentary flash of human panic, she realized he was touching her where her breasts should be, and that she was naked. Then she laughed at herself.

All he sees is a cat. And a scroungy one, at that. But he wants me here. He'll keep me safe.

She butted his arm with her head and rubbed her jaw along his hand. If she had been a woman in body, she would have wept for joy.

Being a cat, she learned to purr.

VIII

Charlie cleaned and bandaged the neglected cleaver wound. Ken brushed her coat free of burrs and insects and she was allowed to eat sparingly.

Through it all, she was carefully obedient and cooperative,

lying absolutely still except for an occasional involuntary wince of pain. Ken commented, with some puzzlement, on her high level of intelligence.

It was near dusk when they finished, and Charlie said, "Don't you think we ought to cage her for the night? Don't forget she found her way out of a city apartment with no trouble."

She laid back her ears and Ken laughed. "Will you look at that? I swear she really *understands* the words we say." He sat on his bed. She jumped up to the foot of it, but he pushed her off. "All right, Lady. I won't ask you to sleep in a cage if you won't try to sleep on my bed. Go on out and make yourself comfortable on the sofa. Go on, now."

Reluctantly, she obeyed. As she trotted down the short hallway to the living room—the one she had seen on television—she could hear their voices.

"I don't think she'll try to leave," Ken was saying. "She seems really happy with us. And no wonder—she's been through quite an ordeal."

"Can we keep her here?" asked Charlie. "What about her owner?"

"I'll *find* a way to keep her, Charlie. She deserves extended study. I've never met a smarter animal."

She jumped up on the sofa and settled down, chewing over an ethical problem which had just occurred to her.

He thinks I'm really a mountain lion. In order to find out why I'm so smart and so trainable, he will redirect his research. It will ruin his career if he can't raise another puma to be as intelligent as . . . Raise another . . . Uh-oh . . .

Charlie put it into words.

"Are you planning to breed her to Sir George?"

"You bet your life. She could be the start of a whole new branch of the cat family."

The world crashed around her—again. She laid her head on her paws and felt like crying.

Well, what did I expect? Did I think Dr. Ken Lawson, he of the honest face and the winning smile, would take one look at me and say, "Here is a woman who just happens to be a mountain lion?"

Would I respect a man gullible enough to accept something as crazy as that?

Of course *he thinks I'm only a special-type cat. And he's a scientist—it's part of his job to breed laboratory animals. For that matter, I* am *a mountain lion, and I suppose if you look at him right, George is quite a handsome fellow.*

So why do I feel as if a gorgeous playboy has just suggested that I go out with his pimply-faced nephew instead?

Ken walked past her to the kitchen, filled and drank a glass of water. As he came back through the living room he stopped to stroke her head. She managed to purr for him.

The least she could do was say good-bye.

When she was sure they were both asleep, she figured out a paw-and-jaw operation to work the thumb-latched front door, and ran out into the night. She knew it was foolish and that it would raise the household, but something compelled her to stop at the gate and call a farewell to Sir George.

He answered her, and as she fled into the brush of the hillside down which she had come—had it been only that afternoon?—she understood why his voice stirred her so deeply. His was a cry of loneliness.

She headed straight through the wildest country she could find, knowing that the jeep could never follow her fast enough. But beyond that, she refused to think about what she had done or why. She ran on, climbing ever higher into the hills, hoping that exhaustion would kill the sense of loss that ached inside her.

Finally she sought out a high and lonely place, a rocky ledge surrounded by the jewelled night. She lay there and let the darkness draw out all the pain and confusion. And into that moment of peace came, with sudden clarity, the memory of what the creature she rescued had said to her:

"You valnish our gratitude and ferdingly a lollom until lunar-solar rejuxtaposition thersh."

One word caught at her: *"Until."*

She lifted her head, the mood of calm shifting into one of controlled excitement.

That's what has been nudging my subconscious all this time, keeping me from committing myself to being a cat. I've known all along that the transformation isn't permanent—I'll change back. Thank God, I'll change back!

When?

She thought of what might have happened if the change

occurred while she was caged with Sir George. *And if there were a child . . .* She dismissed that speculation as useless, since the situation had been avoided. Instead she went carefully over the words she now remembered.

"*. . . lunar-solar rejuxtaposition thersh.*"

Re-juxtaposition.

Of course!

Bless you, Marcia, she thought to her friend and neighbor, *for your interest in astrology! I seldom pay attention to such things—if we hadn't been talking about it at dinner the night this happened, I'd never have known that it was the night of the full moon.*

So . . . the next full moon? Can it be that simple?

Maybe "lunar-solar" means the next time the positions of the earth, moon and sun are exactly the same as they were that night. Marcia mentioned that, too—how often did she say that happened?

She searched her memory, and gasped. *Every nineteen years!*

I won't believe it. I'm going to go with the next full moon. I'll change back into a woman twenty-eight days after the night I changed into a cat. But how much time has already passed?

She tried to remember. The trip south had been a nightmare of fear and hunger; the days ran together indistinguishably. She ended by estimating a total of nine days. That left nineteen.

Nineteen days until I become a woman again. But not out here. I want to go home.

Do you suppose they've quarantined my apartment, or whatever it is they do when they think somebody's dead? They don't have any proof, and they surely can't believe a mountain lion consumed an entire woman—especially one my size—and left no more trace than a blood stain or two on her nightgown.

No, I'll bet they've done no more than lock the place up—or think they have. Bless that tricky balcony door! Unless you know the right combination, it seems to lock securely.

Nineteen days. It took me nine to get here; I'll allow nine to get back. I don't want to spend more time than necessary

*in the City—Marcia may be in and out of the apartment, and
I wouldn't be safe anywhere else.*

*So that leaves me ten days here, free. Ten days free of fear
and confusion. Time enough to learn what I wanted to know
in the first place: how it feels to be a cat.*

IX

In the morning she came down the cliff carefully and began to run through the dry, weedy brush. She wasn't running
from anywhere *to* anywhere. She was running for the deli-
cious scratch of scrubby branches against her side, and for
the power and rhythm of her muscles. She was running for
the joy of the morning.

A jackrabbit bolted away from her path; she veered after it
and caught it by the neck. It jerked and struggled until she
snapped the long, lean body upward and broke its neck.

Resolutely she thrust aside a whisper of human conscience
and settled down to eat the prize she had won. She knew that
this kill had been mostly luck. She expected to get very hungry in the next few days.

On some of those hungry days, she watched Ken or Charlie driving or walking through the hills. They were searching
for her, Ken openly, Charlie with the air of a hunter. But
both were carrying guns now and she knew that if she
showed herself in answer to Ken's appealing voice, he would
take no chances. She would be put to sleep, hauled back to
the Institute, and caged. Probably with George.

So she played a harmless game, hiding from them and following them. Partly she did it for the sake of human companionship, however unknowing. Partly she enjoyed the
challenge to her catness of keeping near them and yet keeping them unaware of her nearness. Only once did she fail that
challenge, and then it was by choice.

Ken Lawson knew these hills well, but he was not immune
to accident. It happened suddenly—he was standing on a
large flattish rock that overlooked a steep slope and most of a
weed-choked valley. He shifted his weight, one of the stones
that was bracing the shelf slid out of place, and the world
tilted underneath him. He twisted as he fell and caught the
upper edge of the rock slab, which was still braced in posi-

tion though now it presented him with a smooth slope almost
as long as his body.

He'll never make it! Kathy thought, as she watched him
digging with his feet for some leverage to get his weight
higher on the tilted rock. The flat stone was too smooth, the
hillside underneath it too soft. *The fall won't kill him, but
sliding down that dry and rubbly slope will be a nasty trip.*

Hang on, Ken!

She came out, then, from a manzanita thicket along the
ridge across the small valley from the struggling man. She
had to climb the other side, as Ken had, and work her way
down to the promontory on which he had been standing. He
was hidden from her sight, but she could hear the sound of
his struggle and an occasional gasping oath.

The bottom of the tilted stone faced her; she could see his
fingers gripping the upper edge, moving, searching for better
handholds. She had hoped that she would be able to stand on
solid footing and put some helpful pressure on the rock with
her forelegs. She saw now that it would be impossible; the
slab of rock had lifted up from too deep a pocket of packed
earth.

His hands were sweating and slipping. She didn't have
much time.

She jumped. For a precarious instant she balanced on the
edge of the stone, all four paws clutching at the hard surface.
Ken had inched his way up until his weight was more evenly
distributed, so that her weight was the deciding factor.

Ken felt the stone's movement, and looked up to see what
was causing it. His face was dark and wet with the strain, but
she wanted to laugh at its expression.

"Lady! I'll be damned! Lady!" he said again as the rock
settled back into place. Once gravity stopped working against
him, it was a simple matter for Ken to pull himself across the
rock and get to his knees. He reached for her, laughing, and
she felt the stone shift a little beneath them.

*You imbecile! Will you get the hell off this stone teeter tot-
ter?* The thought was expressed as a dangerous-looking snarl,
but she couldn't say whether it had more effect than the moving rock.

"All right, girl!" he said to her. "I hear you. Just hold
still . . ."

She did, while he very carefully climbed over her crouching form and scrambled onto solid ground. "OK, Lady," he called. "I'm safe now. Just you be careful."

When she had jumped to safety, he sat down and patted the dirt beside him. She considered. The anasthesia gun was at the bottom of the valley, not irretreivably lost but for the moment out of reach. She lay down beside him and they stayed that way for what seemed a long, still time, just being together.

"Well," Ken sighed, getting to his feet, "I can't sit here forever—I've got work to do. I don't suppose you'd care to come home with me?" She stood up and moved away a few paces. "I thought not." He shook his head. "You are really something, Lady. If I didn't know better, I'd say you had human intelligence.

"One thing's sure—I'll never say a word about what happened today. They'll tell me I OD'd on Lassie when I was a kid." He laughed, dusted himself off, looked at her. "We won't come looking for you any more, girl. You've convinced me you're where you want to be. But . . . our gate is always open. Come and visit."

A part of her longed to go with him as she watched him pick his way down the hill and start home. But that was the hungry part, the old Kathy Christopher who needed security. She stayed right where she was until he was out of sight.

She did manage to catch a couple more jackrabbits as her allotted time was nearly up. She had caught field mice and frogs but had largely subsisted on a varied and unpleasant diet of insects. As she lay in the shade on what she thought of as "the last day" and enjoyed a rabbit deliberately stalked and fairly won, she felt satisfied that she had accomplished her purpose. She had survived. The body she was wearing felt natural and right to her. She was a cat and she felt that she had come to understand catness.

That night she came into heat.

X

Katherine Christopher had not been an impassionate woman nor an inexperienced lover. But this . . .

It was a need she could only compare to what she had

heard of withdrawal from drug addiction. It ate at her from the inside out. It disrupted her sleep. It interfered with her motor functions and concentration. It ached and it itched until she howled and rolled on the weedy ground.

And through the clear night air, there came an answer to her pleading cry.

With the sound came the image of the one who made it—the strong handsome wedge of his head, the way muscles rippled beneath the smooth fur on his chest and along his sides, his affection for his human friends, and most compelling of all, his desperate loneliness.

She wanted to go to him and by submitting to him, conquer the raging need within her. They were alike, they should be together, they could ease one another's singularity in a hostile world. Their mating had been decreed . . .

No! cried out an isolated remnant of rationality. Kathy forced herself to stop, look around her. She had been running, already on her way to the Institute. Landmarks told her that she was near the promontory where she had rested the night she left. As though there were two *personae* trying to control one body, the human Kathy had to struggle to turn away from the Institute.

I can't give in! she thought grimly. *I won't. In a few days I'll be human again. I'm human now! Do you hear that, George?*

I'm HUMAN!

God help us, I can't come to you. Forgive me, George. Help me, God! she prayed sincerely. *Help me keep control!*

She dragged herself to the high ledge and lay there trembling, trying to steel herself against George's mournful voice. Her calmness was precarious and hard-won.

It won't last forever. It was her one consolation. *In domestic cats the heat cycle runs—ah, three to five days, I think. Even in a mountain lion, it can't last forever.*

But it seemed to.

Literally, in that time, she wrestled with temptation. She slipped in and out of conscious control, frequently pulling herself back from halfway down the hillside. She pressed her belly into the stone beneath her, willing its heat or its coolness to flow upward and soothe the terrible itch. She rolled and squirmed and then lay still, exhausted, until she could no longer stand being still.

She could not mark the passage of time. The world grew light and then dark; the only difference was that George's voice seemed to echo plaintively among the stars, demanding and begging. The night called out to the human in her, as well, with delirious visions of romance and scraps of intimate memories to feed the fire she fought so hard to bank. At night the need seemed greatest, the call of the male cougar most persuasive.

And at last—and at night—she could no longer resist it.

She had been days without food or sleep. Her mind was feverish and her body had grown weak. Her movements were erratic as she finally yielded to the need and stumbled down the hillside toward the Institute.

She stood again in the arched gateway between the stone walls. In the bright moonlight, she could see that George had come across the wire-enclosed bridge from his run and into his feeding cage to be as close as possible to her. He was mad with her scent, throwing himself against the wire of the cage.

He'll kill himself for need of me, she thought. *Look how he struggles to reach me—he's bleeding! Forgive me for denying you all this time! I'm here now, George. I'm here!*

She ran to stand beside the cage, pulled at the wire with teeth and claws. George screamed and threw his weight against it. The cage held.

She lifted her pain-wracked voice in a howl of rage and frustration—then choked it off as the beam of a flashlight startled her eyes.

"Lady," said a well-remembered voice. Ken Lawson shut off the flashlight, and in a few seconds she could see again. He and Charlie were silhouetted against the lights of the house and yard, but she could see that his hair was dishevelled, his face haggard.

"Ken, be careful," Charlie warned. "She's nobody's pet now. Let me get the sleep gun . . ."

"I said no, Charlie," Ken answered, keeping his voice low. "Don't ask me why. Please don't ask me why."

Ken came toward her slowly. She backed off a few steps, then stopped and let him approach. George had been startled into silence by the light, but now he renewed his efforts to batter down the wire of the cage. Her attention, however, was all on the man.

Memories flashed before her. The calm sanity of his voice cutting through the panic of a city. The look of him as he welcomed her, and the remembered warmth of his hand on her body. Her fear for him as he hung suspended above the treacherous hillside and the precious moments of peaceful companionship afterward. In all the world, he was the only person who was trying to understand.

He came close to her, and knelt so that he could look into her face.

"Ken, please . . ." came Charlie's anxious voice.

"It's all right. She won't hurt me." Then, to her: "You've had a bad time of it, haven't you, Lady. So has George. And Charlie and I haven't been able to sleep for days."

He reached out and took her head between his hands. She closed her eyes and shivered, rubbed her ear into his palm.

"When you didn't show up that first night, Lady—there's nothing I know of that can make a cat willingly hold out against—I'm not sure what I think—

"Lady, what do you want me to do? Shall I open George's cage?"

She opened her eyes, and a strange silence descended. George had stopped his frenzied leaping and sat panting, watching her. Ken looked at her with an expression of puzzlement and speculation on his face. Even Charlie, who couldn't have heard Ken's quiet voice above the racket George was making, seemed to be waiting for her decision.

Through the confusion of her tormented mind, sudden insight flowed into her consciousness as she looked from the cougar to the man before her.

Her body cried out for the huge mountain lion, exquisitely tortured by his nearness.

He could help me. But only because it is his nature. He would be taking, not giving. Satisfying his own need.

Ken wants to help me. I wish he could. Oh God! How I wish he could!

The cat in me needs George. But I'm not a cat.

She looked again into the man's face, and saw his ex-

pression change to reflect a dawning wonder and belief, as
though he could read her thought:

Don't open the cage, Ken. George would only be a surrogate for you.

She summoned all her human control and wrenched herself
away from Ken's hands. He let her go.

She ran away from the irreconcilable conflict, screaming
with all her soul. Willfully she shut out George's howl of disappointed rage, and Ken's soft words of farewell. She forced
herself to run, focusing all her attention and strength on her
powerful, driving legs. She ran until she fell and couldn't rise
again. Then she sank gratefully into the oblivion of sleep, so
long denied her.

XI

When she woke the need was gone, though the scars remained in her tired mind and exhausted body. She moved
slowly, first finding a stream to slake her towering thirst.
Through that day she rested and ate berries and insects. At
night she was strong enough to hunt, and the next morning
she started home.

She moved as fast as she dared, ate when she could and
when she had to. She tried to keep out of sight; the last thing
she needed now was to be identified and pursued all the way
to the city.

She would not allow herself to doubt that she would be retransformed into a woman when next the moon was full. She
knew that the torment she had just suffered, when not
suitably satisfied, would return again in a few days. That was
a specter she refused to face.

Uppermost in her thoughts was the desire to be at home
when it happened, to let it end in the same place where it began. There was an underlying anxiety caused by the timeless
period of her heat cycle and the broad disc of the moon. Her
earlier calculations were worthless, and she knew the full
moon was very close.

She was still many miles from the City when she lay at the
foot of a hedge near dusk to listen to the newscast of a blaring car radio. This was a station which gave tide information

as a feature of its news; she waited tensely to hear it, mentally urging the boy under the car to quiet his rattling tools.

Her patience was rewarded with the date of the impending full moon. She waited a little longer to hear the current date, then she was on her feet and running.

Tomorrow night! I'll never make it!

I have to make it! This, she thought grimly, *is what I've been training for. I will be in my apartment for the full moon!*

She pushed herself through the night, running for long stretches, then walking until she got her breath back. At dawn she had reached the outskirts of the city. She moved more cautiously then, reluctant to start another hue and cry that might result in her apartment being watched. By noon her endurance was at an end, and she went to cover in a boarded-up warehouse, too tired even to chase the rats that chittered at her complainingly.

She awoke in a panic—it was already dark.

What time is it? And what time is the moon full? What exact time?

She left the building, ignoring the emptiness of her stomach, the decision already made.

A straight line through the city. She figured her position against the location of her apartment, settled on the fastest route. *I'll go for broke, follow that line no matter what. The news can't travel much faster than I'll be going.*

"No matter what" included running across the tops of cars which were stopped at lights or parked along the streets. When necessary, she knocked aside pedestrians with a silent apology—but usually she was given plenty of room.

She was three blocks from her apartment, and her lungs were beginning to labor from the sustained effort. She heard a coughing roar and two policemen upon motorcycles came out of a side street after her.

Are they trying to track me? Or do they have orders to shoot if they can do it safely? Doesn't matter . . . I'm too close now. If I can just elude them for a few minutes . . .

She veered to the right and squeezed through the narrow gap between two houses. The yard sloped upward and ended in a high fence. She lunged up and over it, into the alleyway.

But the policemen had anticipated her. One of them was even then turning into the alleyway behind her, the roar of his engine thundering between the fences. Ahead of her, the other screeched his bike to a stop, lowered it to the ground, and dropped behind it. He was aiming a revolver at her.

She put on a burst of speed and leaped over the motorcycle, not quite missing the policeman. He had the good sense not to fire, with the other policeman right behind her, and now he rolled out of the way as his partner jumped the fallen bike and continued the chase.

Ahead of her was the doorway tree, and she hoped that in the heat of pursuit, the man behind her would not realize he was so near the apartment where the mountain lion had first appeared.

She ran as though to pass the tree, then whirled aside and leaped three yards up the trunk. As she pulled herself easily up the tree and sprang from the wildly waving limb onto the balcony, she heard the bike screech to a halt, rev as though it were talking to itself, then roar around the corner toward the front door of the building.

The round and luminous moon shone down on a cat trying desperately to open a locked sliding door.

My God, I can't get it open! And it's so simple—push toward the sill, pull back slightly, push again and then open! Easy for a woman—but not for a cougar! And—oh, no—not out here. . . .

She felt an oddness, a flowing, and in her desperation to get inside, she finally persuaded the door to open. She fell through it and lay in the full glow of moonlight, trying to remember and savor the strangeness of what she was feeling.

The dawning of color, the dimming of sound and odor. A sensation of liquidity, the beginning of difference. When it was done, she only knew that she had experienced something altogether wonderful.

And she was a woman again.

XII

She stood up . . . and laughed when she realized that she was still crouching on the floor. She exercised remembered control and *really* stood up, a little unsteadily.

How tall she was! She didn't remember being this tall.

All my perceptions will be a little different now that I've seen the world from a different viewpoint.

She went to the mirrored doors. In the streaming light of the just-past-full moon, she saw herself as a woman again. And she was no less amazed than when she had seen the image of a mountain lion in that same mirror.

The woman before her had a great snarled-up mane of hair, sun-bleached, matted and tangled with burrs and weeds. She was thinner—not yet slim, by any means, but all that starving and running had melted off at least forty pounds.

Her skin was dirty and scratched, and a long slim scar ran from her shoulder blade around to her left side. She stared at this new woman—filthy and scraggly and stark naked—and she found herself to be beautiful.

But there was a change on her greater than these physical differences. The eyes of the image, blue-green as she remembered them, shone out with an inner light of confidence and challenge.

"Those are the eyes," she said aloud, "of an *independent* woman." She walked over to the balcony, looked up into the night, and whispered: "Whoever you are, little one, you *valnish* my gratitude. Very much."

Martinique jumped onto the balcony and hesitated.

"It's all right," she told him, reaching down to pick him up and scratch behind an ear with a fuller appreciation of the pleasure she gave him. "I'm me again." She grinned. "Well, not the *same* me, maybe."

She paced around the room, reacquainting herself with perpendicular motion. She talked to herself and to the cat, enjoying the sound of her human voice.

"The police will be here any minute. I'll have to think of something to tell them. Then I'll worry about *how* to break the news to Mr. Lodge. And one of these days," she said, warmth stirring deep inside her, "I'll have a nice long talk with Dr. Kenneth Lawson."

Her voice sounded deeper than she remembered it. *I'm probably still hoarse from all the hollering in the hills.* She smiled at the memory, distance and time and the infinite relief of no longer being a cat giving her room to view the experience more objectively. Then she laughed—a sound no cat could make.

It's a good thing I didn't come into heat while I was still in the city. I'd have been pretty conspicuous being followed by a line of ambitious tomcats!

About Anodea Judith and *Bedtime Story*

Anodea Judith is proof of two points I find myself repeating frequently in this anthology; that writing is contagious—living with writers encourages new writers to start writing—and that almost all artists have more than one talent; creativity can express itself in more than one way.

I first knew Anodea Judith as an artist; her murals of clouds and birds and flowers appear everywhere in Berkeley, including on my bedroom ceiling. She is also (murals being an uneven and chancy way of earning a living) a masseuse and physiotherapist of considerable skill, as the backs of the whole community can attest; tight muscles from bending over a typewriter, or a headache obviously due to deadline tension rather than medical problems, yield readily to her skilled hands. More recently she has been writing a book (nonfiction) on the *chakras,* or energy fields of the human body.

But I had never believed that she had any interest in writing fiction until the following story alighted on my desk.

Why is writing fiction so contagious? Well, I believe that most people who are not writers themselves, believe that "being a writer" is something magical and strange; that "writers" are not really human beings, but some race of supermen. (I still remember when a friend of my daughter's blurted out "But you—you aren't at all like a famous writer, you're like a—a—" and finally she found the right word, "like a *real person!*"

People who live around writers a lot quickly get over that exalted opinion of the writer/superhuman. They find out that writers do not produce their creations full-blown like Athena from the head of Jove, but struggle over them one word at a time, crumple up false starts and throw them into their wastebasket, cuss the job as if they were plumbers or shoe salesmen, and that we generally put on our shoes one at a time like any other ordinary mortals. From that disillusioning realization frequently comes another sneaking suspicion; "Hey—if *she* can do it, maybe I could too."

And frequently, it happens.

And the result is often very amusing and fantastic. Any writer who does a lot of editing, or teaches writing, is often accused of creating a "school" of writing—the hand of John W. Campbell is visible in all his precisely schooled "stable" of *Astounding* and *Analog* writers, and the same thing has been said of the Milford and Clarion workshops—that they create their writers in their own image.

"Bedtime Story" certainly refutes that allegation—it is not the kind of story I ever could have written—but I still think it's a fun story!

BEDTIME STORY
by Anodea Judith

"No! I won't!"

Mother grimaced, smoothed the back of her skirt, with determination. She noticed the cloth was wearing thin, and thought wryly that her patience was wearing much thinner.

"For the last time, Johnny, there is nothing in your closet, nothing under your bed, and nothing but little plastic toys in your toy chest. Now you're just going to have to grow up and accept reality and go to bed, like other grown-ups do."

"You mean I can stay up until midnight like you and Daddy?"

"No!" Mother cried and bodily shoved Johnny down the hall, into his room, pushed him onto the bed and shut the door with a slam. "Now, I don't want to hear a peep out of you until morning, understand?"

There was no answer but a slight, soft whimpering. Mother found this extremely hard to listen to without weakening her position, so she quickly walked away down the hall, muttering to herself something about accepting reality and being a grown-up.

Meanwhile Johnny, being grown-up enough to know when he was licked, turned his night light up to high, said a few prayers to his teddy bear and climbed bravely into bed, pulling the covers over him tightly and completely.

"What does Mother know about reality!' he muttered to himself. "I'll show her these creatures are real and she'll be sorry!"

No sooner had Johnny uttered these fateful words than a chill came over the room, accompanied by a loud creak, and the sound of a young child pulling himself deeper into the safety and security of a down comforter. But unfortunately, the quilt did not provide the comfort its name implied and Johnny, fighting between curiosity and abject terror, soon gave way to the curiosity, telling himself that he must not only accept, but face reality and commending himself on his bravery.

There was a faint stir from under the down comforter. There was another loud creak in the room, this time accompanied by a cool breeze stirring the curtains that hung in front of the closed and locked window. Soon a tiny head poked out from under the blankets, followed by one wide eye, then another, and then a tiny nose, sniff, sniff, sniffing the breeze.

"BOO!" a voice said, and the covers flew frantically, completely covering the small child once again, except, of course for the small feet that now stuck out at the bottom of the bed.

"Do you want to see me or don't you?" a hoarse and creaky voice said, while tweaking one of the exposed toes.

This time, Johnny jumped completely out of the covers, though that was not his intention.

"That's more like it," the voice said, and sat down on top of the toy chest with satisfaction.

"Wh-wh-who are y-y-you?" Johnny stammered, trying to grab the fallen covers from the floor and pull himself back onto the bed with them.

The green scaly creature did not answer at first, but gave a huge yawn, revealing large pointed teeth. He stroked a tentacle or two, crossed one of his many legs, and rested his strange green head upon one scaly, clawed hand, while adjusting his sword to the other hand.

"Well, I was hoping you would tell me! After all you created me!"

"What?" Johnny cried with disbelief.

"Oh dear," cried the creature. "When will I get to work for adults once again? Children have such a hard time accepting reality!"

"Wh-What do you mean?" Johnny cried loudly, feeling that on some level he was about to discover a crucial truth to the nature of the universe, that his mother never told him.

The creature suddenly stood and lunged forward toward Johnny, sword arm outstretched, saying, "Do you want me to cut off thy little head, or just thy tiny ears?"

Johnny flew under the bedclothes once again, this time curled in such a little ball that nothing could possibly stick out.

"Well, answer me, you fool! You did call me, didn't you? I mean I certainly wouldn't *choose* to live in a closet, would you?"

Johnny couldn't decide if this guy was out to harm him or not. He certainly was ugly, but then so were some of the creatures on Star Wars, and they had never hurt him. He decided that he had gone this far unscathed, he may as well follow it through, for no one else would ever explain such mysteries to him if he didn't figure it out for himself. Summoning up his best show of courage, using his best imitation of his father's stern voice, he threw off the covers, sat up proudly and said,

"All right, explain yourself, you, you, you thing you."

"That's more like it," the creature replied. "I mean we don't have all night. You do have school tomorrow, you know."

Johnny nodded obediently, commending himself on just how well he was accepting this bedroom conversation with the ugliest creature he had ever seen.

The creature began, "Well, it seems I was quietly roaming around the world of the oversouls, on my way to a hot date, as a matter of fact," (Johnny wondered who or what would ever want to go out on a date with something *so* ugly, but said nothing, "when all of a sudden I feel this commanding presence ordering me into a closet, and then out again, with some nebulous order about showing myself to some adult female creature. Then I arrive and I am treated *quite* discourteously, and find that I must prove my existence, even to the one who created me! Now it's your turn for explanation! And it better be good, if you treasure your little fingers." This last was accompanied by a snarl that made Johnny tuck his little hands under the covers, thereby releasing his hold on them, and they tumbled and slid to the floor, leaving him quite exposed.

"I didn't create you, you, you, ugly," (the sword arm raised menacingly) "I mean nice, friendly thing you."

And the funniest thing happened as he said "friendly." The creature dropped his sword onto the floor and grinned a great broad, fang-filled grin, and reached out his scaly hand to shake it with Johnny's own small one.

Johnny watched to make sure that the other hand wasn't reaching for the sword again. But the sword had disappeared right into the floor on which it had landed! Johnny was so surprised he extended his hand, not looking at the creature but at the spot on the floor where the sword had fallen.

"How did you do that?" he asked.

"Do what?" the creature replied.

"Make the sword disappear?"

"I didn't do it, you did, you juvenile nincompoop," the creature replied. "If you call me friendly, then that I must be, so I have no need of a sword."

Johnny pondered this a moment, but decided to take nothing on faith; he'd try to prove everything. This was, after all, an experiment in accepting reality. And no reality exists without proof.

"Well, I didn't mean to call you ugly, then. You're actually very beautiful." Johnny had crossed his fingers under his pajamas, for this was the biggest lie he had ever told. The creature looked perplexed. Johnny uncrossed his fingers, then gaped with amazement at what he saw before him.

The creature was changing. The fangs in the grin were growing smaller, the scales were growing smoother, the tentacles were twirling around each other and forming a large single horn in the middle of the creature's green head!

"Is that better now?" the creature asked in a soft, breezy voice.

Johnny was beginning to understand, "I think I might like

you better if you weren't green, and if you had a tail of hair instead of one of scales."

The creature changed accordingly. He was now a bright display of rainbow colors, glistening in the light of the night-lamp.

Johnny nodded approvingly, fascinated by such a display of colors. But as he watched, the colors began to move faster and faster, until in front of him there was a bright blur, and the horselike creature settled into a moonlike creamy white. The creature bowed his head, put his horn in Johnny's lap and said, "At your service, sir. Your wish is my command." This was accompanied by a cross between a whinny and a baa, and a shake of that glorious white coat, glistening in the semi-dark.

"Hmm." Johnny nodded with satisfaction. This was indeed more fun, and infinitely more satisfying, than art class at school. Just think what the other boys would say in the morning when he told them!

This however, suddenly reminded Johnny of his original mission of the night. That no one, not his friends, nor his mother, nor his sister, nor his brother, would believe that he had met a large green scaly creature coming out of his closet and had transformed him into a unicorn. Even Johnny had trouble believing it. "Yes," Johnny sighed to himself, "It is not enough that reality exists, it must be proven to others!"

This, he knew, was no small task.

"Well," he said thoughtfully, "do you think you could stay here and keep me company tonight, so the other creatures in the closet don't get me? And then, then in the morning," he started slowly, then more firmly as the idea ripened in his mind, "go into my parents' bedroom and wake up my mother by poking her with your horn! Don't hurt her, of course, I wouldn't want to go to school without breakfast, you understand, but teach her not to disbelieve me when I say there are creatures in my closet!"

The creature turned around slowly as if considering the task at hand. He couldn't very well put his horn in mother's lap, as she was obviously no virgin, but perhaps he could do a kind of showy leap over the bed, brushing the mother's face with his tail, landing with a pirouette and removing the covers with his horn. Yes, that would be quite fun! He told

Johnny of his plan, and Johnny gleefully agreed, clapping his hands together with delight.

"But," the unicorn said sternly, "you must also do something for me."

"You put yourself at my service," Johnny replied, "I shall also put myself at yours. Name your command."

"You must go to bed, and go to sleep and forget all about what happened here tonight. You may tell no one at school tomorrow, for you won't remember. If you do this, I will make sure that your mother gets a glimpse of me she will never forget."

Johnny agreed, although secretly, he thought he could never in a million years forget the extraordinary experience he was having this night.

"Okay, only I don't want any mess-ups or I'll turn you back into an ugly creature again."

The unicorn shuddered. "A deal's a deal. We're on. Now go to sleep." And with that he shut off the night lamp and tucked Johnny firmly under the covers. Johnny was instantly asleep.

The next morning Mother slept through the alarm clock. Father was already up and out of bed, busy in the bathroom, shaving and getting dressed for the day. Suddenly Mother felt the brush of hair against her face. She said, "Ralph, really, it's too early," then sat up with a start, realizing her husband was not there. She turned to the door just in time to see the unicorn do a flurry of pirouettes, ending with a casual arching of his back and a flick of his horn, tossing the bedclothes onto the floor and exposing the poor flabbergasted woman to the realities of her wrinkled nightgown and cold, sleepy feet.

"Ralph!" she cried at the top of her lungs in a shriek that made the word nearly unintelligible. "Come here quickly! I've just seen a unicorn!"

But as her husband entered, grumbling, into the room, she turned and pointed to empty air and a perfectly closed bedroom door. The room was quiet and everything was perfectly still, except of course for her shaking finger pointing at the empty space beside her bed.

"But I saw it! There was a unicorn in the room!"

"I wish you wouldn't throw the covers on the floor like

that, dear. I'm afraid the cats have been in here, and I don't want to have fleas in our bed."

"But Ralph! I saw it! I felt a brush of hair on my face and saw a huge white animal with a single golden horn, turning circles right there over the hooked rug. Then he turned toward me, stuck out his horn and pulled the covers off! I swear it!"

"Dear, do you know whether I have any clean brown socks to wear to work today?"

"But Ralph! I saw a unicorn! Isn't that more important than your dirty socks?"

"Yes, of course, dear. Why don't you give Doc Gamble a call this morning? It's been a while since you had a check-up, and it would be good to get a clean bill of health before we go on our vacation." Ralph looked in the mirror and straightened his tie.

"Johnny! This must be Johnny's doing!" she cried and slipping quickly into slippers went running down the hall to Johnny's room.

"Johnny, get up this instant, I need to talk to you!" she cried in a voice that was not typical of her at all.

Johnny sleepily rolled over and said, "What time is it?"

"It's time for you to tell me what you've been keeping in your closets, that's what! I just saw a huge animal in my room!"

"You what?" Johnny suppressed a giggle at seeing his mother so distraught.

"I saw a big white animal in my room—pulling covers onto the floor! You've been complaining about things coming out of your closet, I want an explanation."

"Oh that." Johnny sighed. "I decided you were right. There is nothing in my closet that isn't of my own making. None of that stuff really exists. I decided to grow up and accept reality," he said with finality.

"But I saw it!"

"Mother, you're just going to have to grow up and accept reality like the rest of us!" With that Johnny jumped out of bed and went to the closet to get dressed for school.

As he put on his shoes, he noticed the floor by the closet was covered with white fur. "Mother," he called. "The cats have been in my bedroom again!"

About James Ian Elliot and *Wrong Number*

James Ian Elliot, one of the many who pass through Greyhaven, has one of the more bizarre artistic interests; he is a skin decorator, alias a tattoo artist, and bears the signs of this interest literally from head to foot in many colors; he could stand in any day for Ray Bradbury's Illustrated Man.

I did not know he was also a writer until Tracy handed me this little gem.

WRONG NUMBER

by James Ian Elliot

The golden-haired man entered the booth, inserted plastic and dialed. The universe dissolved and he hung in nothingness for several eternities. Then the stars swirled, the world put itself together and the black-haired man emerged.

"Damn!" he said, dialing Repair Service. "Third malfunction this week."

About *The Bardic Revel*

One of the major ways in which the writers resident at, and associated with, Greyhaven share their works with one another, is the Bardic Revel.

Greyhaven gives a party every month—only half facetiously, the residents say that it is the only way to make sure they get the house thoroughly cleaned fairly often. Greyhaven has had every kind of party including weddings and wedding receptions, Regency breakfasts, publication parties, and the annual New Year's Waltz/Ball; but perhaps the most frequent is the Bardic Revel, where the artists, poets, musicians and others share their work.

During a year when I was working for a small local magazine, I was asked to review one of these events for the East Bay Review; and attempted to convey the essence of the Bardic Revel for them. Greyhaven was not identified by name, because of many events of party-crashing in the past, but otherwise everything was exactly as detailed herein.

And since, in presenting many of these stories, I intend to introduce them by mentioning that they were first presented at a "Bardic," it is simpler to describe one of those events as it happened on a certain evening in 1977.

THE BARDIC REVEL
by Marion Zimmer Bradley

(*East Bay Review*, vol. 11, no. 19. © 1977 by *The East Bay Review*)

The closing of the Salamandra and Rockridge Station coffeehouses leaves few outlets for local poets and original musi-

cians to present their work. The Bardic Revel is an event
where such musicians and poets can perform before a large
informed audience of their peers.

The Revel held October 8th at a private home in the
Berkeley hills followed the format devised for the local Society for Creative Anachronism, and had much in common
with the old Scottish *ceilidh* (pronounced "caley" and meaning a sing-song). Participants formed a circle, and the Master
of Ceremonies moved the attention from one to another in
orderly fashion.

The Bardic Revel differs in one important way from the
coffeehouse events; there are *no* spectators. All comers are required to participate. Those few who do not have original
work to read or sing may choose to share a favorite work by
someone else; but read, or sing, they must. Unwritten rules
prevent loud expressions of distaste for someone else's work;
your only defense is to do something better yourself.

Paul Edwin Zimmer was Master of Ceremonies; his long
poem "Logan," about the Native American chief of Revolutionary War fame, is soon to be published by an Albany
(CA) publisher. Zimmer, a bearded, balding redhead who af-
fects the wearing of a kilt, kept the procedures moving with a
genial, but firm hand. (He deals cavalierly with crashers and
disruptive drunks.)

For this Revel there was no announced theme, and at least
three groups, widely varying, were present and performing:
the local coffeehouse-poet crowd; a somewhat more scholarly
group of local writers, mostly involved in science fiction, fantasy or mythology; and a group of singers and actors from
the Renaissance Faire. Surprisingly there was little dissension
and no antagonism among these, perhaps because all three
groups are composed largely of tolerant eccentrics. Quality
ranged from the excellent to the abysmal.

Best known from the "local poets" scene was the triad of
Dierdre Evans, Chris Trian and Paladin, whose collaborative
book *Squids in Bondage* has just been announced; Evans read
an extremely funny excerpt from this book, satirizing current
sado-masochistic pop culture trends. Poets who followed included something for all tastes from the tame to the gamey;
one woman read a poem cramming every Anglo-Saxon ob-

scenity I have ever heard, and some I haven't, into eight lines; at the opposite extreme, there were original poems in Middle English, which the writer obligingly translated for the audience.

Local writers Poul Anderson and Randall Garrett both read aloud, Anderson from a work in progress, and Garrett, departing from his usual humorous fiction, read several unpublished poems. One, for my taste, was the best work of the evening; a long and complex poem, virtually impossible to excerpt for quotation, it compared the creative process, the human condition and hell, in a lengthy metaphor of waiting in line for something no one can see, where any possible reward must be taken on faith.

> "And it is always four-thirty, on a hot afternoon,
>   In Disneyland."

Tolkien enthusiasts (there were many present) were delighted with Chris Gilson's reading and translation of an original poem in one of Tolkien's Elvish languages; those knowledgeable in such things informed me that his use of the language was correct, even scholarly. My own contribution included original music composed to words by Tolkien and Poul Anderson. But all the contributions from the science fiction and fantasy crowd were not scholarly. Amy Falkowitz, a local fan and artist, had the whole room rocking with laughter and singing along on the choruses of an original Star Trek folk song (by Leslie Fish) about a ship that ran out of fuel and made it home on beer. Also on the lighter side were Vicki Heydron's lighthearted epic about a villager cursed to sacrifice to a demon who preferred virgins, where that commodity was unobtainable; and Hilary Ayer, an actor from the Renaissance Faire, who sang bawdy Elizabethan ballads in a small but pleasing voice.

The youngest poet to read his own work was nine-year-old Ian Studebaker, reading an original poem entitled "Dolphins in the Sea," by no means the worst poem of the evening. Seven-year-old Fiona Zimmer, already a three year veteran of Renaissance Faire, performed a brief dramatic dialogue with her mother, Faire dancer and actor Tracy Blackstone.

The number of participants, and the lack of theme, made the proceedings unwieldy; after midnight, when the circle had thinned to a more reasonable number, things moved more quickly, and poems became more personal.

The Bardic Revels were once open to all comers, but crowds of crashers and a few thefts have made them invitational only. The best way to be invited is to show up at the weekly Tuesday night readings in the new Children of Paradise coffeeshop, make yourself visible there, and demonstrate your competence.

From various and sundry Bardic Revels

Many of the stories in this anthology were first presented at Bardic Revels. The Bardics have another purpose, however. In a family group which spreads as far as the Greyhaven circle, composed of many creative individuals, all is not always sweetness and light . . . since each of the aforesaid creative individuals is possessed of his or her own share of artistic temperament, and with a dozen or more prima donnas (or primo tenores) present at one time, there have been some rare old rumpuses. When things are best, however, we tend to make creative and even humorous use of one another's little foibles (as in the poems which follow) instead of heaving the dishes at one another. This doesn't, of course, mean that no dishes ever get heaved (the very presence of day people and night people under one roof is enough to drive each of them crazy in different ways) but it defuses enough energy from dish-heaving to giggling that we are not perpetually reduced to serving Sunday tea out of paper plates and cups.

It should be pointed out for the purposes of the fuller understanding of the following items that (1) Paul Edwin Zimmer is known in Greyhaven and in the S.C.A. as "Edwin Berserk" for obscure reasons, possibly connected with a long-standing admiration for Rider Haggard's *Eric Brighteyes*, (see the introduction to "The Hand of Tyr" elsewhere in this volume) or possibly for his style of fighting; while Robert Cook (see introduction to "The Wood-Carver's Son"

is known as Serpent, and many of their friends know them
by no other names.

SERPENT'S LULLABYE
by Diana L. Paxson

Within a dusty cellar, there lies a lumpy bed
Where, when the day is over, weary Serpent lays his head,
And no matter who may call him, no matter what is said,
Still, Serpent slumbers on!

Outside the wind is howling, and thunder racks the air;
Bitter smoke wreathes round him, and flames are everywhere;
Floodwaters rise above him, but for these he has no care,
As Serpent slumbers on!

The silent darkness shatters at the porcine siren's might;
The clatter of machine guns echoes anger through the night;
The bombs of the invader fill the air with ruddy light,
But Serpent slumbers on!

The hosts of Armageddon stride triumphant through the gloom;
The primal gods go laughing to the charnel feast of doom;
But amidst the desolation there remains one little room,
Where Serpent slumbers on. . . .

(n.b. The events in stanza two refer to a flood and fire which
occurred in the basement when Serpent was living at Gray-
haven itself, through which he slept. . . . The style, particularly of the last stanza, is a pastiche of Serpent's poetry)

MORNING SONG

by Robert Cook

The silence deep like umber lies
Within the manor's several halls;
And every sound there made soon dies
Among the massive, wooden walls.
But day is dying 'round this place;
The shadows creep from room to room.
The night presents its ebon face
To fill the manor halls with gloom.

And then, from out this fastness comes
A roar no distances remove.
It rumbles low like distant drums
Or Mongol armies on the move.
The moments pass; it comes again
Like some great beast of eldritch place
A-hunt on some forgotten plain,
A-rolling, growling, comes apace.

It bursts like thunder through the halls!
Like earthquake! tempest! hurricane!
Its power shakes the very walls
And shatters glass of window-pane!
The servants in their quarters pray!
The beasts with frightened cry take flight!
The very birds take wing! Away!
And vanish in the trembling night.

"My cup! My cup! My waking brew!"
A voice like demons thunders out.
"My throat cries out; my stomach too!
I will no longer go without!"
Our courage flies! Our limbs unnerve!
Our very flesh, like jelly, shakes!
You Gods that man's weak state preserve,
Defend us now! The Berserk wakes!

THE BERSERK AND THE BEAR'S SARK
by Diana L. Paxson

Oh, once there was a Berserk,
People thought him very wild,
For he was very hairy,
And his temper was not mild.
When in the heat of battle
He would gnaw his shield for fun,
And if waked up too early,
He would snarl at everyone.

Oh, the Berserk went out hunting
Just to get himself a bear,
For the winter was fast coming,
And he had no cloak to wear.
He said, "The Bear sleeps through the cold,
Curled in his furry skin,
But I will be out fighting
And I need it more than him."

The sun came up, he climbed a rock,
He saw a furry head,
Belonging to a big brown bear,
Who'd just got out of bed.
"Ah ha!" the Berserk said to him,
"Just what I wished to see—
I'll take it off if you'll not give
Your coat of fur to me!"

"Give you my skin?" the Bear replied,
"Who do you think you are?
This is my best fur coat, besides,
I stronger am by far."
The Berserk aimed his spear at him
To take the skin away,
The Bear he gave a mighty roar
And sprang into the fray.

They fought throughout the morning,
Oh, they fought 'till it was noon.
Trees were uprooted, boulders flew,
It was not over soon.
But when at last the fight was done
And everything was still,
The victor took the skin he'd won
And started down the hill.

He came into the village,
And they thought him very wild,
For he was very hairy,
And his temper was not mild.
He sat at the Berserk's table
And he slept upon his bed,
And no one ever noticed
That it was the Bear instead!

(Even children are not exempted from participation; if they wish to sit and listen, they must take their turn and participate. As stated, the poems by younger people are by no means the worst poems presented. These are two poems by younger-generation members of the Greyhaven household, which proves that writing fantasy is either contagious—or hereditary.

REFLECTIONS FROM A HILL

An eagle flies very high,
Highest up that there is;
A dragonfly flies high too,
Not very high for an eagle
But very high for a dragonfly;
And me, when I'm on the hill,
I'm high enough.

Ian Michael Studebaker, August, 1974
(also published in *A is for Coda-wada*, Geraldine Duncann, Mother Goose Enterprises, 1977).

SAD MEMORIES

I remember the unicorn,
The dragons sweetly singing,
The mermaids deftly swimming
Among the coral seabeds.
But now the legends darken;
Men say now that the unicorn
Kills with her silver horn.
"Dragons eat maidens now!"
They cry. I sigh.
Now sailors quickly warn you
Of the mermaids all forlorn.
The old, Pagan gods die,
As others are reborn.

About Elisabeth Waters and *Tell Me A Story*

This story is entirely fictional and any events in it are entirely the product of the writer's imagination. Names of any real people in the story have been changed to protect the guilty. In any case, names would be superfluous to anyone who had ever been inside Greenwalls or Greyhaven. . . .

Almost every writer I know complains that their important papers, pencils, paper clips and favorite reference books seem to vanish into a time warp or a small black hole on their desk. Lisa Waters, whose function in life seems to be making Order out of Chaos, produced this story at a Bardic Revel (see the relevant article); any writer whose house is filled, like mine, "with the fallout of a thirty-year writing career" would find it hysterical, as I did.

Lisa makes her home at Greenwalls, is a computer programmer by trade, and in the intervals of producing short stories and working on a novel, serves as my accountant, filing clerk, tidier-upper and general buffer (by which I mean she answers the phone when I am at the typewriter.) The editors with whom I deal, not to mention my long-suffering agent (not to mention the agents of the Infernal Revenue) are all much happier since Lisa took over my bookkeeping. I shall be delighted when she establishes herself as a writer (Perhaps with the historical novel about Tudor England?) but what will happen to my chaotic files then is anybody's guess. Because the time-warp is still lurking. . . .

TELL ME A STORY
by Elisabeth Waters

Although I had been making jokes about the time warp for years I never really believed in its existence until the night it grabbed me. Anyone who knows me will tell you two things: (1) that I claim to keep a time warp on my desk for losing important papers into, and (2) that my house is so messy and disorganized that a time warp couldn't find anything in it either. My study is littered with the fallout of my thirty-year writing career—reference books on every available shelf and most flat surfaces, manuscripts slithering gracefully onto the floor, reams of paper stacked in odd corners, all covered with a dusting of paper clips, rubber bands, and pencil stubs—some days it's hard to find the typewriter. Add to this my absent-minded-professor husband and my two teenage children and it's easy to see that a time warp would be quite superfluous. Well, it may be superfluous, but it's there.

It had been one of those days when everything went wrong. I was used to losing pens, pencils, typewriter ribbons, the odd ream of paper and five-year-old manuscripts to the "time warp," but this afternoon I hadn't been able to find the manuscript I had been working on that morning. My husband informed me that I had misplaced it and it would turn up, my daughter assured me that the time warp would return it as soon as it finished reading it, and my son asked for an advance on his allowance. I wouldn't mind if the time warp would swallow my purse briefly at moments like that, but naturally the purse sat in plain sight on the kitchen table. My son would probably figure out a way to get it out of the time warp anyway. And, of course, once he got his advance, my daughter needed money for new shoes, and my husband was running out of lunch money. By the time I gave up and crawled up to bed I was considerably poorer—and I still couldn't find that darn manuscript!

I was dreaming, and I didn't know where I was. I woke up and sat up in bed to orient myself. I was in my own bed, my husband was snoring next to me, and the clock on the bed table said 3:15 am. Then the numbers on the clock started flashing, the way they do after the power has been off, but instead of their usual 12:01 am, they were flashing numbers at random, and, while I was still wondering what was happening, nothingness picked me up and swallowed me.

It was the most horrible sensation—or rather, lack of sensation; I couldn't see anything but a sort of murky grey, I couldn't feel anything at all, not even air against my skin or moving through my lungs, I tried to scream and didn't make a sound, or if I did, I didn't hear it. I thought I must be mad, and then I heard the voice *inside* my head, and I knew I was.

"Go on! What happens next?"

"What!?!" I still couldn't hear myself, but apparently the voice could. An image appeared in my mind of a page of manuscript, the last page I had written that morning. It stopped in mid-sentence.

"The story. What happens next?"

"Who are you?" At that point I didn't even care what happened next in my story; I was more interested in what was going to happen next in my life. "Am I dead?"

"No, of course not. I'm 'the time warp you keep on your desk for losing important papers'—and that's unfair, I've never taken anything important, and I always return the stuff anyway. What happens next in the story?"

I'll say one thing for the time warp; it didn't get sidetracked easily. "How would I know what happens next? I haven't written it yet."

"Yes, you do know. How else could you write it? It's got to be in your mind. What happens next?"

"You're already in my mind. If it's there, why can't you find it for yourself?"

"Because it's in your subconscious and I can't access that far down in your mind. I thought even writers knew that. What happens next?" It sounded like a child, nagging for yet another chapter of his bedtime story.

"I don't know. I can't access my subconscious either, not until I sit down at the typewriter and start typing." Something bumped against me in the grey murk. I reached out and ran my hands over it. It was my typewriter.

"What happens next?"

If it could act like a five-year-old, I could treat it like one. "Do your parents know that you're running around swallowing people and typewriters?"

"Well . . ." pause for thought, "they never said I couldn't!" it finished triumphantly.

I must be making progress; for the first time it hadn't said, "What happens next." Keep trying. "Why did you grab me?"

"So you could finish the story. I've finished all your old stuff, and I've read as far as you've written down on this one, and I want to know what happens next."

"You mean that every time one of my old manuscripts disappeared, that was you, reading it?"

"Yes, but I've finished them. What happens next?"

"And when you took paper, and typewriter ribbons, and pens. . . ."

"I was trying to make stories. But I can't! I'm only a time warp and I can't create! Even with all the same materials, you can create stories, and all I can do is make a mess! If I try really hard, I can return stuff I took near where I got it from, but usually it comes out at random. I need you to make the stories."

"So you grabbed me." An awful thought swept through me. "Can you put me back?"

"But I want a story!" Definitely the wail of a small frustrated child.

"I can't write in the middle of a time warp."

"But you said that a writer, by definition, was a person who couldn't stop writing."

Just what I needed: a small child (I'm using the term loosely) with a retentive memory, among its other retentive qualities, who'd apparently been auditing my writing classes. "There are some things that will stop a writer. No paper, no pencils, no light, no time. I need my desk and my writing supplies, but even more, I need my family, my world, my life, and my experience. I need time, flowing past me in an orderly fashion, giving me structure to hang events on. I need time for these events to stir around in my subconscious, before they come out again as ideas and stories. I can't write in a time warp."

"But I want the story! I have to know what happens next!"

"Then you'll have to let me go. Once I get back home, I

can continue to write, and then you'll have the rest of the story—but you had better give it back pretty soon; my editor wants it too."

"You can give him a copy."

"Only if you don't grab it before I have a chance to copy it. I'll make a deal with you. I'll make an extra copy of everything I write, and I'll put it in the bottom drawer of my desk, and you can take it from there. In return, I want you to stop grabbing everything else."

"You'll give me a copy of *all* your stories?"

"All of them." A higher copying bill is a small price to pay for not being dragged out of bed in the middle of the night like this.

"Okay. But you've got to keep giving me stories. If you stop, I'll grab you again, and hold onto you until I *do* figure out how to tap your subconscious. And I want the rest of this story right away. I really want to know what happens next."

My typewriter slipped away from under my fingers and the grey murk swung around me and turned black. The next thing I knew it was morning, and my daughter was standing over my bed, yelling at me because her alarm hadn't gone off and I hadn't wakened her and now she was going to be late for school unless I got up right that second and drove her to school. And the clock was still flashing.

So I got up and drove her to school, and I came home and reset the clock, and I went to the typewriter and finished the story. And now I'm hard at work on another one. Most writers' deadlines are set by human editors, but mine are set by the time warp.

About Randall Garrett and
Just Another Vampire Story

There is a story Randall Garrett told me once about an obnoxious sixteen-year-old who buttonholed him at a science fiction convention and demanded to know how to write salable science fiction. Randall answered him patiently for several questions, but the kid was uncommonly persistent, and Randall is not known for having a particularly long fuse; so he finally told the kid to buzz off and grow up a little before he tried writing. "But," the kid persisted, "you were selling stories before you were seventeen, weren't you?"

"Yeah," Randall answered, "but I didn't have to ask anybody how to do it, either."

Of course, that story has been told before, about Mozart; but Randall can take almost any *cliché*, turn it upside-down and sidewise, and make of it something fresh and wonderful. His well-known Lord Darcy series, about a police detective in an alternate world where magic works and science doesn't, was born out of his impatience with the "scientific detectives" who went in for lengthy explanations of the scientific gobbledygook by which they tested for poisons, checked fingerprints and established ballistic markings. After reading a number of these, he said flippantly that they might as well do their work by magical spells—and then paused, and in that pause were invented Lord Darcy and his magical sorcerer sidekick, Sean O'Lochlainn, who ascertains if a given gun fired a bullet by working a spell forcing it to return to its origin—"The return-to-the-womb principle," as the magician blithely explains.

More recently, Randall has been working as half the team of Garrett and Heydron (see the introduction to "Cat Tale," in this volume) and together they have written the excellent

91

GANDALARA Trilogy . . . *The Steel of Raithskar, The Glass of Dyskornis,* and the forthcoming *The Bronze of Eddarta.*

Randall has also published a charming volume of humorous tales and parody-pastiches, *Takeoff* (Donning, 1980). And for this volume we have discovered a story never before printed in this country, which starts out to be the usual Vampire story . . . or is it?

JUST ANOTHER VAMPIRE STORY
by Randall Garrett

Did you ever meet a drunken vampire? I mean, *really!* Well, let me tell you. I didn't believe him, you understand; not for a minute. But let me tell you.

It was a couple of weeks ago. A Thursday night. I was feeling, you know, kind of lonely, so I decided to go down to The Flame, which is a very nice bar here in San Francisco, if you like that kind of bar, which I do, and that Thursday night it wasn't too crowded, for which I was thankful. Crowds make me nervous.

Anyway, I just sort of strolled in and looked around, just sort of checking the place out, you know—see who was there. I only saw two people I knew, George and Harry, and they were in a back booth glaring at each other, and I certainly didn't want to get into *that* hassle.

And then I spotted him.

He was an absolutely beautiful young man, with black, very wavy hair, cut long, and pale features that reminded me of a thin, young Lord Byron, if you see what I mean. He was wearing a black turtleneck, black jacket and black slacks. Not leather, you understand; those leather boys are just not my type.

Anyway, he was all by himself, with a nearly empty glass in front of him, at one of the side booths. He didn't look surly or mean, like so many young men do; he had a nice, dreamy smile on his rather too-red lips. (I wondered for a second if he wore lipstick. I hoped not; that would be too much.) I watched that dreamy smile for a while, and hoped he wasn't high on something stronger than booze. Oh, I don't mind someone having a little pot now and then, but I am absolutely down on anybody who uses the hard stuff.

I was wondering whether it would be worth my while to go over and investigate when his eyes caught mine and he smiled a little wider. He didn't take his eyes away, and that was an invitation if I ever saw one. I walked on over to where he was sitting.

"Hello," I said, "my name's Dan. Can I buy you a drink?"

"I'd love one, thanks." His voice was low and sort of husky. A nice voice, I thought. "My name's Boris." He had an accent I couldn't quite place. Russian? Too faint to tell.

I signaled Mickey, who's one of the waiters, and he came over to pick up our orders. Boris ordered a double bourbon on the rocks.

"And I'll have a double vodka, water on the side, Mickey," I said. Mickey knows I don't drink, so he always brings me water in both glasses, but since I pay for them as if they really were vodka, he doesn't mind. I like to be sociable, you see, and I found out years ago that going through that routine about being a reformed alcoholic can be an awful drag. Some sons-of-bitches actually try to wheedle you into taking a drink.

I decided after looking closely that he wasn't wearing lipstick; that was just the natural color of his lips. His eyes were fascinating, too: so dark they were almost black, and it was hard to tell where the pupil left off and the iris began. He had long dark lashes that a person might almost suspect were false, but at this distance I could tell they weren't.

I don't remember what we talked about at first. Trivial stuff, just chatter. You know the sort of conversations people have when they're feeling each other out. After about an hour, I decided we knew each other well enough.

"Boris," I said, "how would you like to come up to my place? I've got some very nice Jack Daniels and it's a lot better than sitting around this crummy place. You said you like Vivaldi? I have some records you might like to hear."

He looked at me. His eyes were still bright, but he was having just a tiny bit of trouble focusing them. "Danny, my boy, you jus' made yourself a deal."

We managed to get a taxi, even at that time of night. By

the time we reached my apartment, he had sobered up a little—but not much. I unlocked the door, let him in, and turned on the lights. He looked all around, weaving a little on his feet.

"*We-e-lll!* This place is all *right!*"

I was really glad he appreciated it. I have put a great deal of hard work into my place in order to make it pleasant and beautiful. "Thank you," I said. "I find it comfortable. The booze is in the Chinese cabinet over there—help yourself."

He did—plentifully. "Have you got any ice? I don't like warm whiskey."

"Sure thing," I said. I went over to the fridge and began filling a bowl from the icemaker. My back was to him when he said: "Dan, how old are you?"

"Twenty-eight," I lied, without turning around.

He gave an odd chuckle as I put more ice cubes in the bowl. "How old would you say I was?"

"Oh, nineteen, twenty," I said as I shut the fridge door.

"What if I told you," he said in a strange voice, "that I was born in 1757?"

I turned around to stare at him, the ice bowl in my hand. "You mean 1957."

"*Seventeen* fifty-seven."

"Oh, come now, Boris, nobody's *that* old!"

"I am," he said, with that same odd expression. The timbre of his voice had changed; it was firmer, somehow, even though the bourbon-induced slur was still there. "You see, I am a vampire."

Well, I just stared at him. I wondered what kind of silly game he was playing. Was he thinking of ripping me off or beating me up? Was he trying to frighten me with his story? Or was he just having a little game? He didn't look dangerous or threatening. I decided I might as well play along to see how far he would go.

"You mean you—you change into a bat? Things like that?"

He laughed softly. "Tha's silly, Dan. Jus' plain silly. Violate all the laws of physics. To say nothing of biology. Can I have some of that ice?"

He was sitting plopped in the middle of the big white bean-bag chair—you know, one of those big polyethelene bags half filled with little pieces of plastic foam. They're a little awkward to get out of, and I didn't figure he would try to jump me.

"Sure thing," I said. I picked up the ice tongs and went over to where he was holding up his glass. As I dropped cubes in, he said: "You're not saying much."

"Well—I mean, really—I mean, it isn't *every* day somebody tells you he's a *vampire!*"

He laughed that soft laugh of his and took a hefty belt from the glass. "No, I suppose it isn't. You don't look very frightened, though. Don'cha believe me?"

"Well, I don't know. What are you going to do, bite me in the neck, or something?"

He looked up at me. "No. But I could." Then he laughed—a real laugh, this time. And I saw those two canine teeth. They were like nothing I had ever seen before on a human being. I backed away without taking my eyes off him. That only made him laugh more. I put the ice bowl down carefully on the Chinese cabinet.

"Are you really trying to tell me you're one of the Undead?"

"Oh, no." He shook his head solemnly. "Tha's all superstition. I'm as alive as you are. Maybe more so. I'm just *different*, tha's all."

"Real vampires are supposed to be afraid of Crucifixes. I have one in the other room. Shall I get it?"

"Go ahead, Dan, if it'll make you any happier. Tha's superstition, too," He polished off his drink. "May I have some more?"

"Help yourself." I moved well away from the Chinese cabinet. "Real vampires aren't supposed to be able to drink anything but blood," I said.

Again that unearthly chuckle as he pushed himself up to refill his glass. He wobbled slightly, then walked over to the Chinese cabinet. "Another superstition," he said. "Jus' plain ol' superstition. Oh, we drink blood, all right—lots of it." He looked at me owlishly as he tilted the Jack Daniels bottle. "I know what you're thinking of: that line in the movie, 'No thank you, I never drink—wine.' " He put more ice in his glass. "Well, tha's all bullshit. A little booze never hurt anybody, even a vampire." He went back over and plopped himself into the beanbag again.

"Real vampires," I said carefully, "are supposed to be able to change other people into vampires."

"Ridiculous! Who could believe such rot? You're either a vampire or you aren't. Do you know what a vampire is?"

"I thought I did."

"Well, you don't. I'll tell you what a vampire is." He drank more bourbon. "Do you know that there are other planetary systems besides this puny little Solar System of yours? Well, there are. Yessir, there are." He waved his hand toward the window and the sky beyond. "Tha's where we come from. Ship got lost, cracked up here seven—close to eight hunnerd years ago. Not many of us left. Thirty-two survived. Twenny-four males, eight females. Not a good balance, not a good balance at all. We breed real slow, we vampires do."

He was silent for what seemed an awfully long time, staring broodingly at his glass.

I cleared my throat. "Even so, in eight hundred years—"

"You think there's more of us now? *Wrong!*" He glared across the room at me. "Earth diseases got a lot. Childbirth killed the women." A genuine tear rolled down one cheek. "My mother died when I was born."

"Real vampires are supposed to be immortal."

"Bullshit. Long life span. Twelve, maybe fifteen hunnerd years. If we don't catch anything fatal."

"Like not being in your coffin between sunrise and sunset?" I asked warily.

"Don' hafta stay in a coffin." There was scorn in his voice. "Stay anyplace where the sun's ultraviolet can't get atcha. Our original sun was much redder than this one. Not much UV. Five seconds can give a vampire deadly sunburn. But a coffin? *Hah!* I once spent a whole day riding the New York subways."

"Real vampires," I persisted, "are supposed to be immune to knives and bullets. I suppose that's superstition, too?"

He grinned wolfishly. "Ohh-*ho*-no, wrong again, Danny boy. Here, I'll show you. Got a knife? Gimme a knife. Or a gun."

"I haven't got a gun," I said. "I'll get you a knife." I went back to the kitchenette and got a small paring knife. I didn't feel it would be too smart to hand him my Danish steel chef's knife. "Catch," I said, and tossed it to him.

He tried to catch it, but it landed harmlessly in his lap.

"I'll show you, my shkeptical frien'," he said. Picking up the knife with his right hand, he stabbed the blade into the palm of his left—clear in to the hilt, so that the blade stuck out the back. He held up his left arm like a schoolboy trying to get the attention of his teacher. There was no blood.

He squinted one eye in an exaggerated wink. "Now, here'sa hard part. Watch. Watch." And he pulled the blade out slowly.

He bled a little. Not much. Then he wiped the blood off, and there was only a thin line of pink, which vanished quickly.

"Only way you can kill a vampire is drain all the blood from his body," he said. "Ol' stake-in-the-heart don' work, either."

Now, I didn't believe he was a real vampire, not for a second, but that was a pretty impressive trick. Still, I've read that it can be done with hypnotism or something like that. And there's some kind of hysteria—I forget just what—that will cause that effect in a human being. It's rare, I guess, but . . .

But I knew he was lying. Those teeth could be false—a specially made plate, maybe. And that story about coming from the stars just didn't sound sensible to me. Maybe I'm old-fashioned, but I just don't believe in all that foolishness.

I just stood there, looking at him, trying to think. What was he up to? Was it just a prank, or was he really trying to frighten me? "Real vampires—" My throat went dry. I swallowed and started again. "Real vampires are supposed to be immensely strong."

He lurched to his feet. I didn't like the look on his face. "Oh, we're strong, all right. I'll show you." I didn't at all like the way he said it.

He started toward me, and I just stood there, watching him. My back was already against the wall, so I couldn't get away from him that way.

"We're immensely stronger than any human being. Immensely stronger," he said.

Then, suddenly he leaped and grabbed my wrists.

At that moment, I believed his story. He was far stronger than any human being could possibly be.

I jerked my wrists out of his grip, flipped my hands, and grabbed *his* wrists.

His eyes opened wide in surprise and terror. He tried to jerk away, but I held him firmly.

Then I grinned, and he was *really* terrified.

"Those teeth!" he shrieked. "What in God's name are you?"

"Just another vampire," I said. "A *real* one."

About Adrienne Martine-Barnes and *Wildwood*

One of the cementing forces among all the people who belong to the Greyhaven constellation of writers is Sunday afternoon tea. And one of the people who help to make tea memorable is Adrienne Martine-Barnes, who once said, "After a morning spent at the typewriter, I have two options. I can pour myself six or seven drinks—bad for my waistline and my working ability—or I can go out in the kitchen and cook up a storm."

The results of Adrienne's "cooking fits" tend to be somewhat variable—like all imaginative people, she tends to experiment at times, and the results cannot be 100 percent perfect—did *you* ever try to eat blue rice pudding? On the other hand, she has devised many memorable and addictive delights; the "spinach walnut bread" she invented for a Darkover feast, the "rabbithorn en croute" ditto, which was probably the world's most elaborate *pate* baked in an antlered pastry shell, and a whole series of puddings and pastries and pies, including some thoughtfully devised for the restricted diets some of us are on. When you consider that she is also an excellent costumer who has won many masquerade prizes, a charming and humorous toastmaster at conventions, and an expert on Regency dancing, one wonders how she has time to write. But write she does; her first mainstream novel, called *Never Speak of Love*, has been acclaimed by at least one critical writer as a fine analysis of the struggle between woman and artist. Her science fiction novel *The Dragon Rises* is now in production, and between such major works she managed to produce a story for *Sword of Chaos* and now this finely crafted tale of a world where magic is commonplace . . . but what *kind* of magic—that appears to be the crisis.

I say "appears to be" because one of the fantasy cliche situations is a world where magic works and science doesn't; but Adrienne, in this story of a struggle between rival systems of magic, seems to be using fantasy as a metaphor for other struggles in our technologically oriented civilization, where rival views of science may destroy one world—or the other.

WILDWOOD
by Adrienne Martine-Barnes

Kera flexed her tired shoulders and took a ragged breath. She gritted her teeth and raised the slender metal rod again, beginning once more the ritual of the rising water. For nearly three days she had been trying to master the water before her, for the Ritual Mistress had locked her in the room and told her she could not leave until the task was accomplished. The words came from her mouth in a dreary monotone as she waved the wand over the silver bowl of water. It stayed as flat as glass, reflecting her strained face, the eyes two orbs of black opaline, flecked with red and gold and blue, her lips a line of carmine against the golden skin. Her grey-green hair hung like weeds against her scalp, damp with sweat despite the coolness of the room, so she saw herself drowned in the water she sought to control.

She stopped and sagged forward, feeling the thick stone walls around her like a living tomb. The thirst was almost unbearable, and she was tempted to drink the water, but that would not have helped. How many times had the Ritual Mistress explained that it wasn't water at all, but the essence, the symbol of water. It was useless. Kera never felt the essence she had been told she would find. Water was water, and she had no desire or need to rule it or order its supposed chaos. The stuff in the bowl was anything but chaotic.

Kera's head ached, and she felt weak and dizzy, a feeling which had been growing along with a curious cramp in her abdomen. At that moment her guts twisted sharply and she doubled over in pain, both hands grasping the wand as she bent. There was another twist in her middle, and she snapped the wand in her hands with a tiny chiming sound. Something warm and sticky touched the warm flesh on her thighs, and she gave a cry. The stones in the wall, blocks of metal made by spells, seemed to moan in answer.

Kera gasped. Four Forge-Mages had spent a year to create that object, and she had destroyed it in a second. She peered at it, seeking some flaw in the metal, for she was sure her strength was not great enough to damage the products of smithery. There was nothing.

A breeze seemed to enter the windowless room, a sweet-smelling draft which rippled the surface of the water in the bowl and swept away the musty dampness of stone and mortar. The perspiration on her brow dried as she looked around for the source of the air. The broken wand in her hands began to feel warm against her palms and she dropped them to the floor, backing away.

Then she saw the tiny spatter of dark red on the floor where she had stood, and watched the stone steam and seeth under it. Blood. She searched her hands for some cut when she had broken the wand, but they were unharmed. Blood was forbidden. The Ritual Mistress had pounded that into her. Only uncultured Woods folk used blood to make magic. Kera felt a cold knot of apprehension in her empty stomach and a strange tickle of something like pleasure at the nape of her neck.

The door behind her was unbolted from without, and a moment later her father, Coran, strode in, followed by Mistress Pelli, who taught ritual, and old Sebo, Forge-Mage and Fire Wizard. Coran, Mage Lord of Derry Keep, had a cut on his forehead and the hem of his white gown was singed, as if he had sat too close to the stove, and he was clearly in a fine temper. Kera loved his rosy complexion, his pale blue eyes and night-dark hair, but the expression on his face boded her no good. If only he would smile at me sometimes, or hug me like old Nurse did, she thought.

Mistress Pelli scowled and pursed her meager mouth as if she had just drunk something sour. Her nose quivered, sniffing the air. Behind her, Sebo tottered and looked faintly witless.

"What have you done!" Coran roared, his ruddy face becoming redder.

"I told you not to try," Pelli answered, before Kera could

speak. "You will be fortunate if the foundation doesn't crack."

Kera regarded the Ritual Mistress with all the dislike of years of mutual animosity. "I hope a stone crushes you, old woman. I hope the Keep kills all of you." The words shocked her. It was as if some dammed up river had burst in her mind, releasing thoughts she had hidden from herself.

"The room smells of blossoms," Sebo muttered, moving his hands in warding spells. "Apples. In Derry Keep. Horrible."

Coran grasped Kera by the shoulders and began to shake her. "What kind of daughter are you, defying me at every turn. I have given you everything—the best teachers, the finest tools. And you repay me with insolence and rebellion. Why?"

Kera felt as if a fire were in her veins, a rushing kind of madness. She placed a hand on his chest and shoved hard. "Everything! You give me nothing but dead stone and dead metal. I hate the feel of them, and Pelli's slimy rites, and you!" Her eyes narrowed. "I must be your tool to command the elements. Pah. I will not do it."

"I told you not to try to tame her, Lord. She is too much like her mother. Oh, no. Look!" Pelli pointed a trembling finger at Kera's bare feet. A thin line of blood coiled around the ankle like a strange serpent. "Ruin!"

"Swallow your tongue, old woman." Kera snapped the words thoughtlessly and wrenched herself away from her father. "Drown in your filthy rituals."

Pelli made a gasping sound and clawed at her throat. She opened her wrinkled mouth and a flood of dark liquid flowed down her chin, staining the rose-hued robe and pooling onto the floor. A stench like a cesspit filled the room, and Sebo gagged.

"Stop that," shouted Coran, pointing at the blood.

"How?"

"Look at your power, child. Feel it, control it. And stop that bleeding. If you don't rein it, the Keep will shatter."

"I did nothing," Kera screamed, terrified at the thrill of energy that seemed to fill her now.

"Don't you see why I trained you, forged you. Unritualized power is terrible, deadly. You might as well be a . . . Woods Witch." Coran made an expression of disgust at the mention of the despised race against whom the Keep Lords had waged a long and wearisome war.

"They are dead and gone. You told me so." Kera had a sudden moment of insight. "Or are they? Remember what you said? 'The last one died before your birth, child. Poor stupid primitives.' You told me that that was why we never leave the Keep, that the world outside was ruined by the war. And you never leave the Keep except at twilight, on a flyer, to go to some other Keep. Your feet never touch the earth. How can you bear the stink of those beasts?" She shuddered, for she hated and feared the huge winged animals who lived atop the Keep. "They are not all dead, are they, or you could walk about without fear. And I live. My mother was no minor Ritual Mistress, was she? She was a Woods woman, and so am I."

"Never. I will kill you first." Coran spoke without heat, as if he said no more than please sit down. Then he frowned. "The wards have failed. You should not be able to think such thoughts. You cannot be bleeding. No! This is not possible." He appeared more distressed by the failure of his magic than by his daughter's discoveries or rebellion. "This is your fault," he said, turning to the Ritual Mistress. "I gave careful instructions. . . ."

Pelli had been sawing the air in ritual gestures in an attempt to stem the tide of stuff from her mouth, and had finally gotten it to slow and solidify. "Your ambition," she choked, a large chunk of brownish sludge slipping from her tongue. "Curse you . . . can't remember . . . finished . . . empty, empty . . . wish . . . choked you . . . cradle." Then she tottered out of the room, leaving a trail of odorous muck in her wake.

"I must agree," quavered Sebo. "The Council was against your idea from the beginning."

"Small-minded bastards. They were jealous of my magic." Coran muttered these words, appearing bewildered now.

"Mistress Pelli and I did our best, but you must bear the responsibility, Lord Coran. We warned you that Kera was starting to show . . . odd talents . . . three years ago. You chose not to listen, and to tell the Council everything was progressing well. What is bred in the bone will come out in the soul. Pelli is right. The child should never have been permitted to live, and now she must certainly be killed. If she gets back to her people with the knowledge she has of our methods, there will be chaos."

"Why was I left alive?" Kera asked. She rather liked the old Forge-Mage, though she hated his fires and the metals that were his life and work.

He gave a shrug and a flutter of wrinkled hands. "Lord Coran thought to train your power to use it against the Woods Folk. He caught your mother one night and brought her here. She was a wild thing, a tangle-girl, but he warded her into submission, for she was nearly a child herself, and not yet in her power. She died the moment you drew breath, but the Lord had what he desired—you. A blending of our kind and hers. It was a cruel thing, but the Woods Folk were upsetting all our plans. It was intolerable. We would beat back the Wildwood in one place, and it would sprout up in another. Even today we must constantly sear the earth around the Keeps, or things will grow. Horrible, disorderly chaos." The expression on his wizened face was fearful.

There was a cracking sound far below and the Keep groaned like a huge beast. Kera slipped past her father and Sebo, nearly slipping in Pelli's noisome trail, and dashed for the spiral stairway. She plunged down the stairs two and three at a time. Coran roused from his reveries and followed her, howling in fury.

"Come back. I have to kill you!"

Kera kept going, cutting bare feet and hands on the unforgiving material of the Keep, brushing past dazed servants and Mages who were milling in confusion along the stairwell. The building rumbled and shook as the bewildered Keep folk tried to stop the breaking of the spells which held the structure together. Kera did not notice how the metal shrieked where her body fluids left any imprint.

She reached the bottom a little ahead of a now pursuing mob, feeling the stone around her struggle with the earth on which it rested. She had never been down this far in the Keep before, and she now knew why. She could sense the power which Pelli had been so careful to keep from her. The ground which had patiently borne its hateful burden of spell-warded blocks pushed eagerly into breeches, rending the foundations apart with sonorous rumbles. One portion of the wall crumbled and Kera saw a light beyond, a golden glow. She pressed herself through the small opening, scratching her body beneath the thin blue shift, and saw the sun for the first time.

It was a bloody orb in a clear blue sky, and she blinked at the unaccustomed light, for the Keep lived in candle and torch-light, ever dim and shadow filled. Before her lay a wide, bare expanse of bleached earth. She reached down and touched the crumbly dirt with a scratched hand, and the tower behind her rumbled ominously. Kera ran, a trail of bloody footprints marking the sterile ground.

Coran ran after her, his longer legs and greater strength shortening the distance between them. Then the Keep gave a final howl, an almost human noise that echoed across the bleached plain, and began to collapse, great stones flying through the air before they crashed to the suffering earth.

Gasping with fire-filled lungs, Kera faltered and looked back. A block whistled past her head. Coran had paused perhaps a hundred strides behind her to stare in horror as the Keep died. The flyers atop the building screamed as they fled their kennels, their huge pinons quartering the sky like black cloaks. The plain was milling with frightened people rushing to avoid destruction. She felt a sense of confusion, that all of this should be her doing.

Mage and Keep Lord that he was, Coran recovered some sense of control. He made a sign in the air and a flyer dove from the sky to land its great taloned feet near him. Coran mounted the beast and spoke a command.

The flyer gave a harsh croak and sprang toward Kera, the leathery wings stinking of decay. For a second, Kera could not believe what was happening. Her mind refused to accept that Coran was really determined to kill her. With a scream of fear and rage, Kera threw her bleeding hand up and smeared them across the parts of the dreadful wing that she could reach. The flyer's croak became a shriek of pain. One great pinon sagged as the blood turned to fire, then to grey ash. The flyer sank to earth, spilling Coran. The man staggered away, barely escaping a taloned claw which flailed in agony.

He sprang toward the girl, but she ran away again. Her legs trembled and she stumbled, but she rose again and went on, gasping. Then a sweet-smelling breeze wafted to her, and strength returned. Kera could not name the scent, except it spoke of home and calm and living.

Coran's cry halted her and Kera turned again. Something was rising out of the dead earth, supple, green, sinuous as a serpent, stong and vital. A living whip coiled around the Keep Lord's legs, and he tore at them, screaming. The plain behind them was churning with tangles, spurting from the ground as she watched. The Keep was a tumble of smashed blocks with creepers sweeping over them like green fire.

Immobilized but undaunted, Coran shouted at her. "You cannot win. Run back to your filthy trees and disordered greenings. Go bed some dirty Woodman and get him children. Then see them burn in our purifying fire. Clean! The other Lords will avenge me. When we are done, no blade of green will soil the world for a thousand thousand years. The fire will consume your kind. There will be order!" The tangle wrapped around his chest, squeezing the breath away. She heard the bones crack.

"I am sorry, Father."

"Sorry," he moaned. "You have ruined all my plans, and you are sorry." Then he died, the green creeper rustling around his head.

Kera bowed her head to torn hands, weary and sickened by the destruction that her ignorance and rage had caused. She felt empty, longing for some thing for which she had no clear conception. Snatches of Pelli's endless rites and ritual filled her mind, the words for birthing and departing, for wedding and beddings, words to make water rise and fire bow. She remembered all the wisdom of a lifetime leaking out of the old woman's mouth at her thoughtless command.

If only they had cared for me a little, if he had even loved for a moment, I would have done what they wanted. I should go. No, not yet. I cannot leave him without his passages. I owe him nothing, and he loved me not at all, but I cannot leave him like this.

After a time, Kera approached the green mound where her father's fleshless skull grinned up at a sun he feared and hated, and began the litany of passing, commending him to air and fire, protecting him from earth and water, an empty spake of words to a body in a bush. She found some meaning

for herself in that last ritual, some final understanding of
what had driven him.

Finally, she said, "Depart, Coran Derry-Lord
By untainted fire
And unblemished air
Speed on flaming wings
Across the darkening world
With no earth to hold thee
With no water to keep thee
To the light that is darkness
To unmoving air
And untrammeled order
Remembering that the reality is nothing
And the symbol is all."

The leaves of the tangle stirred and the skull seemed to
sigh, then crumble back into itself. Kera paused a moment,
then walked away, to seek the Wildwood and her mother's
folk, and the pale blossoms of an ancient apple tree.

About Phillip Wayne and *The Tax Collector*

Phillip Wayne plays an Irish harp, cello, banjo, flute, recorder, synthesizer, and half a dozen other instruments I have forgotten, as well as composing and performing for the guitar. He belongs to the Greenwalls, rather than to the original, or Greyhaven, portion of the extended family. His mundane occupation is that of a computer programmer, and he has created several software programs for the Apple Computer. I still remember one Bardic at Greyhaven when there were eleven Irish harps . . . but that is another story.

Phillip turned up at one of my writers workshops, and at that time wrote his first Gellan Greywolf story, about a harper who traveled with a grey linkwolf . . . a telepathic beast who aided and abetted the roguish Gellan at his pranks. At a later Bardic he read the present story, which I thought not quite up to professional standards; so I hassled and chivvied him until he did a proper rewrite.

Members of the allied households in the "Greyhaven Community" share much more than writing. Phillip did the final rewrite on the last page while I was babysitting with his son Alexander, three months old, (as most people know, when a small baby turns up at a convention, fans make bets about how long it will be till I get it on my lap). I like Gellan Greywolf, and prophecy that this will be only the first of his many adventures.

THE TAX COLLECTOR

by Phillip Wayne

Gellan Greywolf, sometimes called Gellan Harper, wrapped his large musician's hand about the smaller one connected to the street urchin reaching up to the wagon where Gellan sat.

Normally, children filled him with a sense of gleeful innocence, but in this particular case the hand extended to places where it should not have been—the inside of his belt purse. The boy would gladly have pulled it out, circumstances permitting, but the arm was passing through another obstacle.

Tira, Gellan's great linkwolf, had closed her jaws, ever so gently, on the arm attached to the hand. Each time the boy would try to remove the hand from the offending place, Tira would growl at him and tighten her grip.

So hungry! Tira thought.

NO! Gellan thought back.

Since all that could be seen of her was a grey head flopped carelessly over the side of the wagon out from a collection of cloth and canvas, the scene was beginning to draw a crowd.

Gellan smiled sweetly at the urchin, who seemed to take his obvious good will as a threat and began struggling to remove the arm from Tira's gentle care.

"Good day to you, young master," Gellan said as if he were talking to the son of a respected lord, "and what seems to have happened to your hand?" He withdrew it carefully from his purse, pulling the young boy up into the wagon with him.

Tira opened her jaws, but Gellan could hear her thinking how good a little meat would taste in her condition. Since he had saved her some months ago, in the northern woods, their link had always been strong. Now, with her ready at any time to bear the litter that she had barely started then, food was constantly on her mind.

The urchin struggled to remove himself from Gellan's grip,

now that the immediate danger of having the arm bitten off was past, but he found Gellan could hold him easily.

"I am Gellan," he said calmly, "perhaps you could tell me your name?"

"Aelwyn," the boy answered, still struggling. "My father is the butcher, and he will cut you and sell you in his shop if you harm me!"

"Will he now, Aelwyn?" Gellan laughed. "And does your father know that you pick purses for your spending money?"

"My father doesn't know anything, right now," the urchin said, quieting, "Baron Ayenbyte has him locked up because he couldn't pay his taxes. I was trying to find money to get him out."

Gellan clucked, and the dray-beast hitched to the wagon began to move forward as the crowd dispersed. "Wouldn't it have been safer to sell the meat in your father's shop? That would not be nearly so—ahem—dangerous."

"The baron took it all for his feast. He's getting married."

"In three days," said Gellan. "That's the reason I'm here. I'm supposed to play at the wedding. Tira's pups will be here any day now, and linkwolf pups are born starved. They need a lot of meat in a hurry."

"I can show you where there is a lot of meat," Aelwyn said slyly, "if you will help me get my father out of gaol."

"And why shouldn't I ask the baron directly for some meat, little one?"

"Because he wouldn't give it to you," Aelwyn said with such innocence and simplicity that, to his own surprise, Gellan actually believed him.

"Well, then, perhaps I will take you up on your offer. Tell me a little more about your father."

The baron had been taxing everyone heavily in preparation for the wedding. The woman was from a *very* rich barony nearby, and old Ayenbyte had stripped his barony bare to put on a festival which would equal any in her own barony. A doting father was part of the deal, and if daddy didn't like Ayenbyte's preparations, the whole thing might be called off.

Gellan had heard rumors about the state of Ayenbyte's treasury—or rather, its lack of state.

"You don't know the name of the lady in question, do you?" Gellan asked.

"No, but her father is named Orbearn, baron of Form."

Gellan knew Orbearn well. The man was conceited, smooth, and totally untrustworthy. If he was bringing his daughter to Ayenbyte to be married, Gellan was willing to bet that there was more than potatoes in his pot.

Perhaps, Gellan decided, he would help Aelwyn, see what Orbearn was up to and, if possible, help himself to the remains. As he talked with Aelwyn, Gellan found himself liking Ayenbyte less and less.

Gellan took a room that night in an inn called The Simpering Unicorn. It was not the best he had ever stayed in, but at least it was clean, and the innkeeper, Clerry, was a jovial, talkative sort once Gellan had wetted his throat with a few pints.

Clerry had actually been a part of the Ayenbyte household for a few months; when the baron refused to pay him for his services, he removed himself from Ayenbyte's employ.

"The baron," said Clerry, "is a fraud. He has all these heads on his wall—trophies of hunts. Ask him, and he will tell you just how he killed each one, and make quite a tale of it, too. And each one, he killed alone, without anyone about. Isn't that strange? But I know how he got each of those animals. He used to have a forester who could knock the fly off of a horse's rump at a hundred paces. When the baron went into the woods to hunt, the forester would disappear at the same time. Back came the baron, and the forester popped up. Guess who did the shooting?"

"No bets," Gellan said, pouring another ale for Clerry.

"He came in here one night, and we got drunk together. Told me all about it."

"What happened to the forester—what did you say his name was?"

"Marbry, Fletcher's son. Don't know what happened to him. The baron went hunting one day, but Marbry stopped by here for an ale. 'Isn't the baron hunting today?' says I. 'Aye,' says he, 'but he won't bag anything today,' and that's all he would say. Then he got on a horse and rode away. Never did find out why he left."

"And did the baron take any game that day?"

"Now how would I know? But they say he hasn't bagged anything since Marbry left." Clerry threw back his head and laughed.

Gellan joined him, and it echoed through the empty innhouse.

The next morning, Gellan packed the still sleeping Aelwyn next to Tira, and the three of them set off for the Castle Ayenbyte. The first thing Gellan noticed about it was the castle's lack of grandeur. There was the usual moat, even though this particular moat seemed to have been long dry. Inside of the moat was a low stone wall. Gellan was informed by a man who slumped guard (stood, Gellan decided, was not quite the word) that he should ask for admittance at the rear gate.

Inside the wall, the castle was not much better. There was a stable, a small house for the servants, a guardshouse that could hold fifteen men at arms, at most, and a main hall, which was shaped like a round box, and was the tallest structure in the complex, at least two stories.

Aelwyn awakened and joined him atop the wagon. "You're my son for the moment," Gellan said, "if you forget that, we will both have problems like your father. Understood?"

"Yes, father," Aelwyn said.

"Good, and behave yourself until I tell you otherwise. No doubt I shall tell you otherwise: think you can handle that?"

"Especially the otherwise," Aelwyn giggled.

A page brought Gellan into the main hall. It was plain that most of the taxes Ayenbyte had collected had gone into this one building. Rich brocades hung on the walls, framing hand-woven tapestries. Lighting was from sconces, alternately silver and gold, and lace covered the broad tables, already set for the guests with plates of gold, large goblets of the same, and knives of silver.

Gellan's palms itched. *A few of those could easily keep me for a year—perhaps more. I could get Tira's pups all the meat they wanted.*

At the head of the grandeur sat the Baron Ayenbyte, in robes of red and green, so much too long for him that they sprawled from his lap onto the stone floor.

The baron signaled for the page to leave them.

"Welcome to the barony Ayenbyte. We are indeed honored to have with us a bard of your stature for my wedding."

It was only on his feet that Gellan could appreciate the tremendous bulk of the man. *He would make four of me*, Gellan thought. *He couldn't lift a bow, let alone draw it and hit anything.*

"I am honored, your highness, to be in the company of such a great hunter." Gellan gestured to the heads lining the wall in back of the throne.

"Ah, yes, but it has been some time since I have gone hunting," the baron said. "I sprained my back almost a year ago; it has never been quite right since."

"I understand fully." Gellan walked up to the heads, examining each one. "You must have been a very good shot. I can't find an arrowmark anywhere on these."

"Shot through the eye, most of them," the baron boasted. "They make better trophies if the arrow goes directly to the brain."

"True. There was a time when I was such a shot. But not since I have taken to barding have I held a bow. I can sympathize with you, it feels as if I have lost a loved one sometimes."

"Why, that it does!" Baron Ayenbyte said, brightening. "You cannot tell how much it warms my heart to have a kindred soul to speak with. See that bear back there? I must tell you how I got him. I am sure you would like to hear."

The baron then commenced into one of the longest tales Gellan had heard from anyone not a storyteller by trade. *Also*, Gellan thought, *one of the least believable*. But he did his best to keep from looking bored or yawning, a feat more remarkable than the heroic deeds the Baron Ayenbyte recounted with such zest.

When he had finished, he started directly into another, and then a third. Gellan listened, sometimes clucking in sympathy, sometimes wide-eyed in simulated fear. The baron obviously counted himself a master storyteller.

Somewhere in the long series of tales, the baron sent for a barrel of ale. They sat drinking as they swapped tales of heroism in jungle and forest.

"It is a shame," Gellan said at last. "I am truly sorry that

you can't present your new bride and her father with a recent
kill for the wedding party. Orbearn judges men on what they
can do, not on what they have done."

"You know him?"

"Oh, intimately," Gellan lied. "I have sung for him a great
many times. Then a triumphal cornet went off somewhere in
Gellan's head, and he knew what he would do.

Without doubt.

Without qualm.

And without the slightest twinge of conscience.

"If I wanted to impress him," Gellan said, letting the
words flow like syrup from his mouth, "truly impress him, I
would present him with a stag. Not just any stag, mind you,
but one of the Great Whites in Flothen Wood. Not even Orbearn has one of those."

"A wonderful idea," said Ayenbyte, brightening, but then
dimming again. "But there is no way, unless we were to . . ."

"We?" Gellan could see that Ayenbyte was quite drunk.

"I thought you might be persuaded to help me. I can pay
you quite well. I thought . . . we might . . . go hunting. If
we brought down a stag . . . you brought down a stag . . .
we could say it was mine. A harmless little deception . . .
and I could pay you very well."

"Out of the question," Gellan said. But, unless he mis-
judged Ayenbyte, one refusal would only spark more interest.

As he expected, Ayenbyte urged him. Gellan said at last,
"I would give anything to have a good bow in my hands
again. Give me that, and we might go hunting in the morning."

Personally, Gellan doubted that a man of Ayenbyte's girth
could have mounted a horse, let alone go hunting. "But we
will have to get one tomorrow. My wedding is only two days
away, you know."

Baron Ayenbyte collapsed on the table, his face in a gold
plate.

Gellan rose, "Sleep well, Baron," he said. "Tomorrow night
may be somewhat less comfortable."

When he emerged, the sun had set, leaving the courtyard
in a misty fog. He found Aelwyn sleeping near the cart, and
nudged him awake.

He got a quill and paper, and settled on the seat to write a hasty note. Tira awoke and began licking his ear.

I'm hungry, she thought. *The pups will be here soon, and they have to eat.*

There is meat nearby, he told her. *We will take you there late tonight. When will the pups be born?*

Tomorrow night, or the next day, I think.

Gellan gave the note to Aelwyn, and sent him off to Clerry's inn with it. When the boy was safely gone, he lay down next to Tira and slept for a few hours.

It was dark when he awoke. Clouds had formed a thick layer obscuring the moon in the sky. Not even a star lent its light.

Now can we find some meat?

Somewhere near here, there is a whole butcher shop, little mother, Gellan thought. *Maybe more than one. Would you like to have your pups in there?*

Gellan extended a hand to the huge head and scratched behind Tira's ears. Tira purred and stood up.

Even for a linkwolf, Tira was large. She lept down from the wagon, followed by Gellan. When they stood side by side, her shoulders came up to his ribcage.

With that much meat, I can smell it if we get close.

They left the barn, walking slowly about the inner courtyard. Tira carefully held her nose high, sniffing the breezes.

Before the clouds had cleared, Tira found herself surrounded by meat in the castle stores near the kitchen. Gellan felt a wave of relief come over him. Even when they were friends, a hungry linkwolf with pups was a force to be reckoned with.

And when they were enemies . . .

Gellan wondered who would be the first of the cooks to come in the morning?

Gellan slept a few more hours, his preliminary duties done. He would need the extra rest for the coming day's activities.

When he reawoke, it was still dark out. Gellan saddled the largest horse he could find in the stable, also picking one out for himself. When both were saddled and bridled, he went in search of Ayenbyte.

The Baron was still as Gellan had left him.

Gellan shook him awake. "The horses are saddled, your lordship," Gellan said cheerily. "Time for an early start."

Ayenbyte blustered a bit, but finally awake enough to realize what was happening. "The deer hunt," he said through ale-clouded eyes. "We're going to get a stag for my wedding."

"Yes, yes," said Gellan. "We have to start early, if we want to get him today."

"Ah. Quite," the Baron said, looking round him groggily. "Can't go in these, have to get other clothes."

"No time to change," Gellan said, hurrying him out the door. "We have to start the hunt. Every hunt has to start early."

"I know that," the Baron said, annoyance showing in his voice, "I am an expert hunter."

"Of course you are, your lordship," Gellan said.

The Baron held a hand to his head for a moment, muttering something Gellan could not quite hear about the quality of his ale.

Gellan led him to his horse. "Your mount, Baron," he said.

The Baron stared, uncomprehendingly.

"Didn't you ride to the hunt before?"

"Of course I did," the Baron snapped, still holding his head with his hands. "But my back . . ."

"I'll help you mount," said Gellan. Bracing himself, he formed a shelf with his leg that allowed the Baron, still in his soft Castle footware, to mount. "I will need the best bow you have in the armory."

"Not the armory," Baron Ayenbyte said, his voice still groggy. "Look in the main hall, over the lintel." The Baron slumped forward, avoiding a fall by grasping the horse's neck at the very last moment. He let out a loud snore, but seemed to be secure.

The bow was a good one. In the light of the burning candles in the sconces, he could see that someone had been at part of it with a chisel, attempting to remove some runes. The job had not been well done, and the name Marbry was still plainly to be seen.

If Gellan had not found that bow with Marbry's name in it, he might, even now, have relented. But, this man needed a good lesson.

There was more spring in Gellan's step than there had been in a long time as he took the Baron's reins and led him deep into Flothen Wood.

"Page!"

The baron could bellow, as Gellan heard. There was no reaction, as he stirred the coals from the morning fire.

"No pages, Baron. We're on a hunt. Remember?" Gellan said. "Out to get a stag."

The baron shook his head. "No. I don't remember. We got drunk. I remember that. Uhhh," he groaned. "My head feels like my torturer used it for practice."

"He may have, but not since this morning. We rode out here, and I set up camp."

"You . . . set . . . up . . ." The Baron sputtered. "Who gave you permission to . . . oh goddess, I remember now. It was the middle of the night. You kidnapped me. I remember it all now."

"You came under your own power. Meanwhile, I would advise getting out of those robes and into something a bit more rugged."

"I didn't bring anything, damn you. You know that."

"Ah," said Gellan, as if that solved the matter. "Perhaps we could cut those up?"

The Baron ignored the insult as he became aware of the odor of cooking food. "Is that meat? Already?"

"Just a small rabbit I snared," Gellan said modestly. "It's down there in the coals. I thought I might have a good breakfast."

"Wonderful idea," Baron Ayenbyte effused. "I assume there will be enough for you also?"

"Certainly," Gellan said gallantly, "I am going to eat it all. You can catch your own, if you want some."

"I have had people killed for less of an insult than that! Watch your tongue!"

Gellan shrugged. "Perhaps, in your own castle, where you have guards and servants. Out here, we are just you and me. However, if I am feeling magnanimous, I might let you have a taste. It should be nearly done."

Gellan reached in and pulled out a crispy skinned carcass

from the ashes. He blew off the burnt wood and what was left would have done the cooks in Ayenbyte's kitchens proud.

Gellan tore off a haunch and handed it to the Baron. He finished it off in three mouthfulls and growled hungrily for more.

"Not until you've paid your taxes," Gellan said, as if speaking to a little boy. "We can't have tax debtors running loose now, can we."

"What are you babbling about, Harper. I make the taxes in this land, not pay them."

"Ah," Gellan sighed, "but now we are in the middle of the Flothen Wood, and unless I miss my guess, you have no way to get out. You are in my country, and here I make the taxes."

"You couldn't keep me here. My men at arms would come looking for me."

"Will they?" Gellan asked. "How long would it take them to find you in the middle of Flothen Wood, if they come in here at all. You seem to have made the place your own little preserve for quite a while. Now, it's someone else's turn. Pay up, Ayenbyte."

The baron sat down on a convenient log and glared at Gellan without answering.

Gellan busied himself around the camp. He cleared brush away, kept the fire supplied, other small things, more to be annoying than do anything constructive.

The Baron glared.

Noon came. Gellan left for a moment to check another snare he had set, and found it full with two rabbits instead of one.

Whistling for good fortune, he went back to camp, the two rabbits slung over his shoulder.

When he got back, the Baron was no longer there.

He called several times without an answer. He debated with himself if he should wait until he heard a call; finally the possibility of Ayenbyte hurting himself won out and he began to follow the wide swath that the baron left as he moved.

When he finally found him, there was nothing he could do but laugh. The Baron, in all his robes, had somehow scaled a tree and was staring with white rimmed eyes at the little creature below him.

It was about the size of the rabbits he had brought back to camp, but black with a single yellowish-white stripe running along its back.

The little animal looked up at the Baron and hissed. The Baron let out a terrified shriek, batting at it uselessly with his long robe. The robe had torn in several places, and the end of it was in shreds.

"Gellan, help me!" the baron shrieked again as the little animal stood on its hind legs and chattered. "Kill it, quick."

"Don't you mean 'kill it quickly'?" asked Gellan solicitously. "Your grammar should be correct, if you want to be understood. That advice is subject to a grammarians tax."

"Grammarians tax!" Baron Ayenbyte shrieked. "What are you talking about?"

"That is subject to a question tax. Along with the Grammarian's tax, and the bite tax for the rabbit haunch, you are getting quite a tax bill."

The little animal chittered again.

"Alright, I'll pay your blackmail . . ." he said through gritted teeth.

"Uh, uh, uh," Gellan said, shaking a finger, "this is just a little tax on services. I could slap a facts-in-error tax on you for that, but I'm willing to let it slide out of generosity."

". . . tax then. But get this monster away from me."

"I would like to, but you haven't paid your taxes," Gellan said simply.

"How can I pay your damned black . . . taxes when I'm up here in this tree?" he shouted.

"Ah," Gellan said, "I see that is a problem. I really don't know. You have some people in prison for exactly the same offense, and with exactly the same problem. Now, I calculate your taxes to be . . ."

Gellan leaned back his head as if in deep thought. ". . . about 14,000 zalts, plus or minus a few. And of course, that doesn't include any additional taxes I may have to add later."

Baron Ayenbyte went white.

"You're crazy," he said. The little animal chittered at him again.

"Anything," he shrieked. "I will give you anything. Just get rid of that monster."

"I only want what is past due on taxes, plus the interest, of course," Gellan said. "It is nearly 15,000 now, you know."

"I'll pay, I promise," said the Baron. "You have my word."

"Well then," Gellan sighed, "I must chase the monster off then." He picked a stout looking twig from the ground and threw it at the animal. "Shoo!" he shouted.

The animal obligingly skittered off into the underbrush.

"He came into camp after me," Ayenbyte said. "I ran for my. . . ."

He looked sheepishly at Gellan. "You did all this purposely, didn't you?"

Gellan shrugged. "You still owe me quite a bit in back taxes. Why don't you write me a document that will allow me to collect?"

The Baron made several indecent remarks about people related to Gellan, whom he could not possibly have known.

"Come, come," said Gellan, enjoying the situation. "We should at least be sportsmen about this. I could easily have left you in that tree."

The Baron followed him sullenly back to camp.

Lunch, for the sake of propriety, was not subject to the usual set of taxes. However, the sky was beginning to cloud up and they would soon be quite wet if they didn't find shelter.

"I could make a lean-to. That would give us some shelter until the rain stopped."

"But that might not be until tomorrow morning. It could rain all night during this part of the year! Take me back to the castle."

Gellan stretched languorously and lay back in the soft ground. "Why? I like the rain."

"But I'm supposed to be married tomorrow! You can't mean to keep me out here all night! I demand to be taken back at once." The Baron stood up, folded his arms over his chest, and, on his demand, stamped one foot on the ground.

Gellan scratched the tip of his nose with his index finger. "Why, so you were," he said, as if the news were a new and complete surprise to him. "How wonderful if you make it."

"My demands," the baron said, drawing himself up to his full height, "are not to be taken lightly."

"In my land," said Gellan softly, "demands of people in arrears of their taxes are not to be taken at all. And remember—I could have left you sitting in that tree."

For emphasis, he tugged slightly on the tattered remains of Baron Ayenbyte's robe of state. The piece of cloth came away in his hand.

The Baron grew silent again.

"Don't run away again, or I might not come looking for you the next time," Gellan said, and lay back to sleep away part of the day.

When the first drops of rain touched his face, it was early evening. Gellan snapped awake to make sure the Baron had stayed put, which he had.

The rain began to come down harder. It sopped the Baron's head, the water running down his face to mix with dirt already there. It created a muddy caricature of what was once smooth, white skin.

"Here's what I will take, in return for getting you to your wedding," Gellan said. "First, I want a document made out to me for 20,000 zalts for taxes and my expenses. Also, I want your written order that you will close all the tax debtors prisons. Finally, I want the real story of how you got each of those trophies. And no lies. I know all about Marbry and the bow you gave me. If you try to wiggle out of the other two, I will make sure everyone else sees the third one. Remember, it will be in your own hand."

The baron glared at him.

"Have it your way," Gellan shrugged, and went back to sleep in the rain.

It was nearly dawn when Gellan felt a pair of hands on him, shaking him awake.

"The fire went out," the baron said. "I'm freezing."

"So it did," said Gellan. "Too bad. I would have liked to have a nice, warm breakfast. Oh well, not much I can do about it now."

"But I'm *starving*," Baron Ayenbyte said. "If I could only get a little bite of something."

"I'm sure you could, if you would be willing to sign those

little documents we talked about last night. Oh, wasn't something else supposed to happen today, also?"

"I was supposed to be married," the Baron said miserably. "Now what can I do?"

"You could write out the documents."

"I don't have a quill. I will write them out when we get back to Castle Ayenbyte. Is that b-b-better?"

"Oh, my," said Gellan, "you're shivering. You could catch your death out here."

"I promise!" he screamed at the top of his lungs.

Gellan rummaged in his belt purse. "I have a quill in here, and some paper too. Why," he added in mock surprise, "I believe there might even be some ink. But no, I think not. After all, the rain might ruin them. We need a dry place."

"Make a canopy out of my robes," the baron pleaded. "Just get me back to the castle in time for the wedding."

Gellan thought for a moment. "Very well. Take off all your clothes."

"All of them? But I'm so cold already!"

"Off!" said Gellan.

The shelter was put up, and in a few minutes Gellan had all three documents in his pouch.

"Now we run back. It's not really very far at all."

"But my clothes! You can't want me to run through the woods naked."

Without listening, Gellan took off at a slow lope.

Swearing loudly, Ayenbyte followed.

Gellan trotted lightly out of the woods. In front of him stood Clerry, and a group of people from the town. *The boy did a good job*, Gellan thought. *I didn't expect him to be able to round up this many people for Ayenbyte's return.*

Gellan caught Aelwyn up as he dashed through the crowd and hugged the boy hard. "Wonderful! How did you get so many people?"

"I told Clerry," Aelwyn said, "and he got them. What's going to happen?"

"Just watch."

At the precise moment Gellan pointed, Baron Ayenbyte emerged from the woods in all his naked, pristine glory. His limbs were scratched and bruised, his body covered with insect bites and mud. In one hand he held a long stick, which he shook furiously while screaming obscenities at Gellan.

"Your Majesty," Gellan said, bowing low, but holding the purse containing the documents up so Ayenbyte could see it, "you should walk more slowly. Be more dignified in front of your subjects."

Ayenbyte eyed the pouch containing the true story of his kills, as well as the other documents, and slowed.

"Now, isn't this something you would like to read to your subjects?" Gellan asked, drawing out the document freeing the tax debtors and closing the gaols.

"Can't this wait until I have some clothes on?" he hissed *sotto voce.*

"I fear not, your majesty. And you'd better do it fast, because I think I can see your wedding party coming."

Ayenbyte craned his neck to see over the crowd and down the main road that led to the castle; then swore and grabbed the document out of Gellan's hands. He started to tear it up; then thought better of it as Gellan began to reach into his pouch for the confession about Marbry.

He eyed the approaching party, and began reading as fast as he could. At first, the crowd laughed, but soon their laughter changed to cheers for Gellan and, to Gellan's surprise, even for Ayenbyte.

When someone out of the crowd produced a blanket and tossed it to the baron, he was almost reduced to tears in gratitude. That was short lived, however, as the party came closer.

The Baron bolted for his castle. The man who had slumped guard before had now assumed a somewhat more relaxed posture, and was obviously now sleeping guard. The baron had to shout at the top of his lungs to wake the man up.

Gellan followed him in, but as the baron headed for the main hall, Gellan headed for the kitchen. The scene was incredible. There were six cooks, armed with hatchets and cleavers, standing against a huge linkwolf with four pups. The wolf was growling, fangs exposed and claws at the ready for any attack.

In the meantime, her cubs, as all cubs are wont to do, were busily cleaning out the meat locker. Meat was strewn over the floor, each cub with a small pile lying near it. Tira had a piece of steak flank lying at her feet, a chunk of it missing and nowhere to be seen.

"Best to let her be," Gellan said to one cook who seemed to be contemplating adding his own body to the collection of raw meat already on the floor.

To make the point a bit more strongly, Tira drew her upper lips back to show a bit more fang.

"But the baron will be furious!" the young cook quailed. "We were supposed to cook that meat for the feast tonight."

"I'm sure the baron will understand," said Gellan, thinking of the documents that he still had in his purse and smiling a bit. "And, if he doesn't, tell him that I can still read his handwriting."

"What does that mean?" the cook asked.

Gellan winked. "It's a magic spell," he said somberly. "Come on, Tira, we have urgent business on the coast, and I have the feeling the baron's hospitality may turn sour very soon."

Outside the gate, he started to chuckle. It turned into a laugh, and then a howl. Tira picked it up, and then the pups joined in, as they went howling down the road.

About Robert Cook and *The Woodcarver's Son*

I heard many of these stories first at a Bardic Revel at
Greyhaven. As the hour grows late, and casual acquaintances
are thinned out, in the wee small hours of the morning, some
unusual things turn up; and that night, for some reason, we
started reading poems about unicorns. After three of them,
Robert Cook, called Serpent at Greyhaven, read the following
story. I thought, when he began it, that it would be the standard romantic tale about unicorns. Did I get a surprise . . . !

Robert Cook lived at Greyhaven for some years, doing
housework and cooking in return for living space and time to
establish himself as a writer. He called himself "Serpent" out
of a flippant joke about being "Your obedient humble Serpent." He was a poet of considerable local reputation, doing
dramatic readings in local coffee houses; he designed incredibly elaborate masquerade costumes, and one night surprised
the two households, Greyhaven and Greenwalls, with his
Christmas present to us all, an elegant eight-course dinner
catered and cooked with his own hands. He was a tall,
skeletal blond youth, about the age of my own oldest son,
David. He was active in the Society for Creative Anachronism; and from the time she was seven years old or thereabout, my daughter Dorothy was his page and apprentice in
the Society, and his devoted follower and companion. He
designed her first Parade costume—an elegant basilisk—and
constructed the elaborate metal armature for the mask; I
have always thought this influenced her to move toward her
present work—the professional designing of Renaissance
Faire costumes. His wife Cathy, a gifted singer with a local
operetta company, became her guardian and mentor when
she was working as an actor with the Faire. Serpent and
Cathy were virtually surrogate parents to Dorothy during her

early adolescence, when every youngster needs at least three sets of parents to guide and help her during the rebellious years.

In the earliest stages of planning for this anthology, I asked Tracy for "Serpent's unicorn story," whose name I did not remember—though the story itself, and the chill it had given me, remained unforgettable. But the story was out to another market; and about that time I learned that Serpent was gravely ill with skin cancer. After a lengthy struggle with chemotherapy, and the false hope of a cure, he died in October, 1981. He had just completed his thirtieth year. He was far too young to die.

And I think you will agree that, as we lost a cherished friend, the world of fantasy has lost a very gifted and promising newcomer. Yet all our lives are richer for having known him, and for the fine work he left.

THE WOODCARVER'S SON
by Robert A. Cook

published in *Fantasy Tales,* vol. 4, No. 7, Spring 1981

Gretch stared pensively into the bubbling murk of the cauldron; thoughts, faces, and events swirled there in an ever-changing tapestry of grey mist. He blew lightly into the rising steam and waited as the vapors crowded aside to form a pool of emptiness; into this void he sprinkled a few grains of an indeterminate herb, muttering arcane words as he did so.

The heavy liquid bubbled once, swallowing the herb, and the sorcerer waited.

"Come, come, my children," he said after several moments, "why do you fret and tease me so? Come forth that I may know those secrets you guard so carefully."

From all manner of places about the room darted small giggles of laughter, high and tinkling like faerie bells, never coming from the same place twice.

Gretch leaned back a trifle from the cauldron, the corners of his mouth turned up in the beginnings of a patient smile, as he waited for the merriment to subside.

At last, amid a chorus of crystalline laughter, a bright, silvery voice spoke. "What is it you would know, Earth-father?"

"Only how the unicorns fare," he replied, smiling.

A renewed chorus of excited laughter followed; from within came the rustle of many tiny voices, like the breath of a summer breeze through quiet trees.

Eventually, the voice returned, giggling excitedly, expectantly.

"The unicorns are hungry, Earth-father."

The ageless sorcerer considered this for a moment, leaning heavily on his staff; he stared deeply into the void above the cauldron, absently rubbing his chin and frowning.

After a few moments, he chuckled thoughtfully and slowly nodded his head.

"Yes . . . I see." He paused for a moment, then continued. "Very well then, my children; I have an errand for you."

"Yes, Earth-father," the voices giggled in unison, "we hear and obey."

"Excellent. You are good children. Now, get you to the house of Aeol, son of Berchta the woodcarver, and whisper in his ear, as he sleeps, that something very wonderful awaits him in the little valley of the Humber; and he need only go there to have it."

Again the chorus of tinkling laughter broke out around the room; one of them replied, "Yes, Earth-father, we shall." Then, the laughter vanished.

Gretch smiled to himself and went off to look after some matter that demanded his attention. The rising vapors swirled momentarily about, filling the void above the cauldron, and finally settled down into vague, drifting mists.

That night, Aeol, the woodcarver's son, had strange dreams.

Aeol awoke restless and ill-at-ease; the usually secure, if solitary, comforts of his house and shop, nestled safely in the village, were anything but contentment for him today.

It was certainly not his custom to wander about in the lonely hills and valleys of Umberland; sticks and sharp stones were the least of a traveler's worries and pinpoints of light often gleamed furtively out from the shadows. Yet, this day, it ill became him to keep his house and shop. Suddenly, he wanted to know what lay beyond the village, to explore distant places his foot had never trod and behold sights his eyes had never seen.

So, off he went, food pouch at his side, staff in hand, and his footsteps leading him unwittingly toward old Father Humber.

As the sun slipped quickly toward the western hills, Aeol found himself far from the village. On setting out, he hadn't planned to spend the night away from home; apart from those things of the darkness against which he had charms and talismans, there were wild beasts to make the wanderer cautious. Some, it was said, would not shun the flesh of a sleeping man. Yet, despite this, he had no inclination to return, and found, to his surprise, that his food pouch contained enough for two or three days instead of one as he'd planned.

He stopped on a low crest as the gathering gloom hid the faces of the trees and covered the gullies with shadow. He needed someplace to sleep, but he shied from the glades and thickets for what they might contain and from hilltops that would betray him to sinister eyes. For a moment, he hesitated, but the night was not so dark nor its denizens so cruel as to outweigh what he felt he might find there. So thinking, he took a deep breath, gripped his staff a little tighter, and set off down the hill.

At last, he came upon a small dell through which flowed a quiet stream. Angling away from the water was a large rock, a cubit's length taller than himself, that rose gradually into a low hill behind. Together with the stream, they formed two natural barriers and made a small, protected area in which to camp. On the open side, he built a fire and set about making himself secure for the night.

After he had eaten, he leaned comfortably back and gazed about. The fire cast vague shadows in wavering forms on the rock and his imagination made creatures of little comfort from them. Disquieting sound filled the night from the trees and brush about the dell, suggesting the presence of uncanny beasts. He gazed uneasily at the shadows, hoping it was just his imagination.

Suddenly he froze, and fixed his gaze on the white, horse-shaped head that had appeared on the rock above.

The amber eyes reflecting the firelight were gentle; the ivory horn that stood up from its forehead had never drawn angry blood, he knew. Its whole presence seemed one of curiosity, as though it had seen the fire and come to learn its meaning.

He stared at the unicorn for long moments, until his eyes began to water. He blinked once and she was gone. He leapt up to follow, but stopped.

There was no need to chase her through the darkness; when morning came, he had only to climb the nearby hill and descend into the little valley of the Humber. There he would find her.

The dawn found him looking down from the hilltop into the lush valley through which flowed old Father Humber. Everything seemed quiet and serene, yet he had the distinct impression of being watched. Nor was that his only odd feeling. Although he couldn't see her, he knew exactly where she was; and . . . it almost seemed as though she were waiting for him.

At the base of the hill, he entered a dense thicket made nearly impassable with brush and low-hung branches. Twigs caught in his clothes and leaves caught in his hair as he forced his way through; and, more than once, he had to stop to free his foot from a maze of gnarled roots.

At last he came to a place where he could see green fields just beyond the next curtain of leaves. He twisted sideways, pushed the foliage apart and forced himself through. As the thicket closed behind him, he turned his head and looked across the open field.

He stopped; his mouth fell open and he stared as if in a trance. There, at the water's edge, she stood.

Surrounded in a cloud of golden sunlight she was. Purer than the newest fallen snow, shimmering and glistening like gem-woven satin, her coat caught the morning light and hurled it back in a rainbow of crystalline white, while her mane ruffled in the breeze like an unwoven tapestry of feathered silk. Rising straight away from her forehead and tapering to an infinitely delicate point, her single, ivory horn glittered and sparkled like polished pearl. And, from luminescent pools of white, two orbs gazed at him, not crude yellow, not tawdry amber, not even gaudy gold, but brilliant, radiant sunlight.

Whether for moments or ages he stood, Aeol didn't know. Her beauty spun in his thoughts, filling every corner of his mind and leaving no room for anything else. How such a creature could exist was beyond his comprehension. Legend and myth paled beside her and even the gods, themselves, were but shoddily clad mimics in her presence.

How he came to take that first step he didn't know. His mind aswirl with her beauty, he never felt the lush, soft grass beneath his feet. He didn't feel the spring breeze as it gently caressed his frame, drawing him forward. He was deaf to the twinkling whispers that urged him onward step by step. And he didn't see the green of the meadow and the blue of the sky as they lay a path for him to where she stood.

And then he was before her, looking into her eyes. He stood there in unthinking awe, for he could actually feel her beauty, as though it were, itself, a living thing.

He would never have thought to touch the unicorn; nay, by the gods, not he! Not a mere mortal, clothed in the rags of his own shabby world, unfit to praise the blades of grass she bent beneath her hooves! Yet, seemingly of its own volition, his hand rose.

Aghast, he watched as his fingers fell slowly toward the silken forehead. Had he been himself, he would have stopped, but no power on earth could have wielded force enough to stay his hand.

Then, he felt it; like no gosling's down, like no lamb's wool, not calm water, nor new blade of grass, not even spring thistle down. His fingertips began to tingle, sparkling like frozen nerves beginning to thaw. It spread to his arms and shoulders, his chest and legs, countless bursts of ecstasy everywhere at once.

Just as he hadn't been able to prevent that first touch, he couldn't end it; his fingers seemed held there by some uncanny power. Then, his amazement redoubled as he found himself laying his whole hand against her and the ecstasy growing equally.

In utter confusion, he stroked that incredible form. Each caress grew longer; each stroke drawing him farther away from her head, down her silken neck, her mane wrapping and unwrapping about his fingers. And on he went until he found his hand upon her back.

Then, she knelt.

Her intent was quite clear to him, but it wasn't real. His leg swung slowly over and he settled down onto her back.

Again, there was nothing to describe what he felt. It wasn't flesh; flesh is coarse and rough. This was form, perfect form, held in place by her will and shaped as she wished it, fitting perfectly to his own lines and sacrificing none of her own to do it.

Slowly, he felt changes beginning. Could he say it was the bunching of muscles, the tautening of sinews? Not by all the gods! There was no change of form, no altering of curves and lines, no movement at all. It was a gathering of energy, a summoning of uncanny strength and unearthly power . . .

And they were gone!

She didn't rise, she didn't leap. She didn't even seem to move. In one fluid motion they were away, flying with a grace and ease no heaven-sent wind could have. All about him was a mist of green and brown, while beneath him coursed a sea of emerald.

Over the lands they went. Over the hills and brakes, through field and forest and thicket alike, as though in a dream, with never the tiniest breath of a thought.

Aeol the woodcarver's son was no fool. He knew the envies and prejudices of his kind too well, so he dared not take the unicorn back to the village. Yet he refused to leave her alone for fear of losing her. Thus it was that, that night and ever afterwards, he slept with her in one of the many glades and thickets in the woods about Wednestown.

One morning when he awoke, she was gone. He leapt to his feet and ran frantically through the trees, calling and searching. A short while of this brought him around a small knoll where he found her staring curiously at him as though wondering what all the excitement was about. After that, he never again feared losing her.

As the days turned into weeks, Aeol came to love the unicorn as he had never loved anything before. She was unearthly, magical; she made the reality of his life a dream from which he resolved never to wake. Boredom vanished in a world of delight and his dreary life of before faded into an abstract memory which he recalled as though it belonged to someone else.

He abandoned his house and shop in the village to live with her in the woodlands, seldom leaving her side. Every day with her was special; she showed him strange and wonderful sights, bearing him countless leagues away from home, far beyond the boundaries of his knowledge.

She took him to where the land ended, and he, alone of all his kin for a hundred years, watched as the relentless water beat against the sand. In a bright summer sunrise, he stood on the massive wall the Romans had built against the wild North men. And, on a clear afternoon in early fall, he gazed across a wide expanse of water and beheld a land completely foreign to him.

When they were not traveling, they would walk quietly along shaded paths, listening to the sigh of summer winds or watching the scamper of brown squirrels. Sometimes, they sported and played in the meadows where the grass was thick and soft underfoot; and sometimes, they would just lie still in a cool glade, he with his head upon her shoulder, and taste of the quiet.

Gretch waited patiently for the laughter to subside as the steam from the cauldron wove strange tapestries about his ancient, ageless face.

"So, my children," he said when all was quiet again, "how fares our young woodcrafter?"

The days had flown swiftly away; spring had become summer and summer had become autumn. The air had cooled, the days grown shorter and it was All-Hallows Eve.

"Oh, very well, indeed, Earth-father," the twinkling voice replied. "Just yesternight he stole the last gold ring he needed to complete his secret work."

"That is well; all transpires as I expected. Now, I have an errand for you."

The voices giggled.

"Go to Aeol where he naps in a glade with his unicorn and whisper to him that tonight is the night; to delay longer would be folly."

Excited laughter filled the room.

"We hear and obey, Earth-father."

Aeol gazed with pride at the marvelous thing he had wrought; it had taken him half the summer to make it. By night, he had crept into the village to steal what he needed; by day, he had hidden himself away and spent endless hours carving, sewing, and fastening. The result was truly something to wonder at.

He reverently stroked the carvings of the leather straps and delicately caressed the gold rings that held them together. He had labored endlessly and tirelessly so that each part would be perfect, each detail exactly to the measure and meaning of its use. Only this would be proper for what he felt; only this was worthy of the wonderful creature which would wear it. Only this was right for a unicorn ... his unicorn.

He turned in the moonlight and stepped forward, holding out the halter with its reins of carven leather and its rings of pure gold.

"And now, my beautiful one," he said, "you shall wear this thing I have wrought for you. It will be a sign, a mark, that all who look upon you shall know that I am your master, that you are mine."

The horn slid easily into his chest, as though his body were made of air. He tried to back away, but he couldn't move his legs. He hesitantly touched the silken forehead and looked uncomprehending into her eyes; those depthless pools of sunlight gazed back at him softly, tenderly, and without malice.

His vision swayed and the meadow reeled before him, swirling in a maelstrom of midnight grey and silver.

Then, the agony began; not from his chest and spreading outward, but through his entire frame in one instant, spinning and swirling as it grew until it blotted out everything else.

His senses were drowned, obliterated in a raging sea of

pain. Greater it grew, faster it went, faster and greater until it was devoured by darkness, blacker than a moonless night.

And, at last, even the darkness was gone.

"What is this place, Learned One?" the apprentice asked. "And why have we come here on All-Hallows Eve?"

The seasons had spun many times round, but had not greatly changed the appearance of the meadow.

"One of great magical power," the sorcerer replied. "For the spell we have come here to do it will be invaluable."

"How can that be, Wise Teacher? I behold nought but the remains of an old halter and a pile of bone chips."

"Note the advanced corruption of the leather; it has lain here many years. Yet, the bits of bone remain neatly stacked in their cone-shaped pile, undisturbed by vultures and other scavengers."

"You speak truly, Master. A most powerful weird must here abide to cause so strange a thing."

Gretch smiled, remembering the night that Berchta the woodcarver had, at the behest of the Christian monks, led the rampaging villagers over the hill and up the mountain to ravage his home.

"Aye, Gremlet, a most powerful weird, indeed; a unicorn has fed here."

"A unicorn, Learned One? I knew not that they fed at all; what is it that they eat?"

Again Gretch smiled and, this time, chuckled softly to himself.

"Only their masters, Gremlet; only their masters."

About *The Incompetent Magician*

One of the privileges of an editor is to choose one of his or her own stories for inclusion. It is also known as "Rank hath its privileges" or as "Thou shalt not muzzle the ox that treadeth out the grain."

Why did I choose "The Incompetent Magician"?

Ever since I started writing, in the late forties and fifties, I have felt myself barred from writing straightforward fantasy. From the demise of *Unknown*, in the forties, until the rise of the Ballantine Adult Fantasy series in the sixties, fantasy was a much-neglected genre. Every science fiction magazine, in their market reports, said "No fantasy wanted." The best-known writers, Merritt, Kuttner, C.L. Moore, during those years covered their fantasy with a skin, sometimes a very *thin* skin, of scientific rationale; even in *Unknown*, fantasy was covered with a flippant and jocular attitude, as if the agreement were, "Fantasy is fun, but nobody must take it seriously, not in the middle of the twentieth century." In a rational society, no one wanted to face the confrontation with the deeper levels of the subconscious, where the archetypes of fantasy have their eternal hold on the human mind.

All of that changed when Tolkien, Donaldson, the new school of fantasy writers, took the youth of America by storm in the sixties. Now fantasy is a respectable *genre*. . . . and almost too popular. I remember once, when I was reading slush in the DAW office, which I like to do as a way of keeping my editorial skills honed—I found what looked like a fairly well-written novel, and, described it at a tea break to Don and Betsy Wollheim; Don sighed and said, "In other words, the standard first-novel fantasy world." Then he sighed again and demanded, "Isn't anyone writing *science fiction* anymore?"

By the time the fantasy boom came along, I was already established as writing science fiction. I used, not magic wands and magic swords, but the sciences of parapsychology; and while some hard scientists take a dim view of the realities of parapsychology, at least it is a game with very strict rules, and rational assessment of powers. Never in my life had I written about pure magic—the kind where a magician waves his magic wand and all the rules are suspended. Then I was asked to contribute to a Robert Asprin anthology, with a number of other writers—Poul Anderson, Gordon Dickson, John Brunner—and I wrote the first story about Lythande, mercenary-magician and Pilgrim Adept. I had intended only to write that one story; but her ghost persisted in walking, and at present there are several stories about Lythande in the process of formation. I said ruefully, once, that I thought Lythande had become my Jirel of Joiry.

I read the first five pages of this story once at one of my writer's workshops—where I require the workshop participants to write a story *during* the workshop, and I never ask anyone to do anything I am not willing to do myself. Ever since then, everyone who was in the workshop has been asking me what happened to Lythande and the incompetent, stammering Rastafyre the Incomparable; so I finished this story for them.

THE INCOMPETENT MAGICIAN
by Marion Zimmer Bradley

Throughout the length and breadth of the world of the Twin Suns, from the Great Salt Desert in the south to the Ice Mountains of the north, no one seeks out a mercenary-magician unless he wants something; and it's usually trouble. It's never the same thing twice, but whatever it is, it's always trouble.

Lythande the Magician looked out from under the hood of the dark, flowing mage-robe; and under the hood, the blue star that proclaimed Lythande to be Pilgrim Adept began to sparkle and give off blue flashes of fire as the magician studied the fat, wheezing little stranger, wondering what kind of trouble this client would be.

Like Lythande, the little stranger wore the cloak of a magician, the fashion of mage-robe worn in the cities at the edge of the Salt Desert. He seemed a little daunted as he looked up at the tall Lythande, and at the glowing blue star. Lythande, cross-belted with twin daggers, looked like a warrior, not a mage.

The fat man wheezed and fidgeted, and finally stammered "H-h-high and noble sor-sor-sorcerer, th-this is embarras—ass—assing—"

Lythande gave him no help, but looked down, with courteous attention, at the bald spot on the fussy little fellow's head. The stranger stammered on:

"I must co-co-confess to you that one of my ri-ri-rivals has st-st-stolen my m-m-magic wa-wa-wa—: he exploded into a perfect storm of stammering, then abandoned "wand" and blurted out "My p-p-powers are not suf-suf-suf—not strong enough to get it ba-ba-back. What would you require as a f-f-fee, O great and noble ma-ma-ma—", he swallowed and managed to get out "sorcerer?"

Beneath the blue star Lythande's arched and colorless brows went up in amusement.

"Indeed? How did that come to pass? Had you not spelled

137

the wand with such sorcery that none but you could touch it?"

The little man stared, fidgeting, at the belt-buckle of his mage-robe. "I t-t-t-told you this was embarrass-as-as—hard to say, O great and noble ma-ma-magician. I had imbi-bi-bi—"

"In short," Lythande said, cutting him off, "you were drunk. And somehow your spell must have failed. Well, do you know who has taken it, and why?"

"Roy—Roygan the Proud," said the little man, adding, "He wanted to be revenged upon m-m-me because he found me in be-be-be—"

"In bed with his wife?" Lythande asked, with perfect gravity, though one better acquainted with the Pilgrim Adept might have detected a faint glimmer of amusement at the corners of the narrow ascetic mouth. The fat little magician nodded miserably and stared at his shoes.

Lythande said at last, in that mellow, neutral voice which had won the mercenary-magician the name of minstrel even before the reputation for successful sorcery had grown, "This bears out the proverb I have always held true, that those who follow the profession of sorcery should have neither wife nor lover. Tell me, O mighty mage and most gallant of bedroom athletes, what do they call you?"

The little man drew himself up to his full height—he reached almost to Lythande's shoulder—and declared, "I am known far and wide in Gandrin as Rastafyre the Incom-comp-comp—"

"Incompetent?" suggested Lythande gravely.

He set his mouth with a hurt look and said with sonorous dignity, "Rastafyre the *Incomparable*!"

"It would be amusing to know how you came by that name," Lythande said, and the eyes under the mage-hood twinkled, "but the telling of funny stories, although a diverting pastime while we await the final battle between Law and Chaos, puts no beans on the table. So you have lost your magic wand to the rival sorcery of Roygan the Proud, and you wish my services to get it back from him—have I understood you correctly?"

Rastafyre nodded, and Lythande asked, "What fee had you thought to offer me in return for the assistance of my sor-

cery, O Rastafyre the incom—" Lythande hesitated a moment
and finished smoothly "incomparable?"

"This jewel," Rastafyre said, drawing forth a great sparkling ruby which flashed blood tones in the narrow darkness
of the hallway.

Lythande gestured him to put it away. "If you wave such
things about *here*, you may attract predators before whom
Roygan the Proud is but a kitten-cub. I wear no jewels but
this," Lythande gestured briefly at the blue star that shone
with pallid light from the midst of the high forehead, "nor
have I lover nor wife nor sweetheart upon whom I might
bestow it; I preach only what I myself practice. Keep your
jewels for those who prize them." Lythande made a snatching
gesture in the air and between the long, narrow fingers, three
rubies appeared, each one superior in color and lustre to the
one in Rastafyre's hand. "As you see, I need them not."

"I but offered the customary fee lest you think me nig-
gardly," said Rastafyre, blinking with surprise and faint
covetousness at the rubies in Lythande's hand, which blinked
for a moment and disappeared. "As it may happen, I have
that which may tempt you further."

The fussy little magician turned and snapped his fingers in
the air. He intoned "Ca-Ca-Carrier!"

Out of thin air a great dark shape made itself seen, a dull
lumpy outline; it fell and flopped ungracefully at his feet,
resolving itself, with a bump, into a brown velveteen bag, em-
broidered with magical symbols in crimson and gold.

"Gently! Gently, Ca-Ca-Carrier," Rastafyre scolded, "or
you will break my treasures within, and Lythande will have
the right to call me Incom-comp-competent!"

"Carrier is more competent than you, O Rastafyre; why
scold your faithful creature?"

"Not Carrier, but Ca-Ca-Carrier," Rastafyre said, "for I
knew myself likely to st-st-stam-that I did not talk very well,
and I la-la-labelled it by the cogno-cogno—by the name
which I knew I would fi-find myself calling it."

This time Lythande chuckled aloud. "Well done, O mighty
and incomparable magician!"

But the laughter died as Rastafyre drew forth from the
dark recesses of Ca-Ca-Carrier a thing of rare beauty.

It was a lute, formed of dark precious woods, set about

with turquoise and mother-of-pearl, the strings shining with silver; and upon the body of the lute, in precious gemstones, was set a pallid blue star, like to the one which glowed between Lythande's brows.

"By the bloodshot eyes of Keth-Ketha!"

Lythande was suddenly looming over the little magician, and the blue star began to sparkle and flame with fury; but the voice was calm and neutral as ever.

"Where got you that, Rastafyre? That lute I know; I myself fashioned it for one I once loved, and now she plays a spirit lute in the courts of Light. And the possessions of a Pilgrim Adept do not pass into the hands of others as readily as the wand of Rastafyre the Incompetent!"

Rastafyre cast down his tubby face and muttered, unable to face the blue glare of the angry Lythande, that it was a secret of the trade.

"Which means, I suppose, that you stole it, fair and square, from some other thief," Lythande remarked, and the glare of anger vanished as quickly as it had come. "Well, so be it; you offer me this lute in return for the recovery of your wand?" The tall mage reached for the lute, but Rastafyre saw the hunger in the Pilgrim Adept's eyes and thrust it behind him.

"First the service for which I sought you out," he reminded Lythande.

Lythande seemed to grow even taller, looming over Rastafyre as if to fill the whole room. The magician's voice, though not loud, seemed to resonate like a great drum.

"Wretch, incompetent, do you dare to haggle with me over my own possession? Fool, it is no more yours than mine— less, for these hands brought the first music from it before you knew how to turn goat's milk sour on the dungheap where you were whelped! By what right do you demand a service of me?"

The bald little man raised his chin and said firmly, "All the world knows that Lythande is a servant of L-L-Law and not of Chaos, and no ma-ma-magician bound to the L-Law would demean hi-hi-himself to cheat an honest ma-ma-man. And what is more, noble Ly-Lythande, this instru—tru-tru— this lute has been cha-changed since it dwelt in your ha-ha-hands. Behold!"

Rastafyre struck a soft chord on the lute and began to play

a soft, melancholy tune. Lythande scowled and demanded, "What do you—?"

Rastafyre gestured imperatively for silence. As the notes quivered in the air, there was a little stirring in the dark hallway, and suddenly, in the heavy air, a woman stood before them.

She was small and slender, with flowing fair hair, clad in the thinnest gown of spider-silk from the forests of Noidhan. Her eyes were blue, set deep under dark lashes in a lovely face; but the face was sorrowful and full of pain. She said in a lovely singing voice "Who thus disturbs the sleep of the enchanted?"

"Koira!" cried Lythande, and the neutral voice for once was high, athrob with agony. "Koira, how—what—?"

The fair-haired woman moved her hands in a spellbound gesture. She murmured, "I know not—" and then, as if waking from deep sleep, she rubbed her eyes and cried out, "Ah, I thought I heard a voice that once I knew—Lythande, is it you? Was it you who enchanted me here, because I turned from you to the love of another? What would you? I was a woman—"

"Silence," said Lythande in a stifled voice, and Rastafyre saw the magician's mouth move as if in pain.

"As you see," said Rastafyre, "it is no longer the lute you knew." The woman's face was fading into air, and Lythande's taut voice whispered, "Where did she go? Summon her back for me!"

"She is now the slave of the enchanted lute," said Rastafyre, chuckling with what seemed obscene enthusiasm, "I could have had her for any service—but to ease your fastidious soul, magician, I will confess that I prefer my women more—" his hands sketched robust curves in the air, "So I have asked of her, only, that now and again she sing to the lute—knew you not this, Lythande? Was it not you who enchanted the woman thither, as she said?"

Within the hood Lythande's head moved in a negative shake, side to side. The face could not be seen, and Rastafyre wondered if he would, after all, be the first to see the mysterious Lythande weep. None had ever seen Lythande show the slightest emotion; never had Lythande been known to eat or to drink wine in company—perhaps, it was believed, the mage *could* not, though most people guessed that it was simply one of the strange vows which bound a Pilgrim Adept.

But from within the hood, Lythande said slowly, "And you offer me this lute, in return for my services in the recovery of your wand?"

"I do, O noble Lythande. For I can see that the enchanted la-la-lady of the lute is known to you from old, and that you would have her as slave, concubine—what have you. And it is this, not the mu-mu-music of the lute alone, that I offer you—when my wa-wa-wand is my own again."

The blaze of the blue star brightened for a moment, then dimmed to a passive glow, and Lythande's voice was flat and neutral again.

"Be it so. For this lute I would undertake to recover the scattered pearls of the necklace of the Fish-goddess should she lose them in the sea; but are you certain that your wand is in the hands of Roygan the Proud, O Rastafyre?"

"I ha-ha-have no other en-en-enem—there is no one else who hates me," said Rastafyre, and again the restrained mirth gleamed for a moment.

"Fortunate are you, O Incom—" the hesitation, and the faint smile, "Incomparable. Well, I shall recover your wand—and the lute shall be mine."

"The lute—and the woman," said Rastafyre, "but only wh-wh-when my wand is again in my own ha-ha-hands."

"If Roygan has it," Lythande said, "it should present no very great difficulties for any *competent* magician."

Rastafyre wrapped the lute into the thick protective covering and fumbled it again into Ca-Ca-Carrier's capacious folds. Rastafyre gestured fussily with another spell.

"In the name of—" He mumbled something, then frowned. "It will not obey me so well without my wa-wa-wand," he mumbled. Again his hands twisted in the simple spell. "G-g-go, confound you, in the name of Indo-do-do—in the name of Indo-do—"

The bag flopped just a little and a corner of it disappeared, but the rest remained, hovering uneasily in the air. Lythande managed somehow not to shriek with laughter, but remarked:

"Allow me, O Incomp—O Incomparable," and made the spell with swift narrow fingers. "In the name of Indovici the Silent, I command you, Carrier—"

"Ca-Ca-Carrier," corrected Rastafyre, and Lythande, lips twitching, repeated the spell.

"In the name of Indovici the Silent, Ca-Ca-Carrier, I command you, go!"

The bag began slowly to fade, winked in and out for a moment, rose heavily into the air, and by the time it reached eye level, was gone.

"Indeed, bargain or no," Lythande said, "I must recover your wand, O Incompetent, lest the profession of magician become a jest for small boys from the Salt Desert to the Cold Hills!"

Rastafyre glared, but thought better of answering; he turned and fussed away, trailed by a small, lumpy brown shadow where Ca-Ca-Carrier stubbornly refused to stay either visible or invisible. Lythande watched him out of sight, then drew from the mage-robe a small pouch, shook out a small quantity of herbs and thoughtfully rolled them into a narrow tube; snapped narrow fingers to make a light, and slowly inhaled the fragrant smoke, letting it trickle out narrow nostrils into the heavy air of the hallway.

Roygan the Proud should present no very great challenge. Lythande knew Roygan of old; when that thief among magicians had first appeared in Lythande's life, Lythande had been young in sorcery and not yet tried in vigilance, and several precious items had vanished without trace from the house where Lythande then dwelt. Rastafyre would have been so easy a target that Lythande marveled that Roygan had not stolen Ca-Ca-Carrier, the hood and mage-robe Rastafyre wore, and perhaps his back teeth as well; there was an old saying in Gandrin, *if Roygan the Proud shakes your hand, count your fingers before he is out of sight.*

But Lythande had pursued Roygan through three cities and across the Great Salt Desert; and when Roygan had been trailed to his lair, Lythande had recovered wand, rings and magical dagger; and then had affixed one of the rings to Roygan's nose with a permanent binding-spell.

Wear this, Lythande had said, *in memory of your treachery, and that honest folk may know you and avoid you.* Now Lythande wondered idly if Roygan had ever found anyone to take the ring off his nose.

Roygan bears me a grudge, thought Lythande, and wondered if Rastafyre the Incompetent, lute and all, were a trap set for Lythande, to surprise the secret of the Pilgrim Adept's magic.

For the strength of any Adept of the Blue Star lies in a certain concealed secret which must never be known; and the one who surprises the secret of a Pilgrim Adept can master all the magic of the Blue Star. And Roygan, with his grudge. . . .

Roygan was not worth worrying about. *But,* Lythande thought, *I have enemies among the Pilgrim Adepts themselves. Roygan might well be a tool of one of these. And so might Rastafyre.*

No, Roygan had not the strength for that; he was a thief, not a true magician or an adept. As for Rastafyre—soundlessly, Lythande laughed. If anyone sought to use that incompetent, the very incompetence of the fat, fussy little magician would recoil upon the accomplice. *I wish no worse for my enemies than Rastafyre for their friend.*

And when I have succeeded—it never occurred to Lythande to say *if*—*I shall have Koira; and the lute. She would not love me; but now, whether or no, she shall be mine, to sing for me whenever I will.*

If it should become known to Lythande's enemies—and the magician knew that there were many of them, even here in Gandrin—that Roygan had somehow incurred the wrath of a Pilgrim Adept, they would be quick to sell the story to any other Pilgrim Adept they could find. Lythande, too, knew how to use that tactic; the knowledge of another Pilgrim Adept's Secret was the greatest protection known under the Twin Suns.

Speaking of Suns—Lythande cast a glance into the sky—it was near to First-sunset; Keth, red and somber, glowed on the horizon, with Reth like a bloody burning eye, an hour or two behind. Curse it, it was one of those nights where there would be long darkness. Lythande frowned, considering; but the darkness, too, could serve.

First Lythande must determine where in Old Gandrin, what corner or alley of that city of rogues and imposters, Roygan might be hiding.

Was there any Adept of the Blue Star who knew of the quarrel with Roygan? Lythande thought not. They had been alone when the deed was done; and Roygan would hardly boast of it; no doubt, that wretch had declared the ring in his nose to be a new fashion in jewelry! Therefore, by the Great Law of Magic, the law of Resonance, Lythande still possessed a tie to Roygan; the ring which once had been Lythande's own, if it was still on Roygan's nose, would lead to Roygan just as inescapably as a homing pigeon flies to its own croft.

There was no time to lose; Lythande would rather not brave the hiding place of Roygan the Thief in full darkness, and already red Keth had slipped below the edge of the world. Two measures, perhaps, on a time-candle; no more time than that, or darkness would help to hide Roygan beneath its cloak, in the somber moonless streets of Old Gandrin.

The Pilgrim Adept needs no wand to make magic. Lythande raised one narrow, fine hand, drew it down in a curious, covering movement. Darkness flowed down from the slender fingers behind that movement, covering the magician with its veil; but inside the spelled circle, Lythande sat cross-legged on the stones, flooded with a neutral shadowless light.

Holding one hand toward the circle, Lythande whispered: "Ring of Lythande, ring which once caressed my finger, be joined to your sister."

Slowly the ring remaining on Lythande's finger began to gleam with an inner radiance. Beside it in the curious light, a second ring appeared, hanging formless and weightless in midair. And around this second ghost-ring, a pallid face took outline, first the beaky and aquiline nose, then the mouthful of broken teeth which had been tipped like fangs with shining metal, then the close-set dark-lashed eyes of Roygan the Proud.

He was not here within the spelled light-circle. Lythande knew that. Rather, the circle, like a mirror, reflected Roygan's face, and at a commanding gesture, the focus of the vision moved out, to encompass a room piled high with treasure, where Roygan had come to hide the fruits of his theft. Magpie Roygan! He did not use his treasure to enrich himself—like Lythande, he could have manufactured jewels at will—but to gain power over other magicians! And so, the links retaining their hold on their owners, Roygan was vulnerable to Lythande's magic as well.

If Rastafyre had been even a halfway competent magi-

cian—even the thought of that tubby little bungler curved
Lythande's thin lips in a mocking smile—Rastafyre would
have known of that bond, and tracked Roygan the proud
himself. For the wand of a magician is a curious thing; in a
very real sense it *is* the magician, for he must put into it one
of his very real powers and senses. As the Blue Star, in a
way, was Lythande's emotion—for it glowed with blue flame
when Lythande was angry or excited—so a wand, in those magicians who must use them, often reflects the most cherished
power of a male magician. Again Lythande smiled mock-
ingly; no bedroom athletics, no seduction of magicians' wives
or daughters, till Rastafyre's wand was in his hand again!

*Perhaps I should become a public benefactor, and never
restore what Rastafyre considers so important, that the
women of my fellow mages may be safe from his wiles!* Yet
Lythande knew, even as the image lingered, and the amusement, that Rastafyre must have back his wand and with it his
power to do good or evil. For Law strives ever against Chaos,
and every human soul must be free to take the part of one or
another; this was the basic law that the Gods of Gandrin had
established, and that all Gods everywhere stood as representa-
tive; that life itself, on the world of the Twin Suns as everywhere till the last star of Eternity is burnt out, is forever
embodying that one Great Strife. And Lythande was sworn,
through the Blue Star, servant to the Law. To deprive
Rastafyre of one jot of his power to choose good or evil, was
to set that basic truth at naught, setting Lythande's oath to
Law in the place of Rastafyre's own choices, and that in itself
was to let in Chaos.

*And the karma of Lythande should stand forever responsi-
ble for the choice of Rastafyre. Guardians of the Blue Star,
stand witness I want no such power, I carry enough karma of
my own! I have set enough causes in motion and must see all
their effects . . . abiding even to the Last Battle!*

The image of Roygan, ring in nose, still hung in the air,
and around it the pattern of Roygan's treasure room. But try
as Lythande would, the Pilgrim Adept could not focus the
image sufficiently to see if the wand of Rastafyre was among
his treasure. So Lythande, with a commanding gesture, expanded the circle of vision still further, to include a street
outside whatever cellar or storeroom held Roygan and his

treasures. The circle expanded farther and farther, till at last the magician saw a known landmark; the Fountain of Mermaids, in the Street of the Seven Sailmakers. From there, apparently, the treasure room of Roygan the Thief must be situated.

And Rastafyre had risked his wand for an affair with Roygan's wife. Truly, Lythande thought, *my maxim is well-chosen, that a mage should have neither sweetheart nor wife. . . .* and bitterness flooded Lythande, making the Blue Star glimmer; *Look what I do, for Koira's mere image or shadow! But how did Rastafyre know?*

For in the days when Koira and Lythande played the lute in the courts of their faraway home, both were young, and no shadow of the Blue Star or Lythande's quest after magic, even into the hidden Place which Is Not of the Pilgrim Adepts, had cast its shadow between them. And Lythande had borne another name.

Yet Koira, or her shade, knew me, and called me by the name Lythande bears now. Why called she not . . . and then, by an enormous effort, almost physical, which brought sweat bursting from the brow beneath the Blue Star, Lythande cut off that memory; with the trained discipline of an Adept, even the memory of the old name vanished.

I am Lythande. The one I was before I bore that name is dead, or wanders in the limbo of the forgotten. With another gesture, Lythande dissolved the spelled circle of light, and stood again in the streets of Old Gandrin, where Reth, too, had begun dangerously to approach the horizon.

Lythande set off toward the Street of the Seven Sailmakers. Keeping ever to the shadows which hid the dark mage-robe, and moving as noiselessly as a breath of wind or a cat's ghost, the Pilgrim Adept traversed a dozen streets, paying little heed to all that inhabited them. Men brawled in taverns, and on the cobbled streets; merchants sold everything from knives to women; children, grubby and half-naked, played their own obscure games, vaulting over barrels and carts, screaming with the joys and tantrums of innocence. Lythande, intent on the magical mission, hardly saw or heard them.

At the Fountain of Mermaids, half a dozen women, draped in the loose robes which made even an ugly woman mysterious and alluring, drew water from the bubbling spring, chirping and twittering like birds; Lythande watched them with a curious, aching sadness. It would have been better to await their going, for the comings and goings of a Pilgrim Adept are better not gossiped about; but Reth was perilously near the horizon and Lythande sensed, in the way a magician will always know a danger, that even a Pilgrim Adept should not attempt to invade the quarters of Roygan the Proud under cover of total night.

They dissolved away, clutching with murmurs at their children, as Lythande appeared noiselessly, as if from thin air, at the edge of the fountain square. One child clung, giggling, to one of the sculptured mermaids, and the mother, who seemed to Lythande little more than a child herself, came and snatched it up, covertly making the sign against the Evil Eye—but not covertly enough. Lythande stood directly barring her path back to the other women, and said "Do you believe, woman, that I would curse you or your child?"

The woman looked at the ground, scuffing her sandaled foot on the cobbles, but her hands, clutching the child to her breast, were white at the knuckles with fear, and Lythande sighed. *Why did I do that?* At the sound of the sigh, the woman looked up, a quick darting glance like a bird's, as quickly averted.

"The blinded eye of Keth witness that I mean no harm to you or your child, and I would bless you if I knew any blessings," Lythande said at last, and faded into shadow so that the woman could gather the courage to scamper away across the street, her child's grubby head clutched against her breast. The encounter had left a taste of bitterness in Lythande's mouth, but with iron discipline, the magician let it slide away into limbo, to be taken out and examined, perhaps, when the bitterness had been attenuated by Time.

"Ring, sister of Roygan's ring, show me where, in the nose of Roygan the Thief, I must seek you!"

One of the shadowed buildings edging the square seemed to fade somewhat in the dying sunset; through the walls of the building, Lythande could see rooms, walls, shadows, the moving shadow of a woman unveiled, a saucy round-bodied little creature with ringlets tumbled over a low brow, and the mark of a dimple in her chin, and great dark-lashed eyes. So this was the woman for whom Rastafyre the Incompetent had risked wand and magic and the vengeance of Roygan?

Do I scorn his choice because that path is barred to me?

Still; madness, between the choice of love and power, to choose such counterfeit of love as such a woman could give. For, silently approaching the walls which were all but transparent to Lythande's spelled Sight, the Pilgrim Adept could see beneath the outer surface of artless coquetry, down to the very core of selfishness and greed within the woman, her grasping at treasures, not for their beauty but for the power they gave her. Rastafyre had not seen so deep within. Was he blinded by lust, then, or was it only further evidence of the name Lythande had given him, *Incompetent?*

With a gesture, Lythande banished the spelled Sight; there was no need of it now, but there was need of haste, for Reth's orange rim actually caressed the western rim of the world. *Yet I can be in, and out, unseen, before the light is wholly gone,* Lythande thought, and, gesturing darkness to rise like a more enveloping mage-robe, stepped through the stone wall. It felt grainy, like walking through maize-dough, but nothing worse. Nevertheless Lythande hastened, pulling against the resistance of the stone; there were tales, horror-tales told in the outer courts of the Pilgrim Adepts where this art was taught, of an Adept of the Blue Star who had lost his courage halfway through the wall, and stuck there, half of his body still trapped within the stone, shrieking with pain until he died. . . . Lythande hated to risk this walking through walls, and usually relied on silence, stealth and spells applied to locks. But there was no time even to find the locks, far less to sound them out by magic and press by magic upon the sensitive tumblers of the bolts. When all the magician's body was within the shadowy room, Lythande drew a breath of relief; even the smell of mold and cobwebs was preferable to the grainy feel of the wall, and now, whatever came, Lythande resolved to go out by the door.

And now, in the heavy darkness of Roygan's treasure room, the light of the Blue Star alone would serve; Lythande felt the curious prickling, half pain, as the Blue Star began to glow. . . . a blue light stole through the darkness, and by that subtle illumination, the Pilgrim Adept made out the con-

tours of great chests, carelessly heaped jewels, bolted boxes
. . . where, in all this hodgepodge of stolen treasure, laid up
magpie fashion by Roygan's greed, was Rastafyre's wand to
be found? Lythande paused, thoughtful, by one great heap of
jewels, rubies blazing like Keth's rays at sunrise, sapphires
flung like dazzling reflections of the light of the Blue Star, a
superb diamond necklace loosely flung like a constellation
blazing beneath the pole-star of a single great gem. Lythande
had spoken truly to Rastefyre, jewels were no temptation, yet
for a moment the magician thought almost sadly of the
women whose throats and slender arms and fingers had once
been adorned with these jewels; why should Roygan profit by
their great losses, if they felt the need of these toys and trin-
kets to enhance their beauty? And Lythande hesitated, considering. There was a spell which, once spoken, would
disperse all these jewels back to their rightful owners, by the
Law of Resonances.

Yet why should Lythande take on the karma of these unknown women, women Lythande would never see or know?
If it had not been their just fate to lose the jewels to the
clever hands of a thief, no doubt Roygan would have sought
in vain for the keys to their treasure chests.

*By that same token, why should I interfere with my magic
in the just karma of Rastafyre, who lost his wand because he
could not contain his lust for the wife of Roygan? Would not
the loss of wand and virility teach him a just respect for the
discipline of continence? It would not be for long, only till he
could take the trouble to fashion and consecrate another
wand of Power . . .*

But Lythande had given the word of a Pilgrim Adept; for
the honor of the Blue Star, what was promised must be performed. Sworn to the Law, it was Lythande's sworn duty to
punish a thief, and all the more because Roygan preyed, not
on Lythande whose defenses were sufficient for revenge, but
upon the harmless Rastafyre . . . and if Roygan's wife found
him not sufficient, then that was Roygan's karma too. Shivering somewhat in the darkness of the storeroom, Lythande
whispered the spell that would make the treasure boxes
transparent to the Sight. By the witchlight, Lythande scanned
box after box, seeing nothing which might, by the remotest
chance, be the wand of Rastafyre.

And outside the light was fading fast, and in the darkness, all the things of magic would be loosed. . . .

And as if the thought had summoned it, suddenly it was there, though Lythande had not seen any door by which it could have entered the treasure chamber, a great grey shape, leaping high at the mage's throat. Lythande whirled, whipping out the dagger on the right, and thrust, hard, at the bane-wolf's throat.

It went through the throat as if through air. Not a true beast, then, but a magical one. . . . Lythande dropped the right-hand dagger, and snatched, left-handed, at the other, the dagger intended for fighting the powers and beasts of magic; but the delay had been nearly fatal; the teeth of the bane-wolf met, like fiery needles, in Lythande's right arm, forcing a cry from the magician's lips. It went unheard; the magical beast fought in silence, without a snarl or a sound even of breathing; Lythande thrust with the left-hand dagger, but could not reach the heart; then the bane-wolf's uncanny weight bore Lythande, writhing, to the ground. Again the needle-teeth of the enchanted creature met like flame in Lythande's shoulder, then in the knee thrust up to ward the beast from the throat. Lythande knew; if the fiery teeth met but once in the throat, it would cut off breath and life. Slowly, painfully, fighting upward, thrusting again and again, Lythande managed to wrestle the beast back, at the cost of bite after bite from the cruel flame-teeth; the bane-wolf's blazing eyes flashed against the light of the Blue Star, which grew fainter and feebler as Lythande's struggles weakened.

Have I come this far to die in a dark cellar in the maw of a wolf, and not even a true wolf, but a thing created by the filthy misuse of sorcery at the hands of a thief?

The thought maddened the magician; with a fierce effort, Lythande thrust the magical dagger deeper into the shoulder of the were-beast, seeking for the heart. With the full thrust of the spell, backed by all Lythande's agony, the magician's very arm thrust through un-natural flesh and bone, striking inward to the lungs, into the very heart of the creature. . . . the blazing breath of the wolf smoked and failed; Lythande withdrew arm and dagger, slimed with the magical blood, as the beast, in eerie silence, writhed and died on the floor, slowly curling and melting into wisps of smoke, until only a little heap of ember, like burnt blood, remained on the floor of the treasure room.

Lythande's breath came loud in the silence as the Pilgrim Adept wiped the slime from the magical dagger, thrust it back into one sheath, then sought on the floor for where the right-hand dagger had fallen. There was slime on the magician's left hand, too, and the Adept wiped it, viciously, on a bolt of precious velvet; Roygan's things to Roygan, then! When the right-hand dagger was safe again in the other sheath, Lythande turned to the frantic search again for Rastafyre's wand. It was not to be thought of, that there would be much more time. Even if Roygan toyed with the wife who was all his now Rastafyre's power was gone, he could not stay with her forever, and if his magical power had created the bane-wolf, surely the death of the creature, drawing as it did on Roygan's own vitality, would alert him to the intrusion into his treasure room.

Through the lid of one of the boxes, Lythande could see, in the magical witchlight which responded only to the things of magical Power, a long narrow shape, wrapped in silks but still glowing with the light that singled out the things of magic. Surely that must be Rastafyre's wand, unless Roygan the Thief had a collection of such things—and the kind of incompetence which had allowed Roygan to get the wand, was uncommon among magicians . . . praise to Keth's all-seeing eye!

Lythande fumbled with the lock. Now that the excitement of the fight with the banewolf had subsided, shoulder and arm were aching like half-healed burns where the enchanted teeth had met in Lythande's flesh. Worse than burns, perhaps, Lythande thought, for they might not yield to ordinary burn-remedies! The magician wanted to tear off the tattered tunic where the bane-wolf had torn, but there were reasons not to do this within an enemy's stronghold! Lythande drew the mage-robe's folds closer, bitten hands wrenching at the bolts. The Pilgrim Adept was very strong; unlike those magicians who relied always on magic and avoided exertion, Lythande had traveled afoot and alone over all the highroads and by-roads lighted by the Twin Suns, and the wiry arms, the elegant-looking hands, had the strength of the daggers they wielded. After a moment the first hinge of the chest yielded, with a sound as loud, in the darkening cellar, as the explosion of fireworks; Lythande flinched at the sound . . . surely even Roygan must hear that in his wife's very chamber! Now for the other hinge. The bitten hands were growing more painful by the moment; Lythande took the right-hand dagger, the one intended for objects which were natural and not magic, and tried to wedge it under the hinge, prying in grim silence without success. Was the damned thing spelled shut? No; for then Lythande's hands alone could not have budged the first bolt. Blood was dripping from the blistered hand before the second lock gave way, and Lythande reached into the chest, and recoiled as if from the very teeth of the bane-wolf. Howling with rage and pain and frustration, Lythande swept into the chest with the left-hand dagger; there was a small ghastly shrilling and something ugly, horrible and only half visible, writhed and died. But now Lythande held the wand of Rastafyre, triumphant.

Wincing at the pain, Lythande stripped the concealing cloths from the wand. A grimace of distaste came over the magician's narrow face as the phallic carvings and shape of the wand were revealed, but after all, this had been fairly obvious—that Rastafyre would arm his wand with his manhood. It was, after all, his own problem; it was not Lythande's karma to teach other magicians either discretion or manners. A bargain had been made and a service should be performed.

Hastily wadding the protective silks around the wand—it was easier to handle that way, and Lythande had no wish even to look upon the gross thing—Lythande turned to the business of getting out again. Not through the walls. Darkness had surely fallen by now, though in the windowless treasure-room it was hard to tell, but there must be a door somewhere.

Lythande had heard nothing; but abruptly, as the witch-light flared, Roygan the Proud stood directly in the center of the room.

"So, Lythande the Magician is Lythande the Thief! How like you the business of thievery, then, Magician?"

A trap, then. But Lythande's mellow, neutral voice was calm.

"It is written; from the thief all shall be stolen at last. By the ring in your nose, Roygan, you know the truth of what I say."

With an inarticulate howl of rage, Roygan hurled himself at Lythande. The magician stepped aside, and Roygan hurtled against a chest, giving a furious yelp of pain as his knees collided with the metalled edge of the chest. He whirled, but Lythande, dagger in hand, stood facing him.

"Ring of Lythande, Ring of Roygan's shame, be welded to this," Lythande murmured, and the dagger flung itself against Roygan's face. Roygan grunted with pain as Lythande's dagger molded itself against the ring, curling around his face.

"Ai! Ai! Take it off, damn you by every god and godlet of Gandrin, or I—"

"You will *what*?" demanded Lythande, looking with an aloof grin at Roygan's face, the dagger curled around the end of his nose, and gripping, as if by a powerful magnet, at the metal tips of Roygan's teeth. Furious, howling, Roygan flung himself again at Lythande, his yell wordless now as the metal of the dagger fastened itself tighter to his teeth. Lythande laughed, stepping free easily from Roygan's clutching hands; but the thief's face was alight with sudden triumphant glee.

"Hoy," he mumbled through the edges of the dagger. "Now I have touched Lythande and I know your secret. . . . Lythande, Pilgrim Adept, wearer of the Blue Star, you are— ai! *Ai-ya!*" With a fearful screech of pain, Roygan fell to the floor, wordless as the dagger curled deeper into his mouth; blood burst from his lip, and in the next moment, Lythande's other dagger thrust through his heart, in the merciful release from agony.

Lythande bent, retrieved the dagger which had thrust into Roygan's heart. Then, Blue Star blazing magic, Lythande reached for the other dagger, which had bitten through Roygan's lips, tongue, throat. A murmured spell restored it to the shape of a dagger, the metal slowly uncurling under the stroking hands of the owner's sorcery. Slowly, sighing, Lythande sheathed both daggers.

I meant not to kill him. But I knew too well what his next words would be; and the magic of a Pilgrim Adept is void if the Secret is spoken aloud. And, knowing, I could not let him live. Why was she so regretful? Roygan was not the first

Lythande had killed to keep that Secret, the words actually on Roygan's mutilated tongue; *Lythande, you are a woman.*

A woman. A woman, who in her pride had penetrated the courts of the Pilgrim Adepts in disguise; and when the Blue Star was already between her brows, had been punished and rewarded with the Secret she had kept well enough to deceive even the Great Adept in the Temple of the Blue Star.

Your Secret, then, shall be forever; for on the day when any man save myself shall speak your secret aloud, your power is void. Be then forever doomed with the Secret you yourself have chosen, and be forever in the eyes of all men what you made us think you.

Bitterly, Lythande thrust the wand of Rastafyre under the folds of the mage-robe. Now she had leisure to find a way out by the doors. The locks yielded to the touch of magic; but before leaving the cellar, Lythande spoke the spell which would return Roygan's stolen jewels to their owners.

A small victory for the cause of Law. And Roygan the thief had met his just fate.

Stepping out into the fading sunlight, Lythande blinked. It had seemed to take hours, that silent struggle in the darkness of the Treasure-room. Yet the sun still lingered, and a little child played noiselessly, splashing her feet in the fountain, until a chubby young woman came to scold her merrily and tug her withindoors. Listening to the laughter, Lythande sighed. A thousand years, a thousand memories, cut her away from the woman and the child.

To love no man lest my Secret be known. To love no woman lest she be a target for my enemies in quest of the Secret.

And she risked exposure and powerlessness, again and again, for such as Rastafyre. *Why?*

Because I must. There was no answer other than that, a Pilgrim Adept's vow to Law against Chaos. Rastafyre should have his wand back. There was no law that all magicians should be competent.

She laid a narrow hand along the wand, trying not to flinch at the shape, and murmured, "Bring me to your master."

Lythande found Rastafyre in a tavern; and, having no wish

for any public display of power, beckoned him outside. The tubby little magician stared up in awe at the blazing Blue Star.

"You have it? Already?"

Silently, Lythande held out the wrapped wand to Rastafyre. As he touched it, he seemed to grow taller, handsomer, less tubby; even his face fell into lines of strength and virility.

"And now my fee," Lythande reminded him.

He said sullenly "How know I that Roygan the Proud will not come after me?"

"I knew not," said Lythande calmly, "that your magic had power to raise the dead, oh Rastafyre the Incomparable."

"You—you—k-k-k-he's dead?"

"He lies where his ill-gotten treasures rest, with the ring of Lythande still through his nose," Lythande said calmly. "Try, now, to keep your magic wand out of the power of other men's wives."

Rastafyre chuckled. He said "But wha-wha—what else would I do w-w-with my p-p-power?"

Lythande grimaced. "Koira's lute," she said, "or you will lie where Roygan lies."

Rastafyre the Incomparable raised his hand. "Ca-ca-Carrier," he intoned, and, flickering in and off in the dullness of the room, the velvet bag winked in, out again, came back, vanished again even as Rastafyre had his hand within it.

"Damn you, Ca-ca-Carrier! Come or go, but don't *flicker* like that! Stay! Stay, I said!" He sounded, Lythande thought, as if he were talking to a reluctant puppy dog.

Finally, when he got it entirely materialized, he drew forth the lute. With a grave bow, Lythande accepted it, tucking it out of sight under the mage-robe.

"Health and prosperity to you, O Lythande," he said—for once without stuttering; perhaps the wand did that for him too?

"Health and prosperity to you, O Rastafyre the incom—" Lythande hesitated, laughed aloud and said, "Incomparable."

He took himself off then and Lythande added silently, "And more luck in your adventures," as she watched Ca-ca-Carrier dimly lumping along like a small surly shadow at his heels, until at last it vanished entirely.

Alone, Lythande stepped into the dark street, under the cold and moonless sky. With a single gesture the magical circle blotted away all surroundings; there was neither time nor space. Then Lythande began to play the lute softly. There was a little stirring in the silence, and the figure of Koira, slender, delicate, her pale hair shimmering about her face and her body gleaming through wispy veils, appeared before her.

"Lythande—" she whispered. "It is you!"

"It is I, Koira. Sing to me," Lythande commanded. "Sing to me the song you sang when we sat together in the gardens of Hilarion."

Lythande's fingers moved on the lute, and Koira's soft contralto swelled out into an ancient song from a country half a world away and so many years Lythande feared to remember how many.

> "The years shall fall upon you, and the light
> That dwelled in you, go into endless night;
> As wine, poured out and sunk into the ground,
> Even your song shall leave no breath of sound,
> And as the leaves within the forest fall,
> Your memory will not remain at all,
> As a word said, a song sung, and be
> Forever with the memories—"

"Stop," Lythande said, strangled. Koira fell silent, at last whispering, "I sang at your command and now I am still at your command."

When Lythande could look up without the agony of despair, Koira too was silent. Lythande said at last, "What binds you to the lute, Koira whom once I loved?"

"I know not," Koira said, and it seemed that the ghost of her voice was bitter, "I know only that while this lute survives, I am enslaved to it."

"And to my will?"

"Even so, Lythande."

Lythande set her mouth hard. She said, "You would not love me when you might; now shall I have you whether you will or no."

"Love—" Koira was silent. "We were maidens then and we loved after the fashion of young maidens; and then you went into a far country where I would not follow, for my heart was a woman's heart, and you—"

"What do you know of my heart?" Lythande cried out in despair.

"I knew that my heart was a woman's heart and longed for a love other than yours," Koira said. "What would you, Lythande? You too are a woman; I call that not love . . ."

Lythande's eyes were closed. But at last the voice was stubborn. "Yet you are here and you shall sing forever at my will, and be forever silent about your desire for a man's love . . . for you there is none other than I, now!"

Koira bowed deeply, but it seemed to Lythande that there was mockery in the bow.

She said sharply "What enslaves you to the lute? Are you bound for a space, or forever?"

"I know not," Koira said, "Or if I know I cannot speak it."

So it was often with enchantments; Lythande knew. . . . and now she would have all of time before her, and sooner or later, sooner or later, Koira would love her. . . . Koira was her slave, she could bid her come and go with her hands on the lute as once they had sought for more than a shared song and a maiden's kiss . . .

But a slave's counterfeit of love is not love. Lythande raised the lute in her hands, poising her fingers on the strings; Koira's form began to waver a little, and then, acting swiftly before she could think better of it, Lythande raised the lute, brought it crashing down and broke it over her knee.

Koira's face wavered, between astonishment and sudden delirious happiness. "Free!" she cried, "Free at last—O, Lythande, now do I know you truly loved me. . . ." and a whisper swirled and faded and was still, and there was only the empty bubble of magic, void, silent, without light or sound.

Lythande stood still, the broken lute in her hands. If Rastafyre could only see. She had risked life, sanity, magic, Secret itself and the Blue Star's power, for this lute, and within moments she had broken it and set free the one who could, over the years, been drawn to her, captive . . . unable to refuse, unable to break Lythande's pride further. . . .

He would think me, too, an incompetent magician.

I wonder which two of us would be right?

With a long sigh, Lythande drew the mage-robe about her thin shoulders, made sure the two daggers were secure in their sheaths—for at this hour, in the moonless streets of Old Gandrin there were many dangers, real and magical—and went on her solitary way stepping over the fragments of the broken lute.

About Jon DeCles and *Cantabile*

Back in 1962 or thereabout, when I was still living in Texas and my brother Paul was living on the family farm outside Albany with my parents, Jon DeCles came for a weekend visit, and somehow the weekend extended itself into a month, then into a few years, and when I visited the farm for a few weeks, Jon and I somehow agreed that we were brother and sister too. By now I seldom remember that my adopted brother Jon is not my own sibling; which is very confusing to people who know my parents. I seldom stop to say "adopted" when I introduce Jon as my brother. When the farm household broke up, Jon, Paul and our mother came to live with us in Berkeley (before the establishment of Greyhaven proper) and we began doing things together as a family.

While I was still living in Texas, Jon sent me a copy of this, his first published story. It is always a painful trial to read a story by someone close to you. What will you say if you don't like it? Suppose it's perfectly awful, and you have to think of something polite and encouraging to say?

To my immense relief, I found *Cantabile* to be a genuinely warm and touching fantasy, and could praise it without reservation. Most of Jon's later stories have had better reception in England than here, though he has sold a great number of short stories to all kinds of markets; but I still think of this story of the Beast Who Wept, with its poignant bittersweetness, as his finest work. Jon is also a theatrical director, a composer who has had a string quartet and other pieces performed by local musicians, a creator and performer of one-man shows (his impersonations of Mark Twain and Edgar Allan Poe have been much acclaimed) and a painter of considerable distinction; an expert in Japanese tea ceremony, and a genius at landscape gardening.

Yet it seems to me that of all Jon's many talents, he has touched, in his writing, the highest level of universality in this touching little fantasy. I cannot imagine why it has never been anthologized before this; it should be more widely known as the small classic I think it.

CANTABILE

by Jon DeCles

A conjecture: it came from the past. Or: it came from the future. A supposition: It was a bolt shot by a talent great even in chains, shot at a venture because it dared not be shot at a target. As to the nature of the chains, or even the talent—? At all times and in every place, genius lives upon the sufferance of idiots.

In shape it was indescribable, and may for that reason perhaps have escaped notice. Eye may refuse to report to brain sights for which no concepts exist. Almost immediately after its appearance it ceased to be. Its contents were scattered, too small to vex the eye with challenge, and drifted slowly earthward. The surface they settled upon was the stony, inhospitable one of the City; and in seconds most of them were dead for dearth of hosting. One only survived. By a chance perhaps mathematically calculable, but nonetheless remote, this one found its way through an opening—smaller than the diameter of a pin—in the foundation of a quartz glass dome which crowned the skyscraper demesne of a Baron of the City, and drifted into a pond chemically and otherwise balanced to sustain life among its contents: plants, algae, and tiny fish. At noon, in the random nurture of this *de facto* womb, The Beast Who Wept was born. Alone of a mother, or a father, or siblings.

The Beast Who Wept was small when he was born. In fact, at the moment of his creation, he was only one quarter inch tall. For a short time before that he had been a random grouping of protoplasmic cells, propelled from one side of the fish pond to the other by sun-currents. The hot of the summer sun, lingering late into Autumn, brought him forth. He was one quarter inch tall, but this soon changed. With the voracious capacity that life had built in him, he soon found and devoured what food the garden offered. In a week's time he had reached the size of a small dog.

A goodly portion of the time allotted the Beast in that week was spent in observation. By City standards the Garden was not small. To all four points of the compass it reached, going for fifty feet in each direction. There it was cut off by the rigid confines of masonry walls. Across the top of the Garden stretched the sectional expanse of a quartz glass dome, thrust up into the sky to sample the rarity of the cold upper air. Here, high atop the Baronial skyscraper, the Garden was isolated, and like a child, sucked and stored warmth from the glowing breast of the Solar furnace. There were murals on the walls of the Garden, quasi-mosaic pictures in warm earth colors, too soft and blending for the Beast's undeveloped perceptions. But then, the Beast had only the things of the Garden to compare them with, the flowers and fish, the dwarf fruit trees, and the gaily colored birds that fluttered everywhere; and those were not what the murals depicted.

One day, sitting in the lily pool and chewing on lotus seeds, the Beast made a discovery. Reaching out, he seized a goldfish. It squirmed and wriggled, and made horrible sounds when he bit into it. Sitting calmly as he was, he was able to make the observation that living things do not like to be eaten while they are still alive. His memory reminded him of the piercing screams of the birds he had eaten, and how difficult it was to pull away the choking downiness of the feathers.

Considering, he decided not to eat any more things that were alive. As the days passed he found it was a good decision. The animals ceased to fear him, and they afforded him much amusement.

The Beast still required protein, but this he solved by awaiting the deaths of his fellow creatures, and in this way, that which was his natural need was provided. The rest of his diet was on the trees, and in the blossoms of the flowers.

When he was four feet tall he learned to walk on his hind

legs, and he discovered the door. Not of his own agency was this discovery, but part of a change in his environment. The door opened and the Woman came through.

By now the Beast could see the murals, and he recognized her instantly as one of the things depicted in mosaic, all brown in the throbbing warm of the un-filtered sunlight. She did not see him at first. He still sat in the cool water of the pond, still chewed his lotus seeds. The woman tossed off the gold robe she wore and stretched out on the hot, clean sand, putting black cloth shields over her eyes.

The Beast stood slowly and stepped with care from the blue painted bottom of the pool to the flagstone walk. He walked quietly to where she lay, and stood looking at her with an agonizing scrutiny, feeling as if he should act. Yet he stood without moving and gazed over her body, with a longing for something that he was not old enough to understand.

After a while the Woman sensed his presence, and took the shields from her eyes. When she saw him she sat up and clutched for her robe. She even gave a little scream to the still air.

"How did you get here?" she said. "What are you doing here?"

The Beast looked at her differently for a moment. Her voice was not shrill and sweet, like the birds, nor soft and guttural, like the goldfish. She did not chirp the way the insects did.

"Well, answer me!" she demanded.

The Beast made a sound in his throat; he pawed at himself. Her voice had been sharp that time, and it hurt him inside. He turned his back to her. He wept, as he had at the screech of a dying bird, but again he did not know why.

"What's the matter? Can't you talk?" she asked.

The Beast turned back to her and looked into her deep blue eyes. They were moist, like his, but not from pain. The Beast had never seen pity.

"You poor thing," the Woman said. She stood, blushed, wrapped her robe about herself, and came toward him. She made motions, indicating the door.

"You can't go out like that," she said. "Where are your clothes?" She made more motions, trying to indicate her curiosity as to the location of his garments, using her robe as an example.

The Beast stood blank, not understanding.

"Oh, all right. I'll look for them."

As she searched, the Woman talked. Idle chatter mostly, to relieve her nervousness at his presence. A flash, a dark thunder-noise, and a rocket passed across the sky, attracted to space like iron to a magnet. The Woman laughed.

"You know, we *are* like mushrooms," she said, looking under a gardenia bush. "Those rockets, those space ships. I venture that you, that most of the workers, have no concept of what they are. Humans, Mortals, we live at the base of the tree, trodden by the passing bulls, the events of life. Up there, in the branches of the Oak, the spaceships carve out an empire, with no thought for us. No thought for people.

"Only the makers of Laws think of people. They make the laws that keep the empire builders from dropping the fire of the Sun on us, from subjugating us or killing us. They make the laws that limit a man to the use of personal combat, or the hiring of mercenaries. They give us a social sanity that limits a man's grasp to his reach."

She went over every foot of the garden. She looked under shrubs and bushes, even in the pool. When she finished, she was puzzled.

"I can't imagine how you got in here without clothes. For that matter, I can't really imagine how you got in here at all. Its a good thing that no one else found you, or you'd be in trouble. You wait here, and I'll go downstairs and see if I can get some of my younger brother's things for you. Then we'll see if I can get you out of the building. Without anyone seeing you."

She looked at him again, turning her head from left to right, and finally letting it come to rest, tilted at an angle, on her golden shoulder.

"I might not be able to get you out tonight, so I will bring you some food after dinner. I used to eat up here quite often, so no one will think it strange."

The Beast stood looking for a long while at the place where she had lain in the sand. Then, not having understood what she said about food, he went about the Garden gathering his own.

* * *

The Beast did not understand Night. He was born of the gentle rays and hard radiations of the Sun, and when the Sun disappeared behind the concrete confines of the Garden, he curled up in a bed of ornamental hemlocks and went to sleep. Times had been when noises from below jarred him out of his euphoria, and in those times he had seen the stars and the moon. The stars were cold, and the moon made him feel sick, and pale with an emotion he had no reason to know was Grief.

He was asleep when the Woman came again. She waved her hand in front of a glowing metal panel, and the Garden burst, like a fresh blown iris, into an enigma of artificial lighting. The light was not so strong as sunrise, but illumined the room as brightly. As the lights gave no heat, the Woman found the Beast sleeping, curled tightly. At her touch he was awake, looking up at her.

She was pale gold now. The moon washed her with milk. Her hair was moon-blued, not black, yet she was of a kin with the black soil beneath him. Under the still of the moon and the stars, he worshiped her.

"Come," she said. "Put these on. I think my brother is larger than you are, but they will fit."

The Beast stood bewildered. He tried to follow her motions, but to no avail.

"Don't you know how to put them on?"

He was silent. The Woman sensed then that there was something in him she had not encountered before. For a moment the Woman was afraid of him.

"Oh. You don't understand me, do you? Not at all?"

The Woman helped him to put the clothes on, though at his touch, she was embarrassed. His eyes followed her, and from her he breathed in the scent of peppermint, a scent he knew from the bed of aromatics near the bird's fountain.

"You're a nice little boy," she said as she dressed him. "I feel strange near you. Almost as if I were your mother, but not motherly." She laughed. "The way I felt about my dolls when I was your age, or the way I feel about the birds here in the garden. I had a little dog with black spots when I was very young. My father wasn't a Baron then. We lived in a Baron's tower, but my father was only learning his craft. I was allowed to play with the other children, and I knew lots of boys like you. Only, of course, they could talk."

She looked at him with that pity again.

"Well, you look presentable at least, and you shall have a new suit of clothes when you go home. I imagine *that* must be among the workers. Well, never mind, you won't have to go back tonight. I couldn't smuggle you beneath the hundredth floor if my life depended on it. I brought you some food."

She led him across the Garden and handed him a basket of food. He looked dumbly at her, so she opened a flask of beer, spread a cloth on the ground and put pieces of cooked fowl, bread and melon upon it. He still did not eat until she put a piece in his hand. Then he knew it was food.

The Woman sat on the flagstones and watched him eat with his fingers. After a few moments she had the urge to reach out and pet him, or scratch his head, he reminded her so much of her lost puppy.

"You know, if I had this room all to myself, I should keep you here in secret, as a pet. My father forbids me another dog. He says that someone would use it as a weapon against me. I don't have any friends. No one that I can talk with, and naturally, I can't go out of the building. I'm only eighteen, and the Lottery hasn't chosen me a husband, so I've never been in the company of a young man. Oh, *how* I look forward to that day! Someone tall and strong like a warrior, and bronzed as if from working in the fields. He'll be so wonderful and mannerly. He'll take me in his arms, and like a dance, we'll live!"

The Woman's eyes glittered and she saw past the Beast, beyond him, and into the future. The Beast looked into her eyes, past the veils of happy tears, and his own eyes glittered in response.

When he had finished the food the Beast made another decision. He reached out his hand, shiny with cooking oil, and touched the sleeve of her dress. It was a white dress, with puffy sleeves that billowed when she walked. The place where his hand met the softness of her garment was stained hopelessly, but the Woman smiled. On impulse she bent and kissed his forehead, tenderly, as is right to kiss a child.

"You are sweet," she said, and left with the basket and the

white tablecloth. On her way she turned out the lights. The Beast scampered back into his hemlock grove, and was soon asleep.

The families of the Barons were well fed. If the Baron requested a meal that was less than nutritious in itself, the food was carefully processed with the necessary vitamins, minerals, and proteins. Thus the Beast had eaten his first complete and balanced meal. He was, for the first time in his short life, properly fed to stimulate his extraordinary rate of growth. During the night, the Beast matured.

The Sun rose over the concrete walls and began its daily progression from one quartz panel to another, like some obscure piece in a ruleless game of chess. The Beast luxuriated in its warmth. He stretched his golden limbs, and with their first contraction, the muscles firmed and rounded. With his first breath of evergreen and morning oxygen, his lungs gained capacity and his chest expanded. When he stood, it was with a limitless ease, and he perceived that he now possessed a complement of body hair. And, there were other things, things within him, that were different.

The clothes that the Woman had given him were torn, burst by his expansions in the night, and they fell from him. He was divested of their shabbiness by his very nature. The Beast was now an adolescent, or rather, in the last stages of his adolescence.

All morning the Sun moved in its prescribed path, and with the passing of the day the Beast stationed himself before the door. When the quartz glass was stained with sunset colors, the door opened. The Woman was all in yellow, wispy nylon, like jonquils, sunflowers, the high clear notes of a trumpet. She looked at the Beast.

Nothing perceptible passed between them. The Beast stood still. He did not weep now. The Woman stood still. She did not seek in her mind for an explanation, neither did she consider that one was necessary.

"You are the same," she said. "You are the same little boy, and I can tell it. But you are different, not the same, for you are now a Man."

The Beast looked at her and his eyes were not damp nor unfocused. He was strong now, and different.

* * *

When the Sun was down and the stars glowed faintly in a powder-blue sky, the Juno lilies bloomed. They lifted their great white blossoms slightly above the water and strained toward the place where the moon would be. The Beast reached down and tugged at one until its rubbery stem snapped. Droplets of pool water came cascading up at them. The Woman held it to her breast and inhaled its perfume.

She sighed, and from her dark, damp lungs came a returned fragrance of hot summer nights and willow trees. The Beast kissed her, the way she had taught him to kiss her.

She hummed a low, rhythmic air, leaning back on the grass, then began to sing.

"My Prince grew from a Frog," she sang, and the crickets stopped their chirping to listen.

> "My Prince grew from a Frog,
> Who lived in a Silver Well,
> And the Story that I tell,
> Is how I kissed him as he sat
> On a Log. The Frog who was
>   a Prince
> Retrieved my Golden Ball."

She left him before the morning came. Her black hair glistened from the stroke of many caresses. The Beast ate the food she had left for him and went to sleep. The hemlocks were a prickly bower for him, and the lotuses were no longer sacred.

The next week passed. The Beast had a beard of light brown and there were traces of lines around the edges of his eyes. His shoulder-length hair was coarser; his skin was not so soft, his lips were darker and harder than before.

The Woman was not so different, but she had changed.

"I wish this could last forever, My Prince," she said one day when the Sun was especially hot. "But you will not last forever, nor will I. I have seen, in you, a wonder and a miracle: But miracles must pass, as must all things, good or bad, and I fear that the good must often pass sooner than the evil. You have grown quickly—from a child to a man within a month. I think that soon, My Prince, you will die. When you have died, I shall be left alone."

It was the Woman's turn to weep, and the Beast could not comfort her in these tears because he did not understand her speech, and had he, he would not have been capable of dealing with the concepts of which she spoke. In the days of the Woman, the Beast knew only ecstasy.

"You have come here," she said, composing herself and blinking back the tears, "from some place beyond my world, and you have become a world for me. I am glad you came. You have given me something to measure the worth of my life, a standard. . . . I think, perhaps, it is good that you will grow old and die very quickly. If my father discovered you here he would have you put to death. I do not mind so much that you should die. I cannot ask favors of Death. But I would not be cheated by murder."

The Beast was like a man who is middle aged. He was heavier, though, by a mercy of his creation, he did not develop a paunch, nor any of the less pleasant accidents of matter that tend to make a man lose some of his physical pride during that time of life. Had the Beast developed any of these imperfections, he would not have concerned himself with them. His life was too short to allow the learning of social conscience.

They were not so passionate now, the Beast and the Woman. They had settled, in two short weeks, to the kind of relationship that many, even after years of marriage never achieve. They were together constantly, and when they were together, neither was alone.

"These have been days that were of worth," she said. "I value these days as I will none that come after. When a man is chosen for me, I shall be a wife to him, but the Lottery will have failed. Any who is my husband will be sadly put to hold my affections hence."

When she was in a somber mood she told him: "My father is in difficulty with the other Barons. His bill has been rejected in the congress, and he faces expulsion. If that happens, I will be sent away to spend my life as a worker. Father will stay and fight, as is the custom, and everyone in the Tower will eventually be beaten into the ground. If Father goes to war, you will be discovered. This garden is atop the gun turrets, and the floor is underlaid with weapons. Oh, if he is expelled—!"

The time came shortly when the Beast was old. He could not smell the hemlocks in the night, or the pink pearl lilies. His long, straight hair was white, as was his beard. His eyes were deep now, and rheumy. He was bent, and he slept much more than had been his wont.

The Woman had not come to him for three days. The sky outside was cold and grey. From time to time tiny, sharp flakes of snow would jet against the quartz glass and make a rasping noise. The Beast made a decision based on observation, and waved his hand in front of the glowing metal panel. The lights came on, but, blending with the murky daylight, did not cheer him. The red roses on a small trellis, roses that had throbbed with life, roses that had surged up with brilliance to meet the living Sun, were now faded and washed with despondence, purple like the lips of a painted whore.

When the Woman came, it was quickly. She hurried through the door into the dark, humid Garden. It was the first time the Beast had seen outdoor garments, and he was curious about them. The Woman wore a black cloak and hood, and carried a satchel.

The Woman ran and pressed herself to the Beast. She wet his cheeks with tears.

"Good-bye!" she sobbed. "Good-bye, My Prince. This is the last time I shall see you. My Father is expelled, and he is sending me away through the tunnels. There is no way I can save you. My Father and his retainers will all be dead before the morning, and you with them. Will you not now speak to me one word, one good-bye? Say to me once, only once!"

The Beast held her gently to him. Outside, a drone like the sound of bees. Snow stung the quartz glass and melted.

The Beast sensed what she wanted. He made sounds in his throat, rough, harsh sounds, croaking noises . . . but not words. It was beyond his ability, and his lifetime had been too short for the learning.

Like a star, appearing between furtive clouds, an aeroplane came into existence beyond the windows. It was an antique thing, so out of place in this world, with propellers, and a little glassed-in cockpit with a gun. The pilot pulled the trigger and a tight line of bullets shot across the glass. Then the plane was gone and the windows were shattered.

In his arms the Woman hung limp. She had jumped away from him at the approach of the aeroplane, then fallen back into his embrace.

The Beast worked his gnarled fingers to undo the shiny black buttons of her coat. With great and tender care he opened her blouse. He tore away the constricting under clothes and bared her chest. Between her breasts he found a hole. It was bruised, and blood trickled out, and it betrayed no pulse. The Woman was Dead.

He wondered what action he should take. When the animals of the Garden died, he ate them. He wondered if he should do this now. Absently, he leaned his old head down, old in a few weeks, and licked the blood from her flesh. The sweet salt taste in his mouth, he closed his eyes, and when he opened them again, he wept. The Beast wept. He stood, bent with exhaustion, and wept.

Her body was clean and white. Through the broken windows a fierce wind swept down and stirred her glossy black hair. A little curl fell to her forehead.

High, at the top of the sky, at the summit of the Baron's tower, the Garden was gutted. The wind grew wilder and swept into the shell of life, breaking out the remaining glass. The wind tore the petals from the roses and pulled them in a whirlpool, out into the open air, scattering them through the sky. The birds were freed. Chartreuse and blue and white parakeets fluttered up, among the saffron and scarlet petals, to fly away and die in the coming Winter. A peacock blazed into distant oblivion, ever falling.

The snow was driven into the warm little pools and came to rest on the leaves of the lotuses, turning the pond into a bed of seeming giant mushrooms. The orchids blackened at cold's touch. The palms, and the bougainvilleas, divested of their blossoms, shook at the storm's frenzied eddying.

Alone in the heavens, the Beast Who Wept withered. The Sun was veiled in snow, the flowers all were dying, and only the hemlocks did not seem to mind.

About Susan Shwartz and *Dagger Spring*

This is the first of two stories only peripherally associated with Greyhaven. After reading and carefully balancing all the "Greyhaven" stories for this anthology (and two or three of the Greyhaven writers, for various reasons, are absent, because of work on other commitments, oversight, or, as in the case of my son David Bradley, working so hard on a novel that he had no time to produce a short story for this volume) I discovered that I had less wordage than the editor had allowed; and therefore I chose two of the best writers with whom I had been closely and personally associated and who were, I felt, indicative of the kind of talent I liked to discover in associates, and encourage.

Susan Shwartz was a participant in the first Writer's Workshop I gave, in which every writer was expected to plot and create a story actually during the workshop—I have little tolerance for the miscalled "workshops" which are simply hashing over old manuscripts. Nine times out of ten they dissipate into encounter-groups of the worst sort, with the "criticism" either indulging in mutual backscratching, or degenerating into vicious releases of hostility.

Susan, a Ph.D. and (then) a teacher of English literature at Cornell university, impressed me at once with the quality of her work; a first impression which was soon validated by her appearance in *Analog* with "The Struldbrug Solution" and her editing of the anthology *Hecate's Cauldron* (DAW, Feb. '82). When I heard the title for this anthology, I had hoped to see the excellent story she had done for the workshop, "Dagger Spring," somewhere in its pages. Still, her loss is my gain; I believe this story of ancient ritual magic (try contrasting it, for instance, with Barnes's "Wildwood") fits well into the ambiance of Greyhaven stories, and, I sincerely hope, will tend to show that like attracts like. I'm proud to have printed her very first story in "The Keeper's Price," and though she has since appeared in other markets, I'm proud to have her here, too.

DAGGER SPRING

by Susan M. Shwartz

Olwen forced herself up once again from her skinned knees. Her grimy hands plucked some painful burrs from her sandals and tattered cloak. It had been fine once—fit for the Princess of Penllyn she'd been, not the renegade she'd made of herself—but rock outcroppings and clumps of thistles, sere and brown like everything else in Penllyn, had shredded it.

Watching out for another loose stone or exposed root, Olwen worked her way down the Cynfael's banks toward the crags of Talebolion where the river flung itself far below into a boiling tidal basin. Edged with knifesharp flints, Talebolion would keep what it gained forever. If she drowned the royal dagger within it, the queen her mother couldn't turn it on herself in the Beltane sacrifice.

All I want is to save Mother's life. Goddess, why is that so much to ask? What are you, that your daughters must die in the hawthorn nemet?

A cloud veiled the moon, as if the Goddess Modron turned her face away. Olwen's thoughts shaped themselves into a prayer, panted out to the painful rhythm of her blistered feet. Her nails cut into her palms, cut off her chant with awareness of this new pain and the darkness of the moon. Olwen had stolen queensblade, the Goddess Modron's sacred knife, and she bore it now only to cast it away. Daughter of the Queen Blodeuedd, the Mother's Chosen in Penllyn, Olwen had made of herself blasphemer and outlaw, a nothing with no right to appeal to the Goddess.

And she was glad, glad, glad.

Hot tears surged into Olwen's eyes, and the drying riverbed quivered into dark rainbows. She waited for the wind to clear

her vision; the rocks and mud of shrinking Cynfael were
treacherous to walk for a girl whose eyes were blinded with
weeping. Should she fall and break her ankle, here she'd lie
until she starved, unable to save herself. Or to rid Penllyn of
queensblade . . . *queens' bane*, she called it. Olwen rubbed
one hip, bruised and aching from the fall off her pony *(don't
think of Liatha now or you'll cry again!)*. Tumbling clear of
the poor beast's hoofs, the dagger's black hilt had driven so
hard against her flesh that she winced at every step.

If only Cynfael still flowed deep, as it had in her childhood
when it nursed all Penllyn, Olwen might have flung
queensblade into it. But Cynfael, shallow after seasons of
drought, might spew the dagger back on land for someone to
return to the royal maenol . . . and the queen, who would
turn it on herself for Penllyn's sake. But let the sea swallow
it, and only fish would know what had become of it. Let
queensblade have their thin blood as a sacrifice, and welcome!

And afterward? If Olwen tumbled from the rocks, or if she
escaped into one of the manrealms where no bards made
lampoons—well, let the rest come as it might. Never had she
been so weary! Her mother Blodeuedd would live, and in exile Olwen would be spared her grief, and spared the hearing
of the pungent satires Penllyn's clever bards would make:
Olwen the coward, Olwen the thief.

"The hidden spring feeds the hawthorn nemet." Olwen
paused to ransack her three-year-old's memory for the rest of
the Goddess' Law. That was it! She recited it triumphantly
for her mother and the Archdruid. "And the daughter's gift
feeds the land."

"Good, Olwen!" Amergin the Druid approved, scant
praise, but deeply satisfying to the child. Blodeuedd hugged
her and laughed, a sound like Cynfael rippling over rocks under the spring sun. The golden apples which bound her braids
gleamed, but not so brightly as her hair or eyes.

All around Olwen glowed light, firelight on the keys her
mother carried at her glinting silver belt of linked leaves,
green starlight dancing from the bracelets she wore which
Aillel, Olwen's father, had brought before he died from

Varangia, the very-far-away, and a shifting glitter on the hilt of the royal dagger at her belt. Black and silver chasing winked in the firelight, and Olwen, fascinated, reached out to touch it, perhaps even draw the ancient blade.

"Don't," her mother said. Olwen drew back her hands. It was no matter. One day queensblade too would be hers to hold, even to wear. She was Olwen, princess of Penllyn, and from the splendor of the scented fire to the trout leaping in the rivers, her land shone with wonders.

Suddenly her mother looked away, her eyes even brighter. "I wish Aillel might hear her," she whispered. A tear shimmered on her face, was quickly flicked away.

The only father Olwen could really remember was Amergin. "You have me," she offered her mother, trying to remove Blodeuedd's sadness, the only possible shadow on her tiny, fearless world.

Then Blodeuedd smiled and the light flooded back like sunrise over the crest of Eryri in spring.

Last year the crops had failed. At high summer, the wells had run dry. This winter had brought little snow to whiten Eryri's peaks, bringing the spring little snowmelt to freshen the springs and rivers for the planting. Now, when the sky should have been heavy with billowing rainclouds, it was comfortlessly bright. And the moon, the Face of Modron, turned steadily toward the time of Beltane.

Only a few weeks ago Olwen had had her first flow of blood. A sudden panic—*this is too soon!*—had made her cry out, had drawn Blodeuedd to her side, to embrace and comfort her.

"Praise the Goddess," Blodeuedd exulted, "you're a woman now. Now I . . ."

Fearing the rest of Blodeuedd's words, Olwen clung to her mother like a baby, not a princess who'd just passed into womanhood. She didn't feel grown up and she didn't want to! Against her own slenderness, her mother's body felt heavier, softer than she remembered. And her hair, freed from its braids and circlet, was greying.

She's older, Olwen noticed, suddenly terrified. Queensblade —even this early, Blodeuedd wore it belted over her loose bedgown—pressed against her side, and Olwen recoiled into herself. Now she shed blood, and that blood made Modron's Law very real. It meant her death, she understood suddenly . . . and her mother's.

Her pretty room spun and shrank. Now it felt like a prison, or like the cage she'd seen near the high altars where sacrificial beasts, cramped and terrified, lowed as they waited for death in the hawthorn grove. She tore free of Blodeuedd and ran into the garden.

"Olwen!" her mother called. "What's wrong, child?"

What was she supposed to do? Face her mother with this new awareness, look into the fading, loving eyes and know that they were both going to die? When Blodeuedd had been young (*young as I am now,* Olwen thought, shuddering), the bards had called her the woman of flowers. No one would ever say that where Olwen walked white roses bloomed; not one flower could she coax into bud.

That her roses thrive became suddenly the most important thing in all Penllyn. Olwen hastened to the artesian well near the kitchens. Even when all the other wells but this one had dried up in the last terrible drought, this one alone had supplied the whole maenol. Olwen lowered the leather bucket almost to the end of its rope before she finally heard a muffled splash, but she drew up only a little brown, silty fluid.

Perhaps just one rose. . . .

A slender hand on the rope handle stopped her.

"Pour it back," said the Queen. "We cannot waste water on flowers when we need food."

"Mother," Olwen protested, "my garden dies."

"So does mine," Blodeuedd replied.

Olwen's eyes flickered to the black dagger at her mother's belt, then across the shrunken river to the secrecy of the hawthorn grove, most sacred of all the nemets in Penllyn. It was the only one into which iron could—indeed, must—be carried, and in which blood might—and had to—be spilled.

Blodeuedd followed Olwen's eyes and thoughts. "Beltane comes with the full moon, Olwen. If Penllyn is to bear fruit this year. . . ."

"No!" Olwen cried. "You have years left!"

"Olwen, you're the one with the years. Mine are all count-

ed. You'll make a good queen, dear. I've taught you everything I. . . ."

Sunlight glared on queensblade, drew Olwen's eyes the way
an adder draws a fledgling toward its coils.

"You're not going into the nemet with *that*!" she gestured,
revolted, at the dagger. "We can't even be sure that Modron's
Law is truth."

"To question what must be is pointless," Blodeuedd said
calmly. "Sooner or later, I must pass within the Goddess for
Penllyn's sake. That is the law, Olwen. Give me your
blessing, and I shall pass content. Refuse if you will: just the
same, I must go. Daughter, don't you see that Penllyn dies?
The land needs young blood to rule it."

Young blood. After Blodeuedd's blood had glutted queensblade, Olwen would have to wear it till she too aged and the
Law compelled her to turn it on herself.

"Can't you wait—just a little longer?" She bargained for
time. Years ago, she'd bargained so in order to stay up later.
"Maybe till I'm married, even a mother myself? There's so
much yet for me to learn . . . I'm not ready. . . ."

"You're going to have to be," Blodeuedd told her firmly.
Years ago, that same tone had ordered Olwen into bed.

"But it's not fair!" Olwen protested. "Why does Penllyn
need you more than I do? Because Amergin declares that's
the law? I don't trust those Druids. They love their power too
well; they use law like a whip to keep Penllyn in fear.
Modron's law is cold. Any sort of land that wants its queen's
blood—I say it isn't worth it!"

"You blaspheme," Blodeuedd said coldly. "All that we are
is by favor of the Goddess. See you remember that, girl."

Now Blodeuedd was angry with her! It was the last injus-
tice.

"It's all so hopeless!" Olwen choked, and fled as a child
flees after a beating, back to her dusty, dying garden to weep
with her forehead resting against the cool marble of the silent
fountain.

Amergin found her there. "Olwen," he ordered, "turn
around."

She shook her head.

"Stand up and face me!" No one disobeyed when the archdruid spoke in that tone. Reluctantly Olwen stood, her face half-averted and wholly rebellious.

"Your childishness causes your mother great unhappiness," Amergin informed her sadly.

And risks all Penllyn. Olwen bristled more at the words he forbore to speak more than at those he had actually uttered.

"You call Modron mother, Druid?" she accused. "Then tell me this: what sort of mother craves the death of a child?"

The Druid strode forward and grasped her shoulders, as if, Olwen thought, he would shake her into submission to that ghastly law which killed Penllyn's queens for a hope of rain. Then he calmed himself; Olwen felt his hands loosen.

"I thought I'd taught you better. But as always: the careless weaver must weave the same cloth twice. Sit down, and I'll try again."

This new patience humiliated Olwen more than his anger. Her chin quivered, and she bit her lip, turning her face away so no Druid should see a princess of Penllyn cry.

"Because you were born royal, Olwen, did you think that you'd be spared the return of gift for gift? What we most love, we most pay for. Haven't you ever seen a bird or a rabbit run before the hunter to lure him away from her young?

"When I was a young man, I traveled through the man-realms. War had savaged it, and many people fled. I tended some of the refugee women. Some were ill, starving even, but their babies lived because their mothers' bodies had wasted themselves to give their children a chance at life. Even if it cost them their own."

Amergin gazed through Olwen into remembered anguish.

Maybe she could run away now, she thought, but old respect, old love kept her at the archdruid's side.

"If a beggar risk death for her child, how much more should a queen accept for her land? The queen is the Goddess' favorite daughter, but the land's mother. Her fertility is Penllyn's, and as her inner spring dies. . . ."

"No!" Olwen cried. "I can't lose her!"

"Do you think I want to tell you that you must?" Amergin's voice filled with deep pain. "Do you call Druids cold, Olwen? My order's training is submission to what *is*: not what pleases us, nor even what we judge fair, but simply what must be." He looked down at his hands, high-veined, long-fingered, and old. "So now, rather than oppose the goddess' law, I must let even you hate me."

Amergin's voice quavered, and Olwen, hearing the hurt in it, burst into tears. With almost a mother's gentleness, he reached out and stroked her coppery hair. "Olwen, Olwen. Are you ready to be queen? Soon the moon brightens for Beltane. Gladly would I spare you this, but if we are to have any harvest at all, the land must be revived . . . and soon. . . ."

Olwen sat down wearily on a dead trunk that leaned out over the shrinking river. Maybe, in those last frenzied days before Beltane, she'd gone a little mad. For hours she had sat deciphering the faded ogham records for a solution. Instead she had found the story of Ganhumara the Faithless. Centuries ago, Ganhumara, eager to live as queen, refused to die as one when she started to age: Ganhumara, so desperate for life that she'd abandoned Penllyn for a man from one of the manrealms and died of a stillborn son at an age when most of Penllyn's women were grandmothers, not mothers, and when any other queen would have long since passed within the nemet. Until that long-delayed death from bleeding in childbirth had released it, Penllyn had groaned with drought and famine.

To this day, the bards called all traitors "Ganhumara's children." Olwen rubbed her temples, further tangling her hair, as she tried the name out. Olwen, Ganhumara's child. Not Blodeuedd's. But what would that matter to her compared to Blodeuedd's life?

Night after night, the cold moon rose fuller in the sky and Beltane neared. The hawthorn nemet seemed to gleam and quiver in expectation. No one had spoken further of law or queenship to Olwen, but Blodeuedd had taken to wearing queensblade unsheathed.

That was when Olwen's great idea had been born. Ganhumara brought suffering on Penllyn because she had refused to use queensblade. But if *Olwen* took it, stole it, Blodeuedd couldn't use it because she wouldn't have it. Penllyn would be safe, and so would her mother. If Olwen threw the dagger into the sea, never again must any queen die for the land. Not even the Goddess could blame her mother . . . or Penllyn. And since Olwen wasn't sure that there really *was* a goddess, what could it matter to her?

Trudging beside the sluggish river, Olwen cursed herself for a fool. Oh, it had been easy enough to slip into her mother's rooms before Blodeuedd went to dinner, while she was in her bath and the dagger lay unguarded.

Olwen grabbed up a handful of hard green berries, crammed them into her dry mouth. They were so tart she spit them out again, her face twisting at the unexpected coppery taste, like bile or blood . . . or guilt.

Not an hour out of the maenol, and they'd discovered it, had set hunters on her.

How their horns had shrieked, like the Wild Hunt itself! After that, she didn't think that stories of that trail of ghosts on ghoststallions racing the clouds, questing for human blood would ever frighten her again; she'd been hunted, and the reality was more terrible than fireside tales. But she had screamed at those horns, tightened her hands on her pony Liatha's reins till she snorted and reared in terror.

No! She wouldn't be caught and dragged back to the maenol like a naughty child or a traitor. She jerked Liatha's head around and galloped into the deep forest where the hunters' tall horses couldn't break through the low-sweeping branches. Even here, Penllyn's blight had spread: fallen trees blocked her way, forced Liatha away from the road, deeper and deeper into the shadowy haunts of hungry wolves. Horns howled out again, and Olwen pummeled Liatha's sides, urged the old pony to greater haste in the crackling underbrush.

As Olwen twisted in the saddle to check her back trail, a gnarled root caught Liatha's hoof. The pony stumbled and fell with a shrill whinny. Just in time to avoid being pinned beneath her, Olwen rolled free and felt queensblade's hilt crush painfully into her thigh.

For what seemed like endless hours, she lay watching a dizzy, violet sunset whirl over her upturned face. No hunters came. Finally, Liatha, rolling and snorting in pain, recalled her to her senses.

Olwen dragged herself over to her pony. Saddle and stirrups were twisted grotesquely on her flank. "Oh, Liatha," she murmured, "I should never have galloped on such rough ground. It's all my fault."

One glance at Liatha's twisted foreleg told her that her pony would never run anyplace again.

Gently she removed saddle and bridle, then sat stroking Liatha's mane. As the sky darkened, she realized she'd have to move on. But she couldn't just leave Liatha to suffer alone until hunter, thirst—or wolves—killed her. It had been all her fault. If only Gwyn the hostler were here. He'd do what had to be done, sparing Olwen.

But Gwyn was at the maenol, doubtless regretting Olwen's flight as he curried the horses of the hunters who had failed to capture her and queensblade. Liatha couldn't walk, and she must not be left behind to die slowly. So Olwen would have to give her quick death. She looked down at queensblade. It was the only weapon she had.

Flinging her arms about her pony's hot, sweat-lathered neck, she cried and begged Liatha's forgiveness until the pony nickered at her, nudging her with a soft nose. Olwen drew the black dagger, hiding it in a fold of her cloak so Liatha wouldn't see.

"Pretty Liatha, good girl," Olwen crooned, despite the ache in her throat. She blinked tears back; she had to see clearly in order to find the spot Gwyn had once shown her.

With a strength she didn't know she had, she made the quick, merciful cut, and jumped back from the pony's neck. Furiously, she hurled the bloody dagger away. It quivered—a sweet, sated sound—in a treetrunk. As the light dimmed in Liatha's loving, malt-colored eyes, Olwen laid her head against the pony's flank and wept herself out.

Finally she sat up, scrubbed her hands in the rough grass to clean the blood from them, and shivered. Near the pallid horizon, the waxing moon had come out and was watching her coldly.

Well, Goddess, are you satisfied?

The pulse of crickets frayed at her nerves. She hadn't become a thief just to quit here! She retrieved the dagger and wiped it off. Moonlight on its hammered surface (legend had

it queensblade had been forged from the heart of a fallen
star) caught her eyes.

Accept what must be, Amergin had said.

"No!" Olwen whispered. She pushed past Liatha's body
toward Talebolion and the sea.

Later that night Olwen wrapped her cloak about her.
Twigs plucked her hood from her head and snapped off in
her hair; brambles snagged her skirts and scratched her
ankles. And queensblade, Liatha's blood on it too, lay heavy
at her side. Kinslayer, carried by Thief: oh, she could already
hear the riddles the bards would make of her!

A huge Oak, two branches outstretched to grab her,
loomed up on the path, looking like an avenging Druid.
Olwen cowered back, tripped on a loose stone, and crashed
heavily. For a little while, she cried again—for her mother,
her pony, the smart of her scrapes and bruises. But no more
crying! She'd wallowed long enough, too long in self-pity. She
was Olwen and she had to destroy queensblade. That was
what was.

Over and over she chanted name and purpose to herself.
Black clouds whirled away in the cold wind, and the Face of
Modron rose still higher in its path across the sky: brilliant
and reproachful. Under the moon's steady glare, what had
seemed like a high, unselfish deed felt like betrayal. Moon-
fancies! Olwen winced and turned her eyes away.

Cynfael's course emerged from the forest and flowed past a
hill's base. Half cut off from the rest of Penllyn by the river's
channel, nestled a tiny clearing.

Olwen stared at it numbly. She couldn't believe she'd actually escaped the forest! Something darted past her feet and
she staggered against a birch sapling, one hand pressed
against her teeth. If she didn't scream, maybe it would creep
away.

Thirstily the tall grass whispered and rustled. Toward her.
She dared to look down. Almost at her feet crouched a rabbit, its coat matted and dull, its ears flattened against its head,
and its eyes glazed and staring with fear. Why had it run
toward her?

Olwen glanced quickly around. A tangle of grass and fur-tufts softened a nest in which huddled four rabbit kittens, finger-length, blind, and vulnerable. The doe had been using her own body to bait a trail away from them.

"I won't hurt them" Olwen promised. She stooped, extended her fingers, her hand palm out, to the doe, but it jumped back, never taking its eyes off her. "See? I'm going away." Carefully Olwen stepped past the rabbit, past the nest, aware as the grass shifted again, that the doe had rejoined her litter.

Olwen continued down the hill toward the clearing. Years ago, someone must have started to fence it in, then decided it was not worth the effort. A few posts still lurched around a poor house.

At first, Olwen thought it was years deserted, but reddish light worked itself out to her through the cracked hide of its one window and the gaps in the poorly chinked walls. Outside the door, a goat with shrunken teats cropped at dry tufts of sparse grass. What did the people here do for milk or meat?

Olwen too—if she was to walk all the way to Talebolion, she needed rest. And food. Poor as these people were, they were still people of Penllyn. It had always been her country's pride that no stranger ever was turned away without hospitality.

Olwen scrubbed her hands across her face, licked them, and tried again. She thought that her face might even be almost clean now. Then she picked the twigs and leaves from her disheveled braids and twisted her belt around to hide queensblade inside her cloak. Hurt, hungry, and bedraggled, now she would look just like any other lost girl. Even if these cottagers knew the princess had run away, how could they think that Olwen would come to their door?

Now that she saw a promise of rest, Olwen was surprised at just how unsteady her knees felt. She walked up to the door. No rich odor of good stew greeted her: and as she approached, the voices she heard inside hushed fearfully. Almost timidly, she scratched at the warped planks of the door. Even its leather hinges were frayed.

"Hallo, the house?" she called. Her voice rose thinly, then—to her horror—broke. "Please, anybody?"

"Be welcome to this hearth," came a tired woman's voice. Olwen pushed the door open and edged inside.

A few reed pallets lay on one side of a meager fire. On the other side of the hearth, a rough-hewn table and benches were the only other furniture in the cottage. Two children sat quietly, waiting to eat; another, only slightly older than his brother or sister, grunted as he heaved a heavy ax back onto the pegs driven high into the wall to hold it.

Why hasn't Mother . . . then Olwen remembered. Blodeuedd couldn't seek out every cottager in her land to make sure they all starved at the same time. Perhaps, after Olwen threw away queensblade, the Goddess—if she existed—would pity Penllyn.

The woman knelt beside the hearthfire, nursing it with sticks from the pile of wood her son had brought in. In the corners of the room, firelight leaped to the night wind, cast shadow dancers on the crude walls. Behind Olwen the door slammed shut.

"Well, come in," the woman said. Despite her rags and the stoop of her thin shoulders, her voice was friendly. She straightened and gave a last stir to the black pot which hung from a warped metal hook over the fire.

"Come and eat," she said. "You're just in time. The soup is thin, but I let no child at my hearth starve."

Olwen watched the woman's bony hands. Firelight shone through them as she filled the last bowl. Her ladle scraped on the bottom of the battered pot, trembling as the woman's hand shook. There were four bowls, Olwen noticed, and five people now to feed.

"No thank you," Olwen said to the mother. "There'll be food for me at home. I'm already late."

A haze of pity and dizziness blurred the sight of the mother and children staring at the strange girl as Olwen, not daring to trust the voice that might yet break and beg their food from them, backed toward the cracked door.

The wind cooled across her cheeks, which felt reddened as with sun or shame; down Olwen sank by the cottage wall, weeping for the starvelings within. This was spring when Penllyn's fields and orchards should quicken, yet that family had nothing. At that rate, they would never see autumn, much less survive a winter.

She huddled shoulders into her cloak, hand brushing against the serpentine pin which fastened it. The gift of

Amergin on her last name day, it was of precious metal and amethysts. If she left it where the family might come and find. . . .

What then? she thought. *Men have killed for the price of a gem. Or what if someone saw it and cried, "Look! The lost princess' brooch! What have you done to her?" They might be punished, and they are innocent, innocent. . . .*

Her charity might only worsen, hasten their fate. It was not good enough.

Unsteadily, Olwen rose to her feet, regretting the gift she dared not leave them. Her feet lagged on the path to the sea. The wind took on a sharper edge, and she smelled the tang of salt, heard the rush of wave against rock. Her reckoning had been off: she stood nearer Talebolion than she had thought.

An hour's walk brought her out to the end of rock where the sea crashed against the high cliffs and gleamed inquiet under the face of Modron. The wind blew and belled her cloak out from her body.

"Goddess, help me!" she screamed suddenly. There at the horizon she thought she saw sails. Ships from the manrealms!

"No!" Olwen shrieked. "Go back!"

She waved both arms at them, took a rash step forward, but the wind forced her back, blowing the waves into froth and the louds away. Modron's face gleamed on the horizon, revealing a sea empty of ships, holding only the reflection of the Beltane moon.

So bright was the moonlight that Olwen could see her face in the blade—queensblade—that she had unconsciously drawn when she thought Penllyn was in danger. If those ships had landed, Olwen realized, she would have rushed at them—one girl against a fleet—and tried to protect her realm, regardless if her death came to her for it.

Moonlight startled off the blade, spilled down into the sea.

That must be how Mother feels, Olwen thought.

Queensblade trembled with the shaking of her hand. For an instant she tensed, tempted desperately to throw it into Talebolion's cauldron. But she would have used it to save Penllyn. She would have died for Penllyn.

Olwen lowered her hand and sheathed the dagger. She keened, the song of her lament blowing away across the water. Just so would she mourn when, on Beltane eve, Amergin must emerge alone from the nemet to bind her with crown and queensblade to Penllyn's service.

She turned from the smell of brine, the crash of wind and wave, feeling tired, infinitely sad, but clear of mind, like one who had recovered from a fever which led her mind astray down grim, wrong roads.

Olwen was going home.

Her steps quickened, but she saved her strength: Penllyn needed her too much for her to risk herself.

I will be a good queen to you, she promised the weary, sleeping land.

About Patricia Shaw Mathews and *Lariven*

Patricia Shaw Mathews began writing Darkover stories for the Friends of Darkover, and is certainly one of the major talents we have uncovered among them. As all writers do who begin writing in someone else's universe, whether *Star Trek* or Darkover, in the fullness of time she developed the confidence to work in her own universe with her own characters.

"Lariven" uses some of the elements of Darkover—specifically, a dying telepath race, a crowded Terran bureaucracy—but somehow it comes out with its own unique flavor. On the surface, this is the story of the barbarian queen against the civilized and decadent empire; below the surface, it is something else entirely.

Pat Mathews has never been physically present in the Greyhaven or Greenwalls household. Yet I have worked with her long enough to feel very strongly that she is both protégé and friend—and that one day she will be a name to reckon with in our chosen fields.

Pat sold her first stories under the name Patricia Mathews, before becoming aware of the existence of a best-selling author of romances, Patricia Matthews, with two "t"s, and has been advised by that publisher that using the name would create much confusion. Having no wish to infringe on the publicity of Ms. Matthews, Patricia Shaw Mathews, as the younger writer, and in a very different genre, has chosen to alter her by-line in this way.

LARIVEN

by Patricia Shaw Mathews

Korvath the Conqueror had built this castle so that a long terrace faced the mist-shrouded hills across the river, the one land he had never conquered and had come to think he never would. It was a burr under his saddle, and now he told his Terran guests irritably, "No man goes there but by invitation. The people of the lands beyond the river have powers I'd not care to tangle with."

Brooklyn Anderson of the Terran Survey Service bit her lip. "I think we've been invited," she told the warlord, fully realizing how silly it must sound to all of them. Her partner, Ben de Anza, nodded agreement.

One of Korvath's wives, a plump blonde with a local accent, nodded. "They're telepaths," she agreed, her soft face full of awe. The other, a lean athletic redhead with Korvath's accent, gave her a skeptical look, while the Terrans examined their sudden good fortune on all sides for pitfalls.

The Empire badly needed telepaths, for spacecraft communications, for First Contact work, especially with nonhumans, and above all, in navigation; it was only now beginning to be understood how much of the art of hyperspace navigation was actually psionic. But telepaths born in the overcrowded worlds of the central Empire, where a license to have more than one child was a visible certificate of success, went insane or blocked before they could be found. Members of telepathic cultures on other worlds thoroughly disliked the atmosphere of industrialized, overcrowded, bureaucratic Earth, and quit after a year or so. Only the Space-Born could breed reliable telepaths for space work, and the Space-Born held the Empire to exorbitant contracts. If a telepath had called to Anderson and de Anza's Survey team, they would answer at any cost short of an interplanetary incident.

"We've been having dreams," Anderson told Korvath. "A woman, asking us to come. Ash-blonde, very fair, slender, green eyes, delicate features, wearing some sort of robe about this color"—she indicated a russet drapery among the wall hangings—"like this."

Korvath stopped his restless pacing, his mouth open. "Lariven," he said in a hoarse whisper. "Well, that's quite another matter, stranger-guests. If Lariven has summoned you, then I myself will escort you." He beckoned to a servant. "Bid the children of Lariven come, if they will."

"Yes, Lord," the man said, and scurried away.

The red-orange sun drifted behind the mist, for a moment illuminating it like a giant sheet of coral light, while the Terrans thought over the incredible good luck that had given them such easy access to a telepath or telepaths who were willing to talk to, if not deal with, the Empire. This Lariven was obviously of very high rank here, respected, and for some reason she seemed to want to get in touch with the Terrans. Why? And who was she?

She was one of the Seven Queens of the Hills Beyond the River, where no man comes but by invitation. She sat on a low pillar in a moss-floored grove and delicately withdrew her mind from contact. "They are called Terrans," she said, satisfied.

Deliet of the Silver Harp mentally licked her fingers like a cat, as if to remove something sticky. "Below the river among the mind-blind," she said, making a dainty little face.

Ariane of the Wind held out her wine cup to be filled. A halfling of Lariven's house refilled it; Ariane caressed the fragile boy's cheek and he stammered, "Thank you, Mistress."

"You chose to live below the river for a time, did you not?" Ariane asked her sister-queen. "What was that like?"

"Earthbound," Lariven summed up the heavy food and foamy thick beer, the heavy skirts, the endless petty restrictions on her normally free movement, the sullen suspicions of the women bound to Korvath's house, and Korvath's heavy body on top of hers. She thought of her tall, strong, intelligent, passionate son Branoth and wondered how earth—Korvath—and air—herself—could create fire.

The halfling filled her cup; she was lavish in her petting and her thanks. Below the level of her mind that he could sense was the nagging feeling that he would be dead within the year; they were so fragile, so short-lived! At least Branoth and his sister Elidir were no halflings. She could be grateful for at least that much.

She came out of her brooding to pick up a mental exchange between Ariane and one of the others " . . . Deliet is too nice to marry as Lariven did."

"Oh, but you don't understand," Ariane answered with exquisite malice. ,"Lariven let Korvath use her, while Deliet keeps her warrior for a pet."

"I can believe that, for of all the children and halflings she's borne, not one looks in the least like him."

They jerked back to attention and shut off the malice without the slightest pretense of caring. Lariven smiled and put her long fingertips together. "I will go to these Terrans," she said.

"As you did Korvath," all thought but none said openly, for one sister's out-marriages were not for another to criticize, although the gossip was endless. Nothing would be changed by it; nothing ever changed in these hills, beyond the river.

They drifted into the antechamber to pick up their wraps, their mounts, and their men. Neither Deliet's hulking outland soldier nor Ariane's princeling nor any of the others had been consulted; in this matter they had no part. Lariven sat alone, in a house where over fifty halflings waited on her smallest whim, thinking over her family's ghosts. Then she reached out for the Terran minds again.

Korvath the Conqueror, his Terran guests, and the two young people called the Children of Lariven rode through the woods on large mammals Survey merely booked as horse-equivalent until the scientific types could get a look at them. The locals called them lorthum.

Korvath was nervous. The tall, burly orange-haired man was moving and speaking with a jerky irritability he had not shown before. At one point on the ride he said, "I could wish the rest of your band were here. Ling is a sorceress of great power, and Moya is a good man to have beside you with a weapon."

"Moya is only a Survey Apprentice, though, and this is a First Contact mission to an unknown culture," Anderson explained. "Ling's our telepath; she's too valuable to risk on such a mission when we already have a local liaison. Three of them," she added, looking at the children. Which culture did they consider themselves as belonging to?

"So they're watchstanding at the ship," De Anza said.

The warlord laughed, and Anderson remembered this culture's assumption that any man and woman not blood kin would sleep together if the occasion arose. She felt like saying that the size of native families struck a good many Terrans as just the same sort of good-natured obscenity as Terran sex-mixed crews did natives, but refrained; she had training in anthropology and Korvath the Conqueror did not.

Branoth, son of Korvath, was equally edgy, but in a much more quiet way. He was as tall as his father, but of leaner build, with red-gold hair and peacock-colored eyes; he dressed in a richer style and carried a lighter, sharper sword. Elidir the Priestess was as quiet as her brother and much calmer. She seemed to be about fifteen to Branoth's eighteen, with silver hair and silver-blue eyes and silver-white skin.

"Albino," Anderson whispered to de Anza under her breath.

"Functional in this climate," de Anza whispered back. The high clouds of the lower altitudes had become a heavy fog now, making it impossible to judge where they were going. "I'd like to have a look at the seacoast responsible for this," he echoed Anderson's thought.

"I was wondering if the lorthum see infra-red," she whispered back. "I think the girl does." She kept her voice low; sound carried in these hills. She realized she was edgy, too.

Then suddenly Lariven was there, tall and pale, wrapped in russet draperies, surrounded by a golden light. How old was she? It was impossible to tell.

Korvath dropped to one knee. De Anza did too, not altogether out of local etiquette. Lariven held out her hands and Elidir dashed into her arms. Lariven hugged and kissed the girl, looking her over at arm's length like any mother, then hugged her and kissed her again. She opened an arm to Branoth, who came slowly, as if he were beyond mothering. She hugged her son once, then extended the hand to Korvath. "Come," she said, her voice like soft music, almost a burr.

Anderson put out her hand Terran style. "Lady Lariven,"

she used the native title for a ruler of a great house in her own right.

Softly Lariven said, "Welcome, daughter."

Ben de Anza stared at her like a man in a dream. She seemed incredibly beautiful; that her features had an alien cast only made her more beautiful. She was tall and fair and slender and there was wisdom in the very way she moved, her cool reserve, her aristocratic bearing. It was hard to believe she had a grown son. She touched his hand and he swallowed, hard. She touched his cheek with her lips, the barest ceremonial greeting. "Welcome, too, man from Terra," she said.

Benjamin de Anza was in love from that moment.

II

Lariven's palace was an endless maze of low stone buildings, gardens, orchards, and openwork structures with rooms tucked into the corners. She rode into a corner of the maze and left the lorthum with a redheaded man of her own cast of feature, but barefoot, with work-worn hands, dressed in a green tunic of sturdy fabric, well-worn.

She settled Korvath in a luxurious part of the grounds, across a courtyard from his son Branoth, and herself between the two of them and Ben de Anza. She put the two women together in a suite as luxurious as her own and let them make their own arrangements. Then she rode off to take care of the halfling she had picked up along the way.

It had been half a day after she joined them, that she turned off the path and stopped before a hut of green boughs and branches. There stood an obviously sick child, slender far beyond the human norm on this world, with great luminous eyes in a head too big for its body, naked and dirty and possibly a boy. Tears rolled down the delicately boned face.

Lariven dismounted and knelt in the dirt before the child, wiping its eyes with her own scarf. "Weep no more," she said gently. "I, your mistress, am now here to take care of you." She lifted her head, her face imperious. A woman appeared at the door of the hut, a redheaded woman with hair uncut and tangled, barefoot, dressed in a skirt and a tabard like the stableman's tunic. She had a baby in her arms, and the baby appeared normal.

"It was ill-done not to tell me of this halfling," Lariven said with the gentleness of one who never needs to raise her voice.

The woman glared. "The Mothers Themselves bear witness I have done nothing to deserve such a child. I have not lain with any of your breed, halfling or other; none have disturbed my dreams."

Lariven laid a hand on the woman's arm. "Sister, this comes from the gods as well as from our kind, an affliction laid on all our people, for I have seen it everywhere except below the river. Would you keep the halfling, then? He will serve me all his days, and I will take the time to dry his tears."

The woman bit back what she would say even though Lariven could surely read her mind. She only answered, "Ah, he cries for nought, and is enraptured for a trifle. Let his sister cut her finger, and he must howl twice as loud as she."

"It is the way of his kind," Lariven said, and gathered the child to her. "Have you a name, halfling?" The child shook its head; she said "I will call you Arie, if it please you, and take oath before all gods and powers that I will do you no harm, but only good. Does that satisfy you, Mistress?"

Reluctantly the woman nodded, and Anderson wondered how much of that was knowing she couldn't care for the child and how much was that she dared not disobey her lady. Or perhaps, a little of both.

Now Lariven gestured to the Terrans to follow her to the halflings' quarters. She led the way to a wide, grassy space with bushes and trees and the little maze-huts scattered everywhere, widely separated. She beckoned to a slender childlike figure with a face weathered like a man of forty's. "Lemie, tend to this one, named Arie," she said. "Be kind, as I know you will."

"I will, Mistress," Lemie promised, exactly as a child would.

They were served at dinner by halflings, and the Terrans were surprised—a little shocked—to see the caresses she lavished on them as if they were pets. "They remain children all their days," Lariven said. "Arie, I think, is one who will live forever, sterile; it is good they do not all die."

A scream split the night. Lariven's ageless face for an instant looked worn and weary; she rose. "Come with me, de Anza, Anderson, if you would understand."

She led them to halfling quarters, where a fragile girl, unmistakably a girl in the very first stages of puberty, lay on a bed, staring at the moons, her face a mask of pain. She was writhing and clutching her belly. Lariven passed a hand over her forehead; the clenched muscles relaxed somewhat. De Anza looked away. "What's wrong with her?" he whispered.

"The Great Moons have come together in the sky, and she bleeds," Lariven answered, looking at the sky. Then, with contempt, "It is the custom of women among us, Terran. Have your wombs no cycles?"

De Anza looked abashed. "You read my mind. I'm sorry. I jumped to conclusions before hearing you out."

Lariven snorted. "That I am so ignorant I read signs in the sky? Then she who guides your starship is also ignorant, I think. Elidir, how bad is the bleeding?"

"Very bad. Mother, she must be miscarrying. Only I can find no traces of a child."

"There is none; she is virgin." Lariven dipped a cloth in an herbal infusion and passed it over the girl. "It is her time of womanhood."

"Mother maiden!" Elidir swore under her breath in shock.

De Anza shoved forward a little. "Any Survey med kit could make up a painkiller adapted to her biochemistry," he offered. He was speaking the local language with Terran inserts; he started to explain.

"Do it," Lariven ordered, interrupting him.

He took a reading, then frowned. "That can't be right. Brooksie, let me borrow your box."

"What does it read?" Anderson asked.

"Lethal. The amount of dope needed to help her at all would also kill her. Lady Lariven, there's something wrong here. That's got to be more than just menstrual cramps."

Lariven turned away. They could almost hear her thinking, *So much for Terran wisdom.* She turned around. "Give her the box," she ordered.

"I can't," de Anza protested. "It would kill her."

"Give her that much mercy, Benjamin de Anza," Lariven said. The girl kept on screaming, now an unbearable shriek. Lariven laid a hand on her face and took a thin silver scalpel from her own kit of herbs and tools. She laid it in the halfling girl's hand. The girl thrashed around and made a few wild random gashes, screaming in a high, shrill voice. Lariven laid a hand on the girl's throat. "Turn your backs, Terrans," she said. They did, and closed their eyes as well. The screaming stopped.

Three or four of the halflings clustered around the door. "Befie was my friend," said the one with the middle-aged face, crying readily and loudly. He placed a worn fur doll on her bed.

A girl came forward with a harp. "Befie was my friend," she wailed, sniffling. "We made music together."

A boy with a toy animal. "Befie and I would have lain together but Mistress said she would die, so we didn't." His eyes begged forgiveness from Lariven.

"You did well, Nomie," she said, patting his shoulder. "The gods took her at her growing-up."

A few more came in and added their toys to the pile. When they had gone, Lariven closed the door and leaned against the wall. "They live such a short time, the children of men," she said, letting her own tears roll. "She was so pretty; I will never again have one so pretty."

"She was your daughter?" de Anza asked in disbelief, readjusting his thinking with considerable difficulty.

"Born of my body in the year I went back to my own land. Korvath would not care to hear I had borne a halfling of that time. He would swear it was none of his, and it is tiresome to be called liar by the ignorant when," she thought a minute and used a Terran phrase, "whenever I play a game I abide by all the rules." She frowned. "But how could a halfling be his? They are never born of outmarriages such as ours." She shrugged, and gave it up. De Anza's eyes followed her, troubled, as they went back to their interrupted dinner.

When none of the halfling servants were about, Anderson ventured, "Mentally retarded?"

"Sensitives," Lariven said. "No power, but sensitive. As Maevenn Greentree said, they weep if another cuts a finger.

How can they not? It is their pain, too. They can touch minds, lying close together."

She looked at them, her large, luminous eyes unreadable. "The children of the telepath kind," she said. "Born to us or to the children of the land. Only those who marry and live below the river are free of this, but they bear no Children of the Power, either."

"We are dying," she said, and all the hills were silent. "Since my twin brother Larivoe died, I am the only telepath of my generation in this house. There were two of us only because our mother Merith had the power to divide the egg in her womb. She was a telepath of great power, but the only one born in her time. Her mother Baete's powers were small. Only Volsce, Baete's own brother was," she plucked the Terran word from their minds, "a full-spectrum telepath, viable. He went mad, as old males who were once of great power do. The very wind and rain must obey Volsce, it was his right, he grew outraged that they did not. He saw Larivoe as plotting to overthrow him, and would meet him on the killing ground."

In the moonlit hush her clear light voice, infinitely remote, went on, "Larivoe died, Volsce died, the only males of the house. Fifty halflings died in the backlash of Volsce's last rage. Twenty others lingered near death for months, as I did, for Larivoe and I were one. We must even mourn Volsce; he was our father. At that"—she stared off at the twin moons in the sky—"we have fared better than any other house in the land." There was an infinite sadness in her remote voice.

"Now you know why I seek out the Empire."

III

"That's what I want from the Empire," said Lariven. The four Survey Team people stood at the base of their ship, door open. The wind blew chill from the hills, and Lariven stood unmoved by weather in her flimsy draperies. "The wisdom that has given you telepaths without halfling births. Or if you cannot do this, I must see it for myself. In exchange, I as a telepath am yours, to speak to your spaceships for you, and any telepath child I bear of my time with you is yours forever."

She did not wait to hear the answer, but nodded as if giving them permission for a conference, and went over to where her family, what was left of them, stood. De Anza, unable to take his eyes off her unearthly beauty, saw her catch her tall son Branoth in an embrace, and kiss him, and take his hands in hers. She seemed to be pleading with him.

Branoth shook his head, and the wind brought de Anza his words. "I can't, Mother; don't ask it of me. I was not reared as your people are, but in the mold of mine."

". . . Elidir? She is willing, and she, for one, will not let us die without trying this one more. . . . then be blessed anyway, Branoth." She was crying. She kissed him again, then walked back to the Terran spaceship.

The four Survey people nodded to her. Anderson felt impelled to say, "It's a deal. They may not approve it at Sector HQ, but as far as I'm concerned, it's a deal."

Lariven touched hands with her and came up the ramp, moving as lightly as if she were on some moon. Her face and bearing were untouched by any but the lightest feeling. She took de Anza's arm on the way up and let him guide her to her quarters. Brooklyn Anderson watched, troubled.

Ben showed every sign of being in love, on a few weeks' acquaintance. Such behavior wasn't like the Survey man, who had been around long enough to separate shore-leave quickies from the long-term thing. She wondered what Lariven saw in Ben. He was in his late thirties, a little smaller than average but not conspiciously so, with hair of an undistinguished brown, thin and fine and simply worn. He was a good man, sound and intelligent, but not a romantic idol, unless Lariven had stars in her eyes. Spaceship stars?

Lariven was beautiful. She was almost certainly older than Ben thought. He seemed to see her through some sort of romantic haze; he had gone down on his knees to her that first day. Only protocol? Anderson doubted it. Of course, Lariven was a telepath; she could probably pick enough out of Ben's mind to set herself up as the most desirable woman in his world, if she cared to, and if she could carry it out.

The real Lariven, who had bid her son good-bye in tears, was probably more worth falling in love with than the lighthearted, sophisticated creature who now dined with them daily. Or was that just euphoria? She was on her way to what might be the salvation of her people, after all.

Lariven was lighthearted, amusing, and amused, at meals. She had taken the transition into and out of hyperspace well, and found liftoff an interesting experience. She learned her way around the ship with ease, from the plumbing to the wardroom food machines, and its small size bothered her no more than the small size of the mountain peoples' huts. She was not only at ease, but entertaining, with anecdotes and the songs of her people and their traditional stories. She plucked out the interesting bits from other people's customs and shared them. She spoke of her marriage to Korvath with lighthearted candor.

"I went back to my people, in the end," she said, light fingertips on Ben's arm. "Life there was a strain. Yet, I remember his strength. Some of my sisters said he was coarse; whatever it was, I savored it in him."

Moya snorted. "Smart broad," he commented. He was a colonial, an apprentice who functioned largely as a bodyguard and as liaison with men like Korvath. He was a large, hairy man with the manners of his homeworld's backwoods, who capitalized on an apelike appearance when it suited him to do so. Anderson and de Anza both turned warning glances on him that he completely ignored.

Lariven smiled. "I thank you, Tom," she said, almost without sarcasm.

Sector HQ was an outpost three weeks away from Lariven's homeworld. By the time the ship broke into normspace, Lariven and de Anza were an established couple. Ling kept to herself. They had repeatedly solicited her opinion about Lariven and her intentions; Ling, citing professional ethics, refused to pry but did swear that to her knowledge, Lariven was not aboard for sabotage, espionage, or any other nefarious purposes, but only, as she said, for genetic reasons. Moya said nothing, and nobody asked his opinion; only Anderson was uneasy, and kept her eyes open.

As they approached Sector HQ in normspace, Lariven found her head beginning to ache with the telepathic pressure of too many voices inside it. There were only a few thousand people on the outpost base. Worried, Anderson called ahead.

"Not to worry," a brusque voice from Sector answered. "A

BuGen team will rendezvous with you at 1750 hours at Outstation Alpha, repeat, Alpha, that's the backside of the major moon next to the quarantine station. Subject is psi; shielded lab facilities will be provided. Sector out."

Now Ling spoke. "Shielded living quarters would be more to the point," she said with distaste.

Lariven made the face of one dropping a dead rodent into the disposal. "They think not of me, but of the convenience of BuGen," she explained tolerantly.

Moya nudged her. "Now you're learning, sister," he said with a backwoodsman's cynicism about bureaucrats. She smiled at him and nodded.

They docked by Outstation Alpha, inspected the facilities, and decided to stay in the ship. Anderson felt moved to apologize to Lariven for the sterile, temporary look of this, her first sight of the Empire. Lariven's long eyes widened. "Apologize for being what it is?" she asked.

A little brown man in a white coat came aboard. "Joby, BuGen," he said. "Mrs. Lariven Korvath? I'll want to do a complete medical examination as well as the usual gene analysis. You can have a female technician stand by if you prefer. Your culture have qualms about taking tissue samples?"

The lady-with-mouse look came over Lariven's face, very faintly, and she laid the tips of her long fingers together in thought. "You will do what you must," she said in a remote voice, "and I will have these Survey women beside me, and if it is in you to keep your thoughts to yourself, do so."

Several hours later, the BuGen man handed her the Terran clothes her Survey friends had provided for this and said cheerfully, "That wasn't too bad now, was it, Mrs. Korvath?"

"Lady Lariven," she said faintly, standing up and shaking herself like a dog coming out of water. "I have never been seen as a piece of living machinery before; it was a novelty."

The BuGen man consulted a dossier before him. Attached to it was a spacegram flimsy, transmitted electronically from within this system's boundaries, and a printout from the sort of transcriber used by court reporters and telepaths taking interstellar messages. Lariven wondered briefly why she must tell the same tale to a telepath, a machine, and now to a psi-blind man's ears. Ritual, she decided; what is told three times in three different ways would by that be known for the truth.

The BuGen man waved her to a chair, in her own ship where she was guest, and began, "If viable but nontelepathic children are born to your people outside their home environment, and partially telepathic but nonviable ones at home, it's pretty clear we're dealing with an environmental factor as well as an hereditary one. Perhaps the presence of other telepaths makes the difference," he suggested.

Lariven tried to be grateful that her Terran benefactors had the wit to see the obvious, but failed, for the little man was so very proud of himself! "I left Branoth, my son by Korvath, below the river with his father's people for this cause," she said mildly. "He even has a trace of the Power. Reared among my people, he would have been halfling, and this I would not risk."

"Isn't your daughter a telepath?" Ben de Anza said suddenly.

Lariven looked at him and answered mildly, "But she was born to me by Larivoe. We were twins; she should be strong in the Power, as indeed it proved." She turned back to BuGen, who made a note.

"It's plain we're dealing with an unstable hybrid here, Mrs. Korvath," the man said, beaming. "Do you follow me? I assume your father—your grandfather—Volsce represented the mutation in its original pure form. Then I think a little computer analysis could give us one or more stable forms. We've found two already: the aristocracy, with an overwhelming majority of psi genes; and the commoners, with only a trace. Your account of the prevalence of nonviable births at all levels of society proves that both forms are hybrid, I think."

"Beefalo," Moya said suddenly. "My folks raise them. Back on Old Earth they had a kind of wild cattle, big and tough, they kept trying to breed to domestic cattle. Failed miserably. Finally found out a three-eighths wild and five-eighths domestic mixture did the trick. You're saying she's beefalo."

Lariven laughed outright for the first time since they'd known her. "I think you are right, Tom Moya," she said with approval, wondering why the word *halfling* stuck to the roof of BuGen's mouth. She smiled at the man from BuGen. "My children by men of the land were either men of the land, or halfling," she summarized again. "Those by other telepaths

were all halfling, but Branoth; even those by Volsce." A faint
trace of ancient pain was in her voice.

"Out of how many pregnancies, Mrs. Korvath?" the little
man from BuGen asked, all impersonal efficiency.

Lariven shrugged. "Fifteen, twenty, you realize we do not
count halflings. We had counted ourselves lucky, the women
of my line, to have Volsce to breed from, but our luck ran
out."

De Anza was sick with pity for her, gallantly facing a genetic tragedy of such magnitude that it took twenty pregnancies to ensure two living children, and one of them must be
by her own twin brother. Lucky, to be able to breed by an
old megalo-maniac who was her father and her mother's father and her grandmother's brother. He thought of Egyptian
and Hawaiian royalty, who had practiced dynastic incest
without even Lariven's urgency of a mutation to protect. Fifteen or twenty pregnancies, by anybody she could manage it
by, relative or stranger. That's what she had been pleading
with Branoth about, to continue the genetic program, to force
one more generation out of a dying line. With Elidir? Or with
herself?

Lariven turned from a discussion of computer analysis and
artificial insemination, looked at the wardroom machine, and
a cup of coffee came into her hand. "Either, Ben," she said,
politely but with a touch of impatience. "In the long run, of
course, Elidir."

Ben de Anza found himself gagging. He looked at her,
searching, as if to find once more the woman he had fallen in
love with. He saw an alien, a plain, worn, pale woman of
alien features, well past her youth, character on her face telling of a long life difficult beyond anything he could imagine.
An artist would have called her beautiful; so would any man
of discernment. So did he. But not as a beloved woman is
beautiful. He could admire her courage beyond measure, but
he could not love her.

Unable to continue the discussion in the wake of de Anza's
emotional storm, Lariven brought another cup of coffee to
her hand and threw the first one away. She laid one long,
cool hand on his arm. "I'm sorry that I have upset you, Ben,"
she said gently. "Your kind has harsh laws on such matters."
She met his eyes with remote kindness. "Does it matter that

yóu no longer love me? Or that once you did? It is over. I will bear a telepath child for Terra; if I learn to twin the child in my womb, you may have one."

"Now, wait a minute!" he exploded in completely automatic reaction. He had been in the Space Service for years, and one of the first things he had learned was not to let a two weeks' fling grow into a claim on the Empire. The long parade of native spaceport girls hoping to wangle Terran citizenship, acknowledgment, for God's sake marriage and a ticket to Terra, out of a sucker of a native spaceman, blasted through his mind.

Lariven turned to ice, and the whole room felt the chill. She vanished, and BuGen made a neat note on the edge of her dossier "teleport." The Terran clothing appeared in the wardroom disposal hopper, two cups of coffee deposited neatly on top of them. As the brown liquid soaked into the red synthetic fabric, the remains of a half-eaten meal appeared on top, then the contents of Lariven's stomach. Then, at long last, she pushed the button.

Moya gaped at the exhibition and spoke for them all. "What the hell did you say to her, Ben?" he demanded.

IV

Benjamin de Anza's name was mud.

For over four days Lariven had stayed in her quarters, not eating, returning any food or refreshments via the trash dump. She spoke only when spoken to, and not at all to de Anza. BuGen used this time to run lab tests and computer simulations, cheerfully explaining that psis were temperamental, and that offworlders often had bad cases of cultural indigestion at Sector HQ.

Lariven had offered one sentence of explanation, via Ling: "It is no longer to my honor to take any gifts from Terran hands." At Anderson's expression of concern, she had answered with complete indifference "I have gone longer than this without food."

"She's only human," de Anza said defensively at an informal drumhead council of his three shipmates. "I had sort of a crush on her; then, suddenly, I didn't. She's a telepath, she'd pick that up." Pressed harder, he said reluctantly, "I used to see her as beautiful. Well, she is, but not in the same way. I had a look at her looking a hundred years old and all worn out, about as pretty as the Rock of Ages; she'd have picked that up, too."

"She never was any spring chicken," Moya said reflectively, "but she's one hell of a fine lady, and I wouldn't mind being seen with her at all. You know, Ben, you three used to make me feel pretty dumb sometimes, but now I'm beginning to wonder just who is the dummy around here. She's been having men fall in and out of love with her since she was out of diapers if she's as old as she looks and still as pretty as she is now. Men have died," he said unexpectedly, "and worms have eaten them, but not for love. Hurt pride, now, that's another matter."

They looked at him; he shrugged. "All right, all right, I'll shut up," he said.

But that night when Moya got up to go to the ship's one small bathroom, he had the feeling that someone was in trouble. He was no psi, but he had a farmer's sense for when a cow is going to calve or a steer is stuck in a fence; he waited until the door opened and Lariven came out. In the ship's dim night lighting, she looked greyish-white. She wore her native draperies; they looked slept in.

He put out a hand. "Hold it," he said. Startled, she stopped. His arm and hand against the wall blocked her passage; she waited. "Out with it," he said. "Talk."

She looked him over calmly. "I was put to shame; shall I be shamed again by telling you?" she asked reasonably.

"Hurt pride. Yeah." He considered her, an unshaven, unattractive colonial in rumpled ship's skivvies and the slender aristocratic alien, and shook his head. "The trouble is, none of us knows what it is. When a man comes gunning for you, you like to know why. We don't read minds and most of us are getting sick of guessing games. BuGen's coming back in a couple of days. What do we tell him? To hell with saving an entire race, you've decided to pick up your marbles and go home? Makes us look like a bunch of idiots."

"Do what you came to do," Lariven said, seating herself in the wardroom, "then finish your say. It is uncomfortable listening to you now."

With a mocking grin Moya said, "Yes, Mama," went on

in, and closed the door. A few minutes later, he joined her, stopping first to get two beers. She left hers unopened beside her; he opened his and drank. "Spill it," he said.

She sat and thought. He waited, then nudged her. "Your family arrangements turned Benny green," he said. "Not me. I'm a breeder. Beef animals or aliens, it's all the same to me. I wouldn't want that for my own people, but if we were the last human beings on the planet, do you think I'd hesitate one minute to do what you've been doing? And you're a grown-up lady; you're not letting little Benny's hangups send you into a temper tantrum."

"You are a breeder," Lariven agreed, her voice cool in the deserted wardroom. "You bring a guest-gift, such as a beefalo"—a faint smile crossed her face—"to one who claims to have always wanted a beefalo. But when you bring this gift, you are lashed away in scorn with 'the nerve of these beggars, forever plaguing me to buy their worthless beasts.' Would you offer a guest-gift of any sort to that one again? Or play the guest, with your gift thrown in your face! It is to my shame that I must still live under a Terran roof until we return! You speak of BuGen. What have I to offer BuGen? I have nothing for Terra, and Terra has nothing for me."

Moya rubbed his unshaven chin and ran his mind back over the day she had vanished. "The kid," he said. "You offered him a kid. Oh, God." He started roaring with laughter. "And of course you couldn't know . . . don't throw another fit, just listen." He started laughing again, then grabbed her shoulders. "Just listen," he repeated.

Lariven, so shocked her very powers left her for a second, sat still under his hands and thought for some reason of Korvath, and of Volsce before his madman's death. She listened.

"Most of the Empire," he was saying earnestly, "is wall to wall Terrans. You thought Sector HQ is jammed; Sector HQ is a desert, empty. You take out a license to even think of having a kid. To have another, you have to prove to BuGen you're worth more than it costs to feed you. That's why my old man emigrated. He has six and they're all A-plus citizens and one of my sisters is Special Talent, but we couldn't have proved it on Earth. Tell a Terry you'd had fifteen or twenty, and he'll tell you to wash your mouth out with soap. So here you are, you'd give anything for a strong, healthy kid, and decide if you have two you'll show your gratitude by giving the daddy one. Fine for the hills of wherever-it-is, but for an Earthman? Oh, brother."

Lariven was looking at him as if he'd missed the point completely. "A telepath child, Moya," she said patiently. "Does the Empire want telepaths, or not? My Sight has shown me that twinned telepaths of any strength, mindbonded, one reared among his own and one among the mindblind, would at the very least not be halfling, and with any luck would have some Power."

Moya narrowed his eyes. "I never heard a word about this, Lady. When did you tell them? Or did you just make it up now?"

She put her fingers together. "I was telling them when they threw this gift of mine, this telepath child that was to be for the Empire, in my face. Now do you expect me to run after them, whining and pulling at their clothes and begging them to take another look at the worthless beast they would not buy of the beggar queen?"

"They can rot first," Moya agreed.

"You do understand."

Moya spit past her face into the trash disposal. "I understand that we had a deal, and you reneged. I don't think enough of anyone who does that to spit on them. Go ahead, throw all the temper tantrums you want, pick up your marbles and go home, but if you were a man I'd mop up the floor with you."

Anger grew on her face. His heartbeat became irregular and he felt a choking in his throat and chest. He lashed out and belted her across the cheek. "Fight like a man, damn you. Or are you the kind to pull a knife on a man without one?" He gasped for breath and studied her. "Yeah. I'll bet you are. You promised the Empire a telepath, and because little Benny gets you all mad, you go back on your word."

A flash of rage lanced through her and she released her hold on his heart. "You call me oathbreaker," she said, twin daggers appearing in her hand. She offered him one, hilt-first.

"You bet," he said with equal anger, ignoring them. "Now, if you don't want to deal with Benny, there's at least three other people on this ship you know would listen: Anderson, Ling, and what's-his-name. BuGen. *And* not one of them would act like you were trying to slap a paternity suit on them." He snorted. "Benny's been watching too many training films; they went to his head. As for you. . . ."

"Silence, Moya, let me finish thinking."

"I was going to say, put me in Benny's shoes—or between his sheets—and you wouldn't. . . ."

His voice shut off. He finished his sentence and not a sound came out. She watched him, smiling with unfeigned amusement, and tucked one of the daggers into his belt. When he stopped sputtering, she released his voice, saying with a smile, "And it is not to your honor to knife-fight with a woman twice your age and possibly with child; next time, say so outright."

"It'll be a long time before you're either twice my age or big enough to show," Moya answered with at least partial truth, "and you are still one hell of a lady. I was about to say Terra's no place for a telepath kid. New Barranca, now, is wide open."

Lariven took his face in her hands. "Silence, and let me see," she ordered. Her hands were cool and light on his face. "But if I speak to these others and they deal with me as Ben de Anza did, I will kill you, for I do not walk into such shame twice," she said.

"No guts. Too bad."

Lariven started to freeze his voice again and stopped as she caught his thought that he'd be quiet. She floated in the middle of the wardroom as if under zero-*g*, cross-legged, thinking that Moya, at least, had been honest, and had risked the certain displeasure of his teammates to do so. It was only what he should do, but she was moved by it all the same. And he had called her oathbreaker, as if she came to Terra with a promised treasure, not with empty hands.

She would go back to the hills. She looked inward at her womb and saw children slowly dying as they misdeveloped, frail, sickly, simpleminded, incomplete empaths, doomed. She saw her whole line dying, and her race, as the hopes raised at each birth slowly and painfully died. Slowly she thought of what she had done already and would do to avoid this. Give her life? Surely, either in death or in lifelong servitude. Lie with a man she despised? If need be she would tie herself to his bed. Lie with one who despised her? For this, the answer must be yes, a conclusion she could not evade for all that she could not face the sting of de Anza's rejection.

She must. She wrenched her mind away from the whimpers of the dying halfling girl and uncurled herself from the tight fetal position she had fallen into, saying, "I will speak to BuGen, with the Survey women present. You may watch; I would rather de Anza did not."

Moya shrugged. "Suits me." Inside he was cheering.

A year later, Lariven stood in the front room of the Moya ranch and took the child Benita from the arms of Tom Moya's mother. "They are mind-linked; we will always have news of each other," she said, kissing Benita's twin brother Anderson good-bye. "We will probably all be fluent in each others' languages before they cut their milk teeth."

She let herself sense Moya's parents, his brothers and sisters, and the entire ranch, adding her knowledge to the vast storehouse in her mind that held all she had seen of the Terran Empire that year. "He will grow well among you," she said.

Mrs. Moya put out a hand to shake. "I'm glad you think so," she said, bemused. She couldn't shake the feeling that the twins were her son's, her own grandchildren, no matter what BuGen and Lariven had said. BuGen would pay for Andy's education; it was the standard foster-care arrangement. She hoped she could do right by the boy. If he couldn't develop normally at home, why, of course he needed a foster home; it was nice to have a little one around again.

She kissed Benita and shook hands with Lariven. Then Moya and Lariven climbed into the Survey landing craft.

"I'm going back to Koryath when this is over," Lariven said when they were out of the atmosphere of New Barranca. "BuGen has found marriages for the twins, and for Branoth and Elidir—not to each other, to Branoth's relief. Strange to think they need never meet their intended; stranger still to think that a machine thought long and hard about such things for them. Do you think my sister houses will follow my example?"

"I think they'll do as they damn well please," Tom Moya said from the depths of his experience with her. "How do you think Korvath will like being married to Spaceport Control?"

Lariven considered Korvath's other wives. "He's been married to stranger things," she said, and laughed, and they began the long trip back.

About C. A. Cador and *The Ring*

Long before House Greyhaven, or even House Greenwalls, was established, in the long-ago times before Paul married Tracy or Diana married Jon, quite a few of us were still living in a big old house up on Arch street. (It was badly haunted, but that is another story, which some day I may write.)

One day in the summer of 1966, or maybe it was 1967, my son David (who is a writer himself, though he was too busy working on his novel to contribute a short story to this volume) brought home a friend whom he introduced only as Caradoc; who, he said, needed a place to stay for a while. We had extra room, and Caradoc proved an unusually quiet and inoffensive tenant, even cooking his own meals, mostly of brown rice and other macrobiotic goodies. He stayed for a few months, and then moved on, and since it had cost us nothing and given us no trouble to house him, I had half forgotten the episode, though I remembered him as a nice youngster and often wondered what had happened to him.

In 1972 or thereabouts, when the Greenwalls household had been formed as the House of Exile in Staten Island, I made a trip to the West Coast to visit the family, and encountered Caradoc again, discovering that with that offhand hospitality we had made a friend for all time. By that time I knew his real name, but it takes a distinct effort to remember it, for I still think of him as Caradoc; and the more so since, with his first story "Payment in Kind," which appeared in one of Lin Carter's *Year's Best Fantasy* series for DAW Books) he achieved immediate critical attention as a fine serious writer of fantasy. Although his own roots include Native American and Peruvian, his fantasy shows a distinct leaning toward the British/Welsh side of his background. Much of

209

his work evokes the fantastic "Celtic Twilight" tradition of Yeats, Dunsany and Fiona MacLeod, and "The Ring" is most definitely in this manner and style.

THE RING

by Caradoc A. Cador

The sea glowed a dark purple lined in white, rolling in from the sky to the small and stony beach in the crashing of one unending breath. The darkness echoed with the sound of the surf and the calling of sea birds. Fiachra felt its life surrounding him and smiled as though at a friend.

He was alone on the stony shore, his cloak wrapped tight about him against the predawn cold. His hair shone almost white in the light of the waning moon.

Dawn glowed in the east; he knew he should hurry, but could not bring himself to. His brothers would not put out to sea without him, only curse if he was too late.

Their curses would be wasted on him now. He was as immune to them as to the wind's bite.

He stopped and stared out over the glowing width of the sea, remembering . . . Mairi's hair in the firelight, Mairi's laugh.

Almost he hoped his brothers would leave without him; he had so much to tell, and no one to tell it to but his sister Morag.

He had stayed the night in Mairi's village, in the common room of Mairi's family—the first time since they had pledged each other at the May Eve Fire.

Now it was morning, and he walked along the coast of the island, back to his own village and his day's work on the family boat.

Only Fiachra of all the folk of the island ever walked the beach for the joy of it, and the cool clean edge of the wind blowing in over the sea from the world's corners.

In other things, he was no different from any of the others: a fisherman born. For uncounted generations his ancestors had wrested their livings from the sea, and a good living it had been, and a hard dying with a grave marker that covered no body; seldom will the sea give up again that which it has claimed.

That had been the death of his father, and his elder brother . . . but the sea is just: If it gives life, who is to gainsay it in its taking?

No one but he of all the village would be out in the cold hours just before dawn; so it was that the ring came to him.

Beyond a huge rock, he saw the boat, wrecked ribs casting jagged shadows in the moonlight; the ring glinted pale gold at him from a dead hand.

The corpse was badly decomposed—almost skeletal. It lay sprawled on its back, hands flung up over its head; around the horror of its skull hair glinted a warmer, darker gold. From the garments, it seemed to have been a man; more one could not tell.

Almost he left the ring there, but it gleamed so in the moonlight . . . nor was Fiachra so much of a dreaming fool as to leave a thing worth a cow to lie on the beach for fear of a dead man.

And then he thought how fine that would look on Mairi's hand on their handfasting day.

It was loose on the rotted finger; in a moment it was in his hand.

He tested the weight of it for an instant, surprised by a heaviness that told of almost pure metal. Then all such thoughts were lost in wonder as he stared at the ring in the palm of his hand. It was of a pale yellow gold, carved in the shape of two interlaced branches covered with leaves.

Never had he held a thing so fair; it glowed as if with its own light, and the metal seemed almost warm on his calloused hand. It slipped onto his finger, fitting as well as if it had been made for it.

The sky was paling with the imminence of dawn when he turned away from the beach and the wrecked boat. He walked back the way he had come, down the length of the beach and around the rocky point at its end.

Life was stirring in the village beyond. It nestled in a fold of the hills, a cluster of white washed round houses beside the small harbor which was its heart.

The smoke of cookfires rose from the smoke holes and figures moved by the boats with the smooth indifferent speed that comes with long familiarity. Dimly it occurred to him that his brothers would be readying the boat, and that he was needed there, or would be soon; he had no care for anything but to show his mother what gleamed on his finger.

As he neared the village one of his brothers called to him; Fiachra, his back to the sea, walked on unhearing up the dirt road that twisted through the village until he came to the white walls of his home.

It was a snug house, stone walls covered with a fresh coat of whitewash that seemed to glow in the first light of dawn and a freshly thatched roof. Behind it on the hillside, his sisters worked among the neat rows of the kitchen garden.

Inside, tightly woven walls of wicker divided the house into compartments ringing the central hearth-hall. The light was dim—a beam of sunlight from the smokehole and the cookfire on the hearth. The fire warmed him, and made of the house a friendly place, snug against the wind that blew ever from the sea—though not against the wind's wailing on the long winter nights, nor the ever present roar of the waves.

Always it had seemed the fairest place in the world to him, with all of comfort and beauty any could ask; somehow now it seemed shrunken upon itself.

His mother was already at the wheel, humming to the rhythm of her foot on the pedal as her fingers deftly twined the long staples of the wool and fed them to the spinning wheel.

Without a break in the swift motion of her fingers she dropped her song. "How are things with Mairi? And why are you not with your brothers?"

For answer he raised his hand to show her the ring glinting from his finger.

The thread broke in her hand, but her foot still drove the pump. "What . . . where did that come from, boy?"

"From the sea, on a dead man's hand." He laughed nervously at his own words, but the laugh rang false even on his own ears. For a moment he wondered how he could have brought himself to its taking, defying the luck of it so.

His mother's foot froze before he had finished speaking. The color slowly drained from her face. "On a dead man's hand?"

Fiachra nodded, smiling, his moment of confusion over. "Over beyond the point, a boat washed on shore in the night."

Carefully she set the floss she had been spinning down and walked over to him, moving with the slight stiffness of her grey hair.

She bent over his hand to examine the ring. Fiachra looked down at her and laughed; this time there was nothing in his voice that rang false. "Is it not fine, then? A king's ring, it is."

His mother grunted, then straightened until her eyes were level with his chin. She searched his face for a moment, then turned, still holding his hand, and said "Come."

Fiachra followed wordlessly as she led him to the hearth and held the hand that wore the ring close to its glowing heat in purification.

His sister Morag came in from the garden then; the old woman silenced her with a swift gesture that stopped her in the doorway.

When it was done, some of the tension went out of her, but only some. "Very pretty it is, to be sure; the traders will give much for it, and be none the wiser of the dead man's hand."

"Ooh . . . let me see!" said Morag. Freed from her mother's commanding gesture, she stepped into the house. "Is that . . . ?"

"I'll not sell it." Fiachra's words cut her off before he knew he was going to say them. "There's nothing they could give me for it that I'd rather have."

Her mother sputtered for a moment, then turned away to her own tasks.

Morag looked a question across the hearth at Fiachra.

He smiled. "It's gold right enough, gold out of the sea. You can wear it for your handfasting if you like."

Morag's eyes danced. "Can I really?"

"She'll no such thing." Their mother's voice rang with outraged finality. "Would you have her *taken*? At her wedding, is it, with rings from out of the sea on dead fingers."

Morag managed to look simultaneously properly horrified for the old woman's benefit and conspiratorially fascinated for Fiachra's.

Their mother rounded on her. "Have you nothing better to do than stand and gawk, girl?"

Morag rushed back out into the garden, almost visibly swollen with the news she carried.

Fiachra sat down beside the hearth and raised the ring to peer at it in the feeble light, studying closely the fineness of the workmanship with which it had been carved, the perfection of every leaf of the intricately entwined branches and every petal of the half-opened flowers.

Where is it, he thought, *that they have roses so fair as that . . .*

The sound of his brothers' booming laughter jarred Fiachra, pulling him back to his place by the fire through layer after misty layer of dream. For a moment after his eyes flew open, he could not remember where he was, but the sight of his mother rising from the wheel and the glint of the ring on his finger brought him back to himself.

His brothers stooped in through the low doorway; Taggart, the oldest of them, began cursing as soon as he caught sight of Fiachra.

"Hush you," called the old woman. "There will be no fighting in this house."

Taggart shook his head. "Warm beside the fire, is it, with the rest of us out on the cold sea . . . he was not sick, we saw him walking home through the village fit as a lark while we were readying the boat . . . It's nothing to me if he goes down the coast to see his girl, I remember when I was his age, but let him come and work as well, and not leave it all to us."

Yann raised his hand and hard words turned to wonder at the glint of gold.

Taggart whistled low at the sight of it, and nothing would do but for Fiachra to tell the story of its finding again, while his three brothers crowded around like so many trees leaning over a pond.

When at least he was done, Taggart smiled and clapped him on the shoulder. "Good lad . . . when we sell 'er, we'll have to leave off the dead man, though."

Fiachra shook his head. "I'm not selling it."

Taggart sputtered for a minute, then looked to their mother.

"He will not sell." The corners of her mouth twitched downward for a moment. "The whole day he spent staring at it half asleep."

"What good is it to him, next to the two cows we could get from the chief?" His brother Ross scratched at the brown thatch of his beard.

The old woman shrugged. After a few moments the brothers wandered off into their compartments.

Their anger and their wonder Fiachra received alike with smiling indifference.

Later, Morag came to his compartment. "Let me see it." Her voice was almost coy, "Let me see it, Red Ear."

Fiachra shook his head violently from side to side, then stretched his neck, throwing his head up and back like a hound baying. "Anything, my queen."

Quickly he slipped it off his finger and dropped it into her outstretched palm. "It's beautiful." She struck a pose of exaggerated dignity. "Fit for a queen." She barely stifled a giggle. "Would you really let me wear it at my wedding?"

"I would, but the old woman wouldn't, and you know it."

Morag sighed. "It would be so grand, though . . . tell me again how you found it."

That night his sleep was restless, full of dreams that he could not quite recall on rising save as a vague beauty and a strangeness.

Remembered or not, his dreams haunted him, as if in forgetting them there was some great loss, and he struggled against the wall of blankness behind which they hid.

He seemed somehow drawn, and when he spoke, it was as if from a distance. Not until they were well out to sea did he lose the listlessness of that strange sleep, and even then he was tired; it seemed that the day's work could not end too soon.

So it went for many days, his dreams becoming more and more vivid, until the day when he shut his eyes and saw not darkness but a rich plain, green grass strewn with little yellow and white flowers and beyond an apple wood; in the same instant he felt the air grow suddenly warm, and the bitter sea wind became a gentle breeze, smelling not of salt and fish but appleblossom and heather and scents for which he had no name. Among the apple boughs there hung a curious instrument like a many stringed harp from whose strings the wind teased faint harmonies.

When he opened his eyes he was back in the family's boat, tossed on the wind-whipped waves.

From that moment, there was no more forgetting of his dreams.

At night he walked through green meadows of surpassing richness, pasturage such as he had never seen, or forests that seemed to stretch on forever under a sky bluer than any mortal sky.

In his dreams he walked on beaches whose sand gleamed like powdered gemstones beside a sea colored with lapis lazuli and flecked with ivory, and saw a city of crystalline towers linked by arched bridges soaring impossibly over emptiness a thousand feet in the air.

Never did he see those who lived in that land of dreams, but they were there; sometimes he felt them, and sometimes heard their voices, calm and pure as starlight, sometimes calling him and sometimes raised in song.

His family saw how he changed, watching with puzzled worry as he grew ever more listless and distracted.

No longer could he be found listening respectfully in the circle of storytellers, or in his place among those whose feet flew in the measures of the island dances when the makers of music played far into the night.

Though he walked the beaches alone, it was no more with any goal beyond them, and days on days passed without him once speaking Mairi's name.

Many were the eyes that sought him without finding the familiar ringlets of his red and curly head or the strong grace of his youth; he had no time for the familiar occupations of his past. All his life was work and dream, waking or sleeping.

When his brothers sought to speak of it to him, he turned away, saying only that he was not sleeping well, and was very tired.

One there was though from whom he could not turn away: his sister Morag.

She came in the night to his bedside and laid her hand on his. "What is it with you, this last month, Red Ear . . ."

The pet name pierced through the shells about him more keenly than all his brothers' gruff and serious words. He gathered his breath to speak, exhaled with a sigh, gathered his breath again, then burst out, "It is like this, sister. I dream . . . I dream of a place."

She looked more puzzled than ever. "What sort of a place?"

Fiachra ignored her question. "No more just in my dreams, either. I have but to shut my eyes when we are sailing out on the sea, and I find myself there. . . . in a place more beautiful than I can say. The West is no longer empty sea to my eyes; sometimes, I can see it there like a colored cloud just where sea and sky meet. And the sea itself . . ." His voice took on an almost hypnotic quality as he spoke. "The sea has voices, voices like bells, voices that call to me, singing songs that would leave the king's bard with his head hanging in shame or crying for jealousy."

Morag's hand tightened around his. "You will leave us, then, and go to those voices. . . ." Her voice caught in an almost-sob. "Oh, hound, how should I live without you."

Fiachra smiled a dreamy half smile. "Ah, no, my queen, your red-eared hound runs still at your back across the dark spaces of the night."

"So you do, Red Ear, but I fear for you. It is as if your dreams have come for you by day, and eat you alive."

Fiachra only laughed, and rumpled her hair.

His mother was less gentle with him.

One day when they came in from the sea, she greeted him with a barked "Sell the ring, fool."

He stumbled past, eyes half shut, mind full of the glow of his dream land; she caught him by the shoulder and turned him to face her.

"It is the ring that has brought you to this, pale shadow of yourself. Full of the magic of the Other People it is, and ruin for plain simple people. It is a thing for the great and the wise; for us it is death."

Fiachra could not repress his laughter; at the sound his mother's face flushed as if she'd been struck.

"Did I not bid you sell it on the day of its finding? Sell it, or throw it back into the sea better still, and let it rest there forever, else Themselves will surely *take* you, or lure you to your death."

He shook his head and walked past her, but still she spoke on. "Mairi will be at the dancing tonight; they say she walked over from the other side of the island, but it is so long since you have been to see her, she will not come here."

His mother's words were not such as he would heed, and her voice seemed harsh and cracked beside the fair voices he heard now by day as well as by night; what more was she, then, but a foolish old woman who knew not what she spoke of.

The next day he did not sail with his brothers, but kept to the house, as if waiting.

A little after noon, Huil, Mairi's elder brother, came to call. Fiachra knew him first by his voice; he stood in the courtyard calling until the old woman let him in.

"No need to be so formal with us, Huil dubh, calling for admission like we was strangers," she said as she ushered him in. "Can I offer you something? A drink? or some oatcake?"

While she spoke, Huil scanned the chamber until he found Fiachra; smiling thinly, he shook his head. "No indeed, it is not so very great a walk as all that from the other side of the island . . . though judging by how seldom your son has walked it of late, it might be beyond the Black Gates."

She nodded. "Oh, well, he has been poorly of late, you know, and I've been telling him not to go out walking so much as he used, for fear he'd chill."

"Was it a chill he might catch at the dancing last night? When Mairi walked over to see him, if he would see her?" Huil's face lost the edge of its good nature.

He walked across the room, stopping in front of Fiachra and looking up and down his almost supine body. "I had heard, but I did not believe the tales. Not two months ago, when last I saw you, you were strong and eager, full of youth and hope. Now you seem shrunken, grown in upon yourself, nor do I like the light I see in your eyes. Have you roused the wrath of some wizard of spell-weaver? Truly you are under some enchantment."

Fiachra laughed hollowly. "No enchantment, only that I

see what you cannot. And what have I to do with wizards, who walk only among the great?"

Huil shook his head. "Be that as it may, while this curse is on you, you are no fit husband for any woman, nor will you be one to my sister. She will find a better man than you, one free of madness and spells." Huil paused; Fiachra's mother seized his hand and started to speak, but he waved her into silence. "It grieves me, and my sister as well, for this marriage was of her own seeking. So must it be, unless the spell that binds you be broken."

The old woman's shoulders sagged.

Fiachra fought down the momentary twinge of regret, shutting his eyes for a moment to refresh himself in the sight and sound of the land of his dreams before replying. "So be it, then, and on your head be the burden, for it is none of my doing. I will find a fairer one than Mairi; now get you gone."

Many and bitter were the words Fiachra's mother said to him that night, so that his brothers walked on the beach, fearing the storm within more than the bitter cold or the damp sea wind. At the last, seeing that her words were to no avail, she went to her bed, weeping.

A while after his mother left him, there came a familiar scratch against the wickerwork wall, and a low voice called out "Red Ear . . . are you awake?"

He muttered a reply, and in a moment she was beside him. "Why did you do it, hound. . . . Did she mean so little to you?"

Fiachra laughed softly, almost to himself. "Mairi? She was a dream, no more, an image gone from my mind, yesterday's storm."

"You loved her once, courted her, wrote a song for her and played it festival night. Now even the music you play on the harp is different . . . everything's changed." There was the sound of tears in her voice. "Oh, hound, what will become of us?"

"You? You will marry, and a fine man will he be, and lucky with it, and you will bear children, and have a fine house and a dozen cows at least, and maybe someday forget running the night with your red-eared hound."

"Never. . . ." She was sobbing now. "Never, Red Ear.

Not until salmon nest in the trees and eat nuts. I could never forget you."

"No, of course not, my queen." Gently he stroked the back of her neck.

Fiachra's dreams possessed him wholly, now; he was scarce able to work, and his sleep was something other than sleep, in which there was little rest. He felt himself being pulled westward in an almost physical way; it was always a hard moment when the boat turned again homeward at the end of a day's fishing.

Stronger and stronger the compulsion grew, and daily he found himself longing more to yield to it and sail to the uttermost west to seek there the land of his dreams.

The more real that land became, the more did his life as a fisherman seem illusion.

With Morag's reluctant help, he began stealing food from the larder and secreting it in his room: cheese, smoked and salted fish, cracker bread. . . . food for a journey of a few weeks. Surely the land in which he had so often walked was no farther than that.

Finally he thought it enough. He rose in the night from his sleepless bed and crept to where his sister slept.

He stood over her bed in the darkness, looking down into the shadows among which she lay. He longed to wake her, to hear her voice once more, but in the end only flourished his hand in salute to her sleeping form and whispered "Farewell, my queen."

His cached provisions wrapped in a blanket, he stole silently out the door and made his way down to the harbor.

He took a small boat, little more than a dinghy, he had made for himself years before and loaded on it his food and a water barrel. Then hoisting its single sail, he turned her bow to the west.

It was as if a great burden dropped from his shoulders. He sang as the boat swept forward like a living thing, exulting in its speed, mingling his voice with the voices of the otherworld as he steered straight away from the dawn.

But on the already far distant shore his sister stood and sang the ancient lament for the sea-dead.

*   *   *

On and on he sailed in a waking dream, sailing out from the midst of the islands into the west. Little did he eat or drink, yet his supplies dwindled.

Finally one morning he saw before him in the farthest distance a land that he knew could be but one, and as he beheld it, it's name came to him as if remembered from half-forgotten tales: The Land of Dreaming Youth.

Swift the boat, over wild waves sweeping, skimming froth milk-white from the sea-crests, yet the gleaming shore came no nearer.

In the distance he saw what seemed to be great birds flying; when one of them flew nearer, he saw that it had the head of a woman.

He turned a little from his course to sail toward the birds, great wings carrying them spiraling slowly up and down above the silver surface of the sea. As he approached he could hear them singing, weaving rhythms and harmonies that matched the complex interlocking figures of the spiral they danced.

Closer still, and the sound of their singing was a fire in his veins, burning with an ancient joy and an ancient sorrow. Which was the harder to bear he knew not, for both were greater than the joys and sorrows of men.

Still the shore seemed to recede before him, as if taunting him. The voices of his dreams rang in his ears, and sometimes it seemed he could hear the low sound of a silver bell.

His finger grew oddly slender as the days passed, so that he feared the ring might slip from his hand. Around his neck he tied it on a cord.

How long he had been sailing he neither knew nor cared; it was enough to see over the boat's bow the coasts of the western land. Days had passed since he had slept; he felt poised on the knife's edge between night and day, waking and sleeping. On life and death he looked as if he were neither.

Once he saw a barge sail past, its hull gleaming silver and its sail the purple of twilight; from it came the sound of a harp and the light crystalline laughter of those who come never to old age or death.

He called and called, but it glided on past him and vanished wakeless in the distance.

His food and water were gone, and day by day he grew weaker; he took a rope and tied himself to the tiller.

It seemed that suddenly he beheld a woman of beauty like the stars on a moonless night or the first fresh grass of spring standing before him beckoning.

He reached out for her hand with his own. Strength poured into him from her touch, and he felt it lift his feet.

He blinked, for the boat was nowhere in sight; instead he stood in the doorway of a hall of lights and music. Around him the voices of his dreams rose in welcoming song; the rough wool fell from his shoulders. . . .

Around his boat the birds with the heads of women flew in stately circles, singing a song that was half welcome and half mourning for the dead. It is sung that none born of woman may come living to the halls of the Uttermost West.

In time a wind arose and blew the boat back, back into the water of mortal lands, where a boat sails with a wake behind it, and gulls ate the flesh from off his bones. After much time, it was driven ashore.

In the midst of the wreck he lay, the ring glinting gold against his breast bone.

About Paul Edwin Zimmer and
The Hand of Tyr

I was thirteen when my brother Paul was born, and already scribbling long incoherent novels in school notebooks. I married for the first time, and moved to Texas, when he was seven years old, leaving him to discover my old collections of fantasy novels, fanzines, even my old hectograph. I don't think I ever doubted for a minute, so young and naïve I was, that Paul would grow up the right way—that is, a science fiction fan, and more than that, a fan who aspired to be a professional writer.

He started out, actually, as a painter, having a two-man show at a local gallery in Albany, New York, and later, when he moved to Berkeley, earning himself something of a reputation as a coffee-house poet; at one time he had trained as an actor, and his decidedly dramatic delivery of his own work made him one of the most sought-after poets of that city—which is somewhat over-provided with poets of all descriptions, from the excellent to the execrable.

From time to time he showed me short stories or the beginnings of novels, none of which I took very seriously. His major interest during these years seemed to be acting as Earl Marshal (a sort of weapons expert and combat referee) of the Society for Creative Anachronism. It's not easy to be objective about someone you've lugged around on one arm; remembering youthful foibles (such as the time Paul commented, I believe seriously, that Edgar Rice Burroughs should be accepted as an important figure in world literature, and that my own writing would be improved by more adherence to Burroughs' standards). But I was impressed by Paul's growing importance as a poet, and even more by his skills as a martial-arts expert.

Our collaboration began that way; when I signed the contract for *Spell Sword*, I went to Paul, as the best-informed person I knew, and asked him to provide me with continuity for the fighting sequences. I believed that these would be bald scenarios explaining the moves, in the style of the old radio prize-fight narration before TV; "A right to the jaw—the champ is against the ropes—the challenger recovers with a quick left to the body, a right to the jaw . . ." etc.

Instead, to my pleased surprise, after lengthy discussion of the points involved, Paul provided me with fully written chapters, almost all of which, because of their clarity and excellence, as well as the deft characterization involved, I managed to incorporate almost word for word into the growing manuscript of *Spell Sword*. He was especially helpful in the creation of the character of Dom Esteban—who was, by mutual consent, based on our father. After this, I felt no hesitation in asking Paul to create the fight sequences of *Hunters of the Red Moon*. Paul wrote almost a third of the final manuscript of that novel; when people asked us about our collaboration, we made a joke that Paul put in the violence and I provided the sex. To this day, royalties for *Spell Sword* and *Hunters* are divided with Paul, and by right his name should appear on *Hunters* as a collaborator, though, since he was an unknown, *Hunters* was published under my name alone.

Survivors, the sequel, was written as a frank collaboration, and his name appeared on the book. We wrote this one differently; after discussing chapters and outline, Paul would write a fast first draft, and I would rewrite it, sharpening up the characterization and the interpersonal interactions somewhat. The splendidly original creation of the Kirgon slavehound, and the Kirgon himself, were Paul's without any amendation by me. And in both books, the character of Aratak, with his constant invocation of the wisdom of the Divine Egg, was more Paul's than mine. I still have not lost hope that some day we may revive Dane and Rianna and Aratak for another journey through weaponry of the universe.

But it won't be for a while; because, shortly after the completion of *The Survivors*, Paul met Sharon Jarvis at a convention, and managed to interest her in the novel he was working on; and Sharon bought it for her own publishers.

Since then, whenever I have broached the subject of another collaboration, Paul has been working on *The Dark Border,* a novel almost as long as my own *Mistress of Magic.*

I seldom see Paul except in the dim overlap where the night meets the day. Paul is so markedly a Night Person that some people have facetiously suspected him of Vampire blood. If he must venture out in daylight, for even the most eccentric of individuals must visit dentists and banks and so forth, he shields his sensitive eyes in the darkest glasses to be had. He rises about four o'clock and staggers about Grey-haven half asleep until seven or so, when several cups of coffee have done their vivifying work. He begins to shine about eleven in the evening, at a party or Bardic Revel—just about the time that I, a Day Person absolutely, have begun to collapse and turn into a pumpkin. However, like a true Day Person, I am always wide awake by five in the morning. In that pre-dawn time, I used to go to Greyhaven. Paul and I would sit in the kitchen, hold our conferences on the current work and drink coffee. . . . after which I would bid him good night and go to start my day while he crawled into bed at the close of his.

And it was at one of these Bardic Revels that I heard him read *The Hand of Tyr.* I have always bent over backwards to be hypercritical of Paul's work—and he, for his part, is highly sensitive to the idea that he might be regarded only in the light of MZB's younger brother, and eager to stand alone; I have not even been allowed to read the manuscript of *The Dark Border,* since he says he wants me to read it for the first time as a fully professional, independent work of art.

So when I asked him—or rather, asked my sister-in-law Tracy, who is also Paul's agent—about *Hand of Tyr* for this volume, she told me that Paul wanted to sell this one independently, and it was out to another market. I kept nagging her for it, saying that I wanted Paul to be represented in this anthology by his very best work—otherwise I might be accused of buying a story Paul could not sell elsewhere! The logic of that finally struck her, and she agreed that even if the story sold elsewhere first, I should have the first anthology rights.

I think this story is Paul's finest work. I wish you could all hear it first, as I did, declaimed in a rich, strong bass voice—

with adequate training, Paul could have made any operatic
basso or Shakespearean actor look to his laurels—of—which,
when he reached the conclusion, stunned even applause and
kept his listeners in a held-breath silence for a full minute before the storm of cheers began. But even on the page, I think
it retains that power. It's a pleasure to hail the "kid" as an independent artist—for no one on earth could say this story
was of the "school of Marion Zimmer Bradley"—and to
salute him as an equal or better.

—Marion Zimmer Bradley

THE HAND OF TYR
by Paul Edwin Zimmer

*Father Odin sent forth from the Hall of the Slain that hero
who is called Farin among the Einherior, although he has
had many another name on earth. All-seeing Heimdall
watched as he crossed Rainbow Bridge, and Blessed Freyja
and Mother Frigg helped him to find his way into a mortal
woman's womb, and safely out again in due season.*

*But of course, he had forgotten his mission, and who he
was.*

Roger Hogg crumpled up the poem he had written and
tossed it across the tiny apartment. He shook his head; small
wonder that no one appreciated his poetry, when he could
not make sense of it himself!

Sunlight poured through dingy windows. A mattress on the
floor (sheets and blankets carefully made up), and a few old
orange crates, turned on their sides and stuffed with books,
were the only furniture, except for the home-made sword
rack which supported his only valuable possession; the two-
hundred-year-old Samurai sword which a friend had sold him
for forty dollars, though it was probably worth a couple of
thousand. . . .

No matter how poor he was, he would not part with that.

He sighed. For a while he had thought that perhaps in poetry he had found his place in life—but it looked like that, too, was a blind alley. Like nearly everything else.

All his life he had had this crazy obsession, the feeling that there was something he *must* do. He had emerged into manhood with the driving need to find some purpose in life, and an odd surety that whatever it was, he had not yet found it.

Maybe it was just loneliness. He had never had many friends. His parents, unable to understand this odd cuckoo hatched in their nest, had at last washed their hands of him, secure in their conviction that *they* had done their duty.

Just loneliness. In his mind ran the hateful chanting that had followed him up from kindergarten— "Roger is a hog! Roger is a hog!"

But that explained nothing; every Hogg for generations must have heard much the same rhyme. But no other Hogg had turned out like him. . . .

His eyes slid caressingly over the lacquered scabbard of his sword, the one thing he loved, the one purpose that had not failed him. Romantic daydreams had led him early into fencing, and then on into Judo, Karate, Aikido, and at last to the sword forms, Kendo and Iai. Now, at least, he could make a precarious living teaching the martial arts.

That seemed closer to the mysterious purpose he sought in life than anything else had, but still not *right*. . . .

Strange, the way a sword, any sword, seemed to fit in his hand, to become a part of him. He had taken to the martial arts—but to the sword in particular—instinctively, as though he had spent long lifetimes learning.

He knelt where he was, closing his eyes in meditation, striving to clear his mind of all thought. He had early abandoned the distant god to whom his parents prayed, and after a brief flirt with atheism had turned to yoga and zen, hoping to find some meaning outside the vast wasteland of everyday life.

He tried to erase his memories, wipe away his scarred emotions, forget past, present, and future in that quietude which is the sound of one hand clapping. . . .

Redness before his eyes, thickening. He felt his heartbeat speeding up as an odd excitement stole over him. He breathed slowly and deeply, trying to breathe peace into his mind, to fall into the White Light. . . .

Redness, thickening, flowing, congealing—like blood. It *was* blood, blood that pulsed from a severed wrist, a bloody stump that pointed at him with white splinters of protruding bone . . .

Then, with a gasp, he was on his feet, staring at the wall, studying the white plaster intently. There was nothing there. There *could not have been* anything there.

A hallucination, then. . . .

Or a vision. . . ?

He had seen a man—an ancient warrior with blazing eyes—pointing at him, pointing with an arm that ended in a mangled redness of chewed flesh and bone.

As his pounding heart quieted, and his gasps softened into more normal breathing, a name rose into his mind.

Tyr, the Viking war-god!

The Norse legends had always held a peculiar fascination for him; many of his poems were drawn from them. That curious story of the binding of the Wolf, most of all. . . .

A part of his mind was rummaging frantically through his scraps of psychology, trying to root out the cause of this fantastic hallucination.

But another part stood rapt in a wonder of belief, asking what the God of War could want with *him?*

War. It was a dirty word to his generation: his romantic leanings had not kept him from that. He thought of the sleek, deadly rockets nestled in deep pits in the earth, waiting for the button of Ragnarok; remembered lying awake as a child, listening to the planes overhead, sick with the fear that this plane would be *the* plane, and expecting each moment to hear the whistle of the falling bomb that would end everything . . .

(But it was the *Wolf* that was to bring Ragnarok, and Tyr had *bound* the Wolf . . .)

He had always rather fancied himself a "Visionary," but if this was a real vision. . . .

Was it a summons? Was there something he should do?

I'm cracking up! said that part of his mind which was still trying to explain away the hallucination. *They always said I was crazy, and they were right! Paranoia—not only do I see things, I have to interpret them as messages from the gods, too!*

Joe. It had always seemed an unlikely accident that he and his radical friends had moved in just down the hall. . . .

If it *was* a real vision, it scared him stiff. . . .

Joe had been hinting that if he really wanted to help straighten the world out—there had been a time when the two of them had talked of nothing else—there were things that might be done, things that *he* was doing. That the Movement could use somebody like Roger. . . .

His hand shot out and lifted his sword from its rack. *Action!* Was this his purpose, at last? He slid the sword from its sheath and held it out, watching the light ripple on the polished blade.

Joe had always been talking about the world of peace and love and plenty he wanted, and of the struggle necessary to bring it into being. Perhaps that was what Roger had been born for. Perhaps that was what this Vision had meant. . . .

Delusions of grandeur, yet! the other part of his mind jibed at him. *Brother, are you cracked!*

He sheathed the sword and placed it gently on the rack.

A wolf-age, a wind-age, ere the world ends. . . . suddenly the line from the *Voluspa* was ringing in his head as he left the apartment, and he found himself muttering the words under his breath.

He'd met Joe in college—they'd taken the same Karate class. They'd had little enough in common—a mutual discontent with the world as it was, and a certain unpopularity with their peers. But Roger had had few friends, and now Joe was the only one he had any contact with—and that only because of the curious chance that had brought Joe and all his new friends to take this apartment.

He knocked on the door. *A wolf-age, a wind-age, ere the world ends.* . . . The door opened, and a bearded face glared at him suspiciously.

"Joe here?" he asked. The bearded face vanished, and there was a low mutter of voices. Then the door widened just enough for Joe's skinny frame to slide through, then closed firmly behind him.

"Hi, Roj. What's up?" his blue eyes were wide and innocent. Roger looked at the floor.

"I was thinking about what you said last week." He hesitated, wishing the real story weren't so—silly. "About—you said—about my being useful—you know—the movement and everything. I'd like to be useful."

"Hey, that's great!" Joe's teeth flashed, and even the vague eyes smiled. A sense of acceptance warmed Roger like coffee on a frosty morning. Then Joe's eyes unfocused again, and with a worried frown he ran his fingers through his uncombed black hair.

"Wait here a minute, Roj. I gotta—gotta talk t' the other guys a minute." His head bobbed in what might have been a mysterious gesture, and he turned and banged loudly on the door.

Again, it opened barely enough for Joe to slide through, and Roger heard the lock click as it closed.

He stared at the blank grey panel. Behind it he could hear the indistinct murmur of voices, even after a moment, muffled shouting.

Well, he couldn't expect them to trust him all at once, could he?

Suddenly, he remembered that it was Tuesday. Tuesday—Tyr's day! Maybe that was why. Maybe that was *all* there was to it. . . .

The door swung open—wider, this time.

"Come on in," said Joe.

Bright lights, and a smell of old chili. A piled chaos of clothing, books and bedding, as though several more people lived in the small apartment than could really fit.

In one corner, some blankets had been hastily thrown over something that might have been a large oil drum, as though to keep him from seeing it. Well, that was only to be expected . . .

Then he was surrounded by six or seven young men, who all moved aside for a tall, oddly neat figure in black jeans and turtleneck.

"Uh, Ivan," Joe was saying, "this is Roger. . . ."

Ivan? A cold blue stare through thick glass walls, and a practiced smile that never left the mouth. His blond hair was the shortest in the room, almost a crew cut.

"Roger, yes. Joe has been telling us about you." There was a professional, over-sincere warmth in the voice. "You're the Black Belt, right? Yes, we *need* people like you in the movement. 'Course, we've got to be careful—you understand."

The smooth, practiced voice went on, barely hesitating over the implied threat, and began to introduce the others.

Mick looked shorter than he really was, with door-filling shoulders and dark, kinky hair. He looked fat from the front, but lean from the side, and his hands looked like he crushed rocks with them. He was the only one who wore a jacket, and a slight bulge under one arm told Roger why.

Johnny's hair was blond, like Ivan's, but fell to his thin shoulders. Duke was small and furtive, with dark, unkempt hair, a neatly trimmed moustache, but with at least a day's stubble on his cheeks. The bearded face that had peered around the door was introduced as Bob.

There was Steve, Dave, and El Adrea. The bewildering mass of faces milled around him, faces black and white, bearded and shaven, talking, planning; all his new friends, comrades, the little band with whom, shoulder to shoulder, he would face the hostile world.

A week passed. Tuesday came round again; and once more Roger knelt, as he did each day, in meditation.

Once again, redness, bright blood-color, forming before his eyes.

He pressed his eyelids more tightly together, but it did not go away. He fought down the fear that burst from his mind, separating it from his being; trying to drive away thought. It had happened before, it was not new. . . .

But it was.

The redness was barred with lines of white.

The teeth of the Wolf.

He was seeing down the open jaws, past the tearing fangs into the slick redness of the devouring gullet; and he felt its hot breath and the dripping slather on his extended hand . . .

Roger leaped sweating from the floor, stifling a cry.

He stared at the bare plaster of the wall, struggling to breathe deeply and control the shaking in his throat. . . .

The *Wolf!*

Of the three Children of Loki, Fenris Wolf was the most fearsome. The Midgard Serpent the gods had thrown into the depths of the ocean, and Hel had been given her own domain in Niflheim. But Fenris dwelt still in Asgard, and grew stead-

ily greater in strength and in evil. And when the gods tried to bind him, knowing he would otherwise destroy the world, he broke every chain they put upon him, boasting no fetter could hold him.

Then the Gods got from the dwarves the marvelous fetter Gleipnir, slender and smooth as a silken thread; made of six impossible things.

As though in sport the gods bade the Wolf to suffer himself to be bound with the light ribbon, to test his strength, but, suspecting a trick, Fenris vowed that he would consent to the game only if he had in his teeth the hand of one of the gods.

The gods were hesitant, looking on one another, but Tyr Warrior stepped forward calmly, and placed his hand in the Wolf's mouth.

The boastful Fenris allowed them to bind him, and then put forth his world-destroying strength. But in vain. The fetter held for all Fenris' struggles, and all the gods laughed.

All but Tyr. He lost his hand. . . .

Roger shivered as the story ran through his mind. He had *felt* the breath of the Wolf on his *extended* arm. . . .

He shivered at the memory. He did not understand.

Frantically he tried to turn his mind away from this madness. He was supposed to teach Karate today. That was all Joe's friends were interested in. He had to give them a lesson today. A lesson. He clung to that. It wasn't quite time yet, but they wouldn't care if he was early . . .

He headed out the door. In his head was booming the terrifying line from the *Voluspa*, prophesying Ragnarok: *the fetter must burst and the Wolf run free.* . . .

Ragnarok, and the deadly rockets, sleek Offspring of Loki, crouched in their pits, waiting for the breaking of the ancient bonds, when *the fetter must burst and the Wolf run free* . . .

He shook his head savagely, trying to clear it. What was this nonsense?

The Vikings hadn't had Atom bombs! Maybe he really *was* cracking up.

He had become a Revolutionary because of the—hallucination, or whatever it was—last week. Now this. What could it mean?

It means your mind is going, he told himself. *Don't start looking for any other meaning, or you'll wind up on a street-corner waving a "Repent" sign. Or in a straightjacket. . . .*

His hand was shaking as he lifted it to pound on the door.

It opened the usual crack and Joe's face peered around it.

"It's Roj," he said over his shoulder, and pulled the door open.

There was a sudden scurry as the others pulled the sheet up over the stuff in the corner. He caught a brief glimpse of some miscellaneous electronic gear and something large that looked like an oil drum, with a black and yellow design on its side, but he looked pointedly away. If they didn't want him to see whatever was in that corner, that was fine with him.

Ivan glared at Joe, and muttered some very short word under his breath. Joe looked defiant.

"Well, now that you're here, what do you want?" Ivan snapped.

"We're supposed to do a Karate lesson today." Roger met Ivan's eyes calmly, as he would have met those of an opponent in a match. Something about the hostility was good: it was real, it was ordinary, it gave him something to hold onto and struggle with. . . .

"You're early."

"Sorry." Roger shrugged. "I can come back later."

"No, no," Ivan said, with a nervous glance at Mick. "No, we'll—we'll get to it, man. Later. Siddown."

Roger sat. They were all terribly nervous about something.

But what the hell, they had plenty to be nervous about. If he knew all their plans, he'd probably be as jumpy as they were . . .

He sat down, and wished they would stop glaring at Joe, and sneaking looks at him. He leaned back in the chair and closed his eyes . . .

The Wolf! The great jaws yawning to swallow the world . . .

He sat bolt upright. They were all staring at him, but he didn't care. The Thing was *here!* He didn't dare close his eyes again, or even blink. He shuddered at the overpowering sense of its living presence, all around him . . .

This was ridiculous! Sweat was rolling on his skin. He sat very still. Ivan and Steve were whispering very quietly in a corner. Bob was intently scribbling in a notebook. Mick was ostentatiously cleaning his gun. They kept looking at him:

quick suspicious glances when they thought he wasn't looking. What the hell was the matter with them?

Well, what was the matter with him?

Joe came over and sat down on the arm of his chair.

"Don't mind them," Joe whispered. "They're kinda nervous."

"I noticed."

"Well, they got reasons." said Joe. "This is big. There's always agents around, and, y'know, the guys don't know you
yet."

"Yeah," Roger nodded. "I understand that. . . ."

There was a sudden pounding on the door that made everybody jump. Ivan slipped it open its usual crack, and then
the rest of the way. Duke came bustling in. As the door
closed behind him he was speaking, excitement shrill in his
voice.

"I've found the perfect place. Get the bomb ready. Just
down the street at the supermarket, around the back, there's
a . . ." he caught sight of Ivan's frantically waving hand, and
stopped, his eyes following Ivan's hand to Roger's chair.

Roger blinked. A *supermarket?*

In the brief darkness behind his eyelids the open jaws
gaped. . . .

All their eyes were on him now, but their hostility was less
disturbing than that single, brief glimpse of the Wolf.

He felt the question building inside him, and after a moment felt his mouth opening to let it out.

"Why a Supermarket? Why not City Hall? Or the Police
Station or something?"

"It won't matter," said Joe. "Not with this bomb."

"Shut up!" yelled Ivan.

"It's an Atom Bomb." Joe said, with a defiant glance at
Ivan.

The light of the room glimmered on the teeth of the Wolf.

"Loudmouth," Ivan snarled. "Yeah," he said, glaring into
Roger's shocked face. "An Atom Bomb. The People's Bomb.
Why not? We stole the plutonium, and we know how to put
it together. If the Pigs don't go along with us and do what we
tell'em, then bang! This whole town goes sky-high!"

The fetter must burst and the Wolf run free. . . .

"Roger's no fink!" Joe was snarling. "I told you! He's with us! He's committed!"

"Is he?" said Ivan, very quietly, his eyes riveted to Roger's pale face.

Am I? Roger wondered.

"Look," Duke interrupted. "Whatever we decide about him, we've gotta get busy. And we haven't got enough gear for everybody."

Ivan frowned, then nodded.

"All right. You go back to your place, Roj. Mick"—the big man looked up—"you go with him. Sorry, Roj. We can't take any chances."

"Yeah," Roger said, nodding.

Mick ostentatiously slid the clip into his pistol.

Back in his own room, Roger sat on the floor, staring at the wall. Mick wandered around for a while, and looked curiously through the bookcase, and finally sprawled out on the bed, watching.

They did not speak.

There were children playing in the park, Roger thought. All around them were thousands of bustling, unsuspecting people, unarmed, harmless and helpless. . . .

He closed his eyes and looked down the red gullet of the Wolf.

He controlled his fear, and breathed in, deeply and slowly. He must think this through. Slowly, calmly he breathed out. These were his *friends.* . . .

The Wolf's jaws yawned wide.

Suddenly, something stirred, another presence, like the sharp, joyous pulse of trumpets in the heart.

The God kneels. Into the mouth of the Wolf he thrusts his hand. As the magic bonds tighten, the great teeth clamp savagely on the wrist . . .

Roger *felt* the pain of the God of War as the terrible jaws closed.

His eyes opened. His mind was clear. Out of his mind a phrase bubbled up, from what forgotten past he could not have told: *Glory to the God Tyr, Sole Binder of the Wolf!*

He slid smoothly to his feet, lifting the scabbarded sword from its rack.

"Hey!" Mick pushed himself up from the bed. "What do you think you're gonna do?"

"Kill you." said Roger, calmly tucking the scabbard through his belt. Mick's eyes widened and his mouth dropped open. The gun came up—

The sword whipped from its sheath like a rattler striking. The gun never went off.

Roger jerked the sword up and snapped it down, shaking off the blood as calmly as he might have shaken rain from an umbrella. He *could* call the police now, let *them* take the risks . . .

Instead he slid the sword carefully back into the sheath, opened the door and walked down the hall.

He did not knock, but tried the handle. Locked, of course.

His vision blurred, and it seemed as though a huge, scarred hand—*not his*—reached out and touched the lock, and the door sprang open.

And then he stood, staring, trapped in nightmare. . . .

The Wolf was there. Its glaring eyes and grinning jaws filled the doorway. It was *here,* it was *now!*

And through the dripping fangs he saw, as though through fog, another nightmare. Weirdly suited figures like astronauts from some other world, clustered about an olive drab central cylinder, with a black and yellow device like an evil three-petaled flower blossoming on its side.

His mind told him what this thing in the wolf's throat must be—a shielded container for transporting plutonium—but the ravening wolf filled his mind and stunned his senses; the open jaws were waiting to receive him. . . .

He heard a voice saying, ". . . but it was *locked,* dammit . . ." and saw the misty, alien figures staring at him.

He strode between the dripping jaws, and in the sudden glaring light spoke a single word.

"No."

The weirdly armored figures were spreading out. A gun turned toward him, but the apartment was too small for that. His sword whistled and the gun went off as the man fell, the bullet driving deeply into the floor. Two more guns came up, but only one went off, the bullet whining harmlessly over his shoulder as he struck.

He wondered which of them had been Joe.

Then the last two were cowering back against the wall. One held a lead cylinder with a pair of tongs, and the other reached over and pulled it open.

"*Get back!*" It was Ivan's voice. "This stuff is hot! Come a step closer and we'll take it out. It'll kill you!"

Roger shrugged his shoulders and lifted his blade.

The deadly metal fell to the floor, and Roger's sword whispered twice in the poisoned air.

He wiped the blood from his sword and sheathed it. He heard a siren in the distance, and wondered if one of the neighbors had called the police because of the shots. It was probably just coincidence, he decided. He'd have to call the police himself. He didn't want to, but somebody had to clean this up. And he'd have to warn them about the radiation.

The plutonium lay on the floor, so innocently, invisibly, killing him. It should go back into its shielding. He shrugged, sadly, and reached down to pick it up.

As his hand touched it, he saw the Wolf's jaws close on his wrist.

They buried him in a lead-lined box, with the ancient, radioactive sword laid on his chest.

And back over the Rainbow Bridge the Valkyries bore Farin of the Einherior—he who had been Roger Hogg—and with them strode One-Handed Tyr, laughing gigantically.

All-Father Odin's single eye flashed approval at his returning hero. But after the rejoicing Valkyries had passed, with Farin and with Tyr Warrior laughing in their midst, War-father joined Heimdall upon Bifrost, gazing with his single, all-seeing eye upon the world where, bound in the hearts of all men, the Grey Wolf watches the dwellings of the gods.

EPILOGUE:
A Footnote on Story Selection

Some people would have you believe that editing an anthology is just a matter of reading the stories that come in, buying the ones you like, rejecting the ones you don't, and sending the manuscript off to the printer. *Et voilà!*

And of course they would believe that in an anthology as narrowly defined as this one, "stories by Greyhaven writers," it would be even simpler; ask everybody for his best unpublished story, write a few cute little anecdotes about the characters who are so well known to the editor, and again, there you are!

If I had ever had any such idea, it vanished when I saw the first heap of stories lying before me, all written by people associated with Greyhaven in one way or another. I could, for instance, have overloaded this anthology with seven or eight twelve-thousand word novellas. I could have produced an anthology so slanted toward the grim, grotesque, and horrible that the reader would believe that Greyhaven stood somewhere in the suburbs of night-haunted Arkham or Innsmouth. Or the anthology might well have shaped up like an issue of the old *Weird Tales*, with the reader free to imagine us as a kind of real-life *Addams Family*, with a vampire to the right of us, a werewolf to the left of us, while ghouls and rats gibbered away in the cellar, and our typewriters rattled like old skeletons in our closets.

Instead I strove for a balance. I carped and chivvied and bounced stories back at the Greyhaven people until I had not only stories which chilled the spine, but a few which tickled the funny-bone as well. For every *frisson* of horror I demanded at least a giggle, if not a belly-laugh. And while it was a temptation to rove in the Celtic twilight (we are all addicted to serious high fantasy, and most of our Bardic revels, as detailed herein, show a distinctly Irish melancholy in the stories, songs and poems we sing and tell) I tried hard to balance fantasy with science-fantasy, magic with rational thought, sorrow with laughter, and, not least, novellas with short-shorts. Only three stories had been specifically selected for this volume when I signed the contract; Diana's "Kindred of the Wind," Paul's "The Hand of Tyr," and Serpent's "The Woodcarver's Son"; and I had to fight to get these, because every one of these writers had written a story which he, or his agent, thought was better, and which was longer. Everything else was the result of tradeoffs and arguments, and an attempt to balance the effect on the reader. ("No, no, Tracy, I can only take *one* Celtic Twilight story. . . .)

Not to mention that my family talk back to me more than they would to most editors, and argue the merits of one story more than another. I had to justify my choices of every story I chose. . . . not to mention justifying every rejection! No doubt, someday they will forgive me for the stories I printed—and perhaps, a long time from now, for the stories I rejected!

I would also like to thank belatedly those members of Greyhaven and Greenwalls who made my task easier by NOT being writers; Walter Breen, who writes only technical nonfiction, my daughter Dorothy, busy with her dancing, and our dear Tracy Blackstone, who serves as agent for many of the writers herein and earnestly argued the merits of one story over another, managing to keep her usual unflappable good temper even though I know she very seldom agreed with my choices. Tracy seems the happy exception to the comment I have made often in these pages, about the inevitable contagion of living in a household of writers; she is an intelligent reader and very helpful critic, but firmly maintains that she has no ambitions *whatever* to be a writer—"Nope, never!"

Likewise free of that troublesome ambition is my helpful secretary Linda Crowe, who sings at Bardic revels in a pleasant voice, playing and composing her own works, and—so far—little Alex, son of two of the writers represented in this volume, whose major talent so far is to soothe frazzled nerves by being cute and cuddly as he goes from lap to lap.

But give him time. After all, he's only four months old, and even I didn't get the ambition to write until I was nine years old. And in this household, I firmly imagine that, a few years from now, he'll come up and tell me he's writing a novel . . .

But sufficient unto this anthology are the writers thereof.

Marion Zimmer Bradley